"Have you nev...
s...

Ash stared at the teenager. "Emily, what are you talking about?"

The girl rolled her eyes in that expressive way she had. "Like anyone with half a brain couldn't have figured it out. There's going to be a baby! *Your* baby. *Mel's* baby!"

"Oh my God." Ash wondered if this was how it felt to be in shock.

"Now I suppose you're going to hyperventilate?" Emily snatched her milk glass off the table and stalked to the sink. "Get a grip, for cripes' sake. People have babies all the time. Especially when they fall in love. If you can't figure out what to do next, well, I give up."

"Next?" He was supposed to *do* something. But what? Buy insurance? Baby formula? Cigars?

"Next. As in, go after Mel and make nice." She rolled her eyes again. "Do I need to write a script here?" She took Ash by the arm and turned him in the direction Mel had run. "Go. Now. And repeat after me, 'Mel, I love you.' And work on your delivery while you're looking for her."

All Ash could do was follow orders and try to steady his heart.

Melinda *and* a baby. Could he really be that lucky?

Dear Reader,

Welcome back to Hope Springs, Virginia.

I hope you're enjoying the people of Hope Springs as much
as I am. I love small Southern towns. I love the people and
the way they rally around when you need them. I love the
sense of tradition. I love the colorful names and the quaint
shops and tree-lined streets.

My heroine in *All-American Baby* doesn't know much about
small-town U.S.A., but she wants to. She wants to find that
sense of community, a place where she can feel a family
connection with everyone she meets. She hasn't experienced
much of that in her life and she is determined that her baby
will grow up with all the things she missed.

Thank you for joining me on another visit to Hope Springs.

Regards,

Peg Sutherland

Books by Peg Sutherland

HARLEQUIN SUPERROMANCE

*780—BABY BOOM
*807—A FATHER'S VOW

*Hope Springs titles

ALL-AMERICAN BABY
BABY
Peg Sutherland

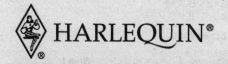

TORONTO • NEW YORK • LONDON
AMSTERDAM • PARIS • SYDNEY • HAMBURG
STOCKHOLM • ATHENS • TOKYO • MILAN • MADRID
PRAGUE • WARSAW • BUDAPEST • AUCKLAND

ISBN 0-373-70845-9

ALL-AMERICAN BABY

This edition published by arrangement with Harlequin Books S.A.

® and TM are trademarks of the publisher. Trademarks indicated with
® are registered in the United States Patent and Trademark Office, the
Canadian Trade Marks Office and in other countries.

Look us up on-line at: http://www.romance.net

Printed in U.S.A.

ALL-AMERICAN
BABY

PROLOGUE

Hope Springs, Virginia

"TOOD GRUNKEMEIER, you're ornery as an old rattlesnake today."

That was Whiskey Rowlett, a regular at Fudgie's Barbershop whenever he wasn't out for a few weeks pursuing the interests that had earned him his nickname.

Tood eyed Whiskey. Whiskey wasn't known for his sweet disposition, either, so it was no surprise Tood's complaints about the heat had struck Whiskey the wrong way. "Rattlesnakes don't bother you if you don't bother them," Tood pointed out.

"Besides, Tood's right," said another of the regulars, who liked to keep peace at Fudgie's because his daughter-in-law and three grandkids had moved in with him and the missus, making peace a scarce commodity in his life at the moment. "It's too dang hot for May."

"'Specially if you've got a houseful, eh, Eb?"

Eben Monk nodded ruefully and conversation drifted off to kids and approaching summertime. Tood's attention strayed. He didn't know much about kids. The last kid he knew anything about was his nephew and he'd had bad news about the boy this very day, from the detective hired by Tood's attorney. His nephew was dead. Found in an abandoned warehouse in Omaha, dead from an apparent drug overdose. Thirty-four and he'd already beat his old uncle to the promised land. And the capper was that nobody seemed to know what had happened to the boy's teenage daughter.

"Lookie there!"

Everybody in the barbershop turned in response to Whiskey's excitement. Whiskey was pointing at the TV mounted in the corner, its sound muted to a low murmur. On the screen, a dark-haired young woman was being scurried from a jet to a limousine waiting across the tarmac.

"That's Melina Somerset," Whiskey said.

Eb and Fudgie took two steps closer to the television.

"Naw. Can't be."

"The devil it's not." Whiskey grabbed the remote and inched up the sound.

"How do you know?" Eb asked. "Ain't nobody seen a picture of her for I don't know how long— fifteen years, maybe."

"I know 'cause I seen it on the noon news outta Roanoke. Announcer said it was her."

"Then what's she doing here?" Fudgie said.

"She ain't here, you old fool. She's in San Francisco."

"What for?"

"Well, now, if I knew that, I reckon I'd be putting

up with Jerry Springer's fool questions instead of yours, wouldn't I?''

''You're cross, Whiskey. Just as cross as can be. You ought to go off on another one of your benders. You know that? We're tired of listening to you.''

Then the barbershop grew quiet as the camera zoomed in for a close-up of the young woman. She was dark and thin, with eyes too large for anyone's face beneath the brim of a man's gray felt fedora. The collar of her raincoat was turned up, but neither it nor the hat had managed to hide her delicate beauty.

Someone in the barbershop whistled low as one of the men surrounding the young woman moved in to block her from the camera. She disappeared into the limousine and the camera panned to a female reporter who did not look nearly as elegant in her raincoat.

''Dang! Imagine that,'' Fudgie said. ''Melina Somerset. How old's she now? 'Bout twenty?''

''Musta been more than a dozen years since they wiped out her mother,'' Eb said. ''She was just a little one then.''

''Her mother and her sister,'' Whiskey said. ''She's twenty-six now. Said so on the noon news.''

''Low-life scum.'' Fudgie sat in the empty barber chair and linked his fingers behind his head. ''Never did catch 'em, did they?''

The debate raged about whether justice had been done for the people who had killed Melina Somerset's mother and sister, but Tood didn't much care. Oh, he knew how the country felt about the mysterious young woman who had apparently arrived in San

Francisco the evening before. Melina Somerset, daughter of computer magnate Tom Somerset, was like America's royalty. And all the more intriguing because she'd lived in seclusion, her whereabouts shrouded in mystery, ever since the tragedy had struck her family. Tom Somerset had paid a big price for his enormous wealth.

At least, Tood thought, Somerset had his daughter. Whereas Tood had nobody.

Seventy-one and a bad ticker marking his days and not a soul in the world to care. The only one on God's green earth who even shared his blood was a runaway fourteen-year-old. He supposed he could send the detective off on her trail now. But he had about as much chance of ever seeing her again as he had of seeing Melina Somerset walking through the door at Fudgie's, that's what Tood reckoned.

Yep, he was going to die alone. That was about the size of it.

CHAPTER ONE

San Francisco, California

ASH THORNDYKE FELT the first stirring of lust as his gaze lingered on the diamond-and-emerald pendant pointing the way to the perfect breasts of the Hollywood agent's young bride.

The breasts were clearly *faux* and interested Ash not in the least.

But the diamonds and emeralds were the real thing. Magnificent specimens. Ash could almost feel them in the palm of his hand, their cool ice, their weighty heft. His breath grew a little quicker and he forced himself to look away.

"A lifetime of training doesn't vanish overnight," he muttered to himself.

"Beg pardon, sir?"

The black-tied waiter balancing the silver tray of champagne flutes paused, a questioning expression on his young face.

"Oh. I... Nothing."

The young man gave Ash a quizzical smile, then seemed to remember that it wasn't his job to analyze this mob of well-dressed, well-heeled, well-known revelers. "Champagne, sir?"

Training. "Not for the moment, thank you." Not while working. Ash had learned that at his father's knee. Never drink on the job.

Ash scanned the crowd. He no longer even had to school himself to look as if his perusal of the gala gathering was casual. It wasn't, no matter how blasé he managed to look. As always at this kind of bash, Ash Thorndyke was working.

Tonight, however, he wasn't on a mission for the kind of expensive baubles worn by the agent's trophy wife. Tonight, Ash Thorndyke had been hired to kidnap Melina Somerset.

Ash's stomach cramped. Maybe he should have that champagne after all. Maybe he should get the heck out of Dodge. Kidnapping beautiful young heiresses wasn't his cup of tea, as Grandfather Thorndyke would say. Cat-burglary—safecracking, pulling off heists that always made the papers but never made the court dockets—was Ash's specialty. It was all a part of the family business. Each member had a specialty. Counterfeiting was what his dad, Bram Thorndyke, did—a skill he'd passed on to Ash's brother, Forbes. Confidence games targeting the sinfully rich, that was Grandfather Thorndyke's forte. For four generations, the Thorndykes had been running their circumspect little family business.

Kidnapping, however, didn't sit right with Ash. The very idea violated his moral code. In this instance, however, family was more important than anybody's moral code.

"Anything for family," he said quietly to the canapé he snagged from a passing silver tray. His payoff for tonight's distasteful little caper was his father's freedom. And Ash was prepared to do anything to ensure that his dying father didn't spend his final days in prison.

The men who had hired Ash promised him that much. They worked for the government, at least that's what their identification said. And Ash had surely been around enough phony papers in his day to recognize a fake when he saw it. Of course, there was always the chance that he was being fooled, but it was a chance he was willing to take. Anything for family.

His quarry had not yet made her appearance. When she did, Ash was certain, she would be hard to miss, even though he couldn't recall having seen a picture of her since a family funeral more than a decade earlier. The family was reclusive, everybody knew that, which made their sudden appearance in California all the more intriguing. Somerset was apparently developing some new technology for the film industry and was here to network and to research the project. Of course, the national media vultures had managed to catch the Somersets' arrival in San Francisco, but Ash made it a policy never to watch television. Now, he just needed to be patient. The rich, headstrong heiress was waiting until a fashionably late hour to make her grand appearance at the gala in her father's honor. Ash would know her from the stir she would create in the crowd.

"Rich women," he said. "A pain in the backside."

Another young waiter was at his elbow. "Champagne, sir?"

Ash's mouth felt a little dry. His nerves were beginning to get the better of him. Bubbles rose lazily to the top of the elegant crystal flute. He could taste them, a sweet, tart explosion against his tongue.

He could also imagine those delightful little bubbles fuzzing his brain and slowing him down just as the time came to execute his plan.

He shook his head.

At midnight, when he turned over Melina Somerset to the government agents who had hired him to confiscate her, he would find a bottle of the finest bubbly in the city by the bay and relax in style. Then, tomorrow, he would be on his way East, to retrieve his father. At last. It had been a long four years since his father's incarceration, far too long.

Ash sidled through the crowd, engaging in only the briefest of conversations with the people he passed, making sure he didn't stand out from the crowd. In fact, his appearance was one of Ash Thorndyke's greatest assets in his line of work. He was nondescript. Average-looking. Tall but not too tall. Average build, with a slight tendency to be too lean. Light-colored hair a shade past blond but not quite brown, worn too long to be called short and too short to be called long. Eyes that might be described as gray. Or green. Or hazel. Depended on who you talked to. Ash looked like the young attorney who drew up your will or a representative of the investment company that managed your finances. He looked like your daughter's best friend's husband, whose name you never can remember.

There was no doubt that Ash Thorndyke's ability to blend in with the crowd was one of the things that had made him so successful.

That, and a sharp wit, unflappable nerves and fingertips that could feel the tumblers working in a safe lock. Ash Thorndyke could romance a safe the way some men could romance a woman. He was the best.

Had been the best, he reminded himself. After tonight, it was all over. That was the deal. His deal with himself.

He kept moving. Kept listening. Kept watching. He saw Tom Somerset, who looked as anxious as Ash felt. Ash overheard the excited chatter as the cream of California society anticipated Melina's appearance. No one knew quite what Tom Somerset had in mind, finally bringing his cloistered daughter out into society. But they were greedily excited to be a part of it. Ash could smell their agitation.

He backed against a wall near the corridor leading to the kitchen and continued to survey the room. He registered every detail. Bits and snatches of conversation floated in and out of his mind.

"...to marry her off, and I personally am convinced that the only man in Hollywood worthy of her..."

"...career as a model. Have you seen that bone structure? Darling, she's a natural."

"...get our hands on her and get her out of the country, half our problems will be over."

"...say she runs away about twice a year. Can you

imagine? Everything one could ever want and all she can think to do is behave like a spoiled…''

Ash frowned. What was that? A snippet of conversation about getting our hands on her? Getting her out of the country? He began to cast about in the din of gossip for that particular conversation. He located it and realized it was coming from the corridor behind him.

"…a plane is waiting."

"And then?"

"Then she disappears for a while."

The voices goaded Ash's memory. He strained to place them, but he'd heard too little. More disturbing, however, than their faint but unidentifiable familiarity, was what they were saying.

"For a while?" the second man said. "But not for good?"

There was a silence. Ash could almost see the first man shrugging and it was then he pinpointed their voices.

He was listening to the two men who had hired him. And the scheme they were discussing sounded alarmingly unlike the innocuous plan they'd outlined for him. A headstrong young woman, a worried father who wanted nothing more than to keep her safe during her stay in the U.S., and government officials with orders from way up the food chain to do anything to keep Tom Somerset happy. That's the way it had been explained to Ash, by the two men claiming to be government operatives.

Something wasn't adding up and Ash couldn't decide exactly what it was. Was the government pulling a fast one on Tom Somerset? Was Somerset the one with the extra card up his sleeve? Was the government playing Ash Thorndyke for a fool?

"Hard to say," the first man replied. "We can't anticipate every eventuality."

"Can we trust this Thorndyke character?"

"To get the job done? Sure. We've got what he wants, right?"

The two men laughed. There was little humor in the sound.

They began to move away then, their voices retreating. Ash remained still. Never act rashly, Grandfather Thorndyke always said. Make a plan. Then execute it.

Maybe the men who'd hired him were feds and maybe they weren't. Maybe Tom Somerset knew what was happening and maybe he didn't. Maybe Melina Somerset was in danger and maybe she wasn't.

All that really mattered to Ash was the one thing he did know for sure. He'd been duped. Nobody duped Ash Thorndyke.

He located Tom Somerset again and began to make his way through the jungle of dueling perfumes and clashing voices. Somerset, when Ash reached him, was encircled by fawning men, men who rarely fawned over anyone, movers and shakers in business and entertainment and government. But Tom Somerset had more money than Hollywood had phonies and that meant everyone loved him.

Ash eased up behind the circle of people, planning his approach, knowing that getting the man alone long enough to ask about his daughter and her safety would be one of Ash's more difficult heists. But as he studied the problem and formulated a plan, two gray-suited men whom Ash pegged instantly as private-security types came up behind Somerset and captured his attention. Ash moved in closer.

"...insists she's coming down."

Somerset looked like a man with dwindling patience. "Then lock her up. God knows what she'll say if we let her out. I won't have her exposing..."

A peal of laughter drowned out the rest of it, but the tenor of that exchange curdled Ash's guts. For someone labeled America's princess, Melina Somerset was not receiving royal treatment at anyone's hands. Something was wrong with this picture, and Ash didn't have enough information to figure out what it was.

He told himself the best thing he could do was walk away.

Then he remembered his father. What if those men who'd hired him really could help his father?

Thinking of his father made him think of something else, too. Honor. Both Grandfather Thorndyke and Bram Thorndyke had taught Ash and his brother a code of honor. And Ash was fairly certain there was something in that code about damsels in distress.

Shrugging it off as not his problem, Ash headed for the foyer. He would walk away. He reached the foyer about the time the two men who'd spoken to

Tom Somerset reached the top of the marble stairway leading to the second floor.

"...break her pretty little neck."

The words echoed in the cavernous foyer. Both men laughed. Ash told himself it was just the kind of flippant remark that family employees would make. Not a serious threat at all.

But after what he'd heard tonight, could he really be sure of that?

IN HER SECOND-FLOOR SUITE, Melina Somerset stood at the bank of windows overlooking the city of San Francisco. The city was built on hills, and this mansion was obviously atop one of them, for the view was panoramic and spectacular. To her left was the Golden Gate Bridge, shrouded tonight in fog and the mystique of legend. As her gaze swept right, she saw Coit Tower, then the lights of the city.

It had been more than a dozen years since Melina had set foot in America. After her mother and sister were killed, she and her father had moved to Europe, moving from one isolated town to another. Eventually, he'd placed her in private school under an assumed name. Then another. And another. Melina had missed the country of her birth. She had missed having a home, any kind of home.

She tried to imagine all the fun that was to be had beyond these walls if she could only make her way from this elegantly appointed suite—one more in a long line of luxurious prisons—to the places where all those lights twinkled.

Out there somewhere were hamburgers and French fries. Stores where blue jeans could be bought. Friendly coffeehouses where people wore those jeans and talked about movies and music and the baseball season. And somewhere, beyond all the lights, were split-level brick houses in the suburbs. Although Melina had missed all that went with being young and free, and regretted that, she now had different priorities. She was ready to grow up.

"Someday I'll get a station wagon," she said wistfully to the faint reflection of her own face in the window. "I'll eat at McDonald's every day and have my chauffeur drive me to aerobics class in my very own station wagon. I'll be just like normal people."

But tonight, she was still a prisoner to her father's success, hostage to his fears. Tonight, she'd been locked in her room because she'd wanted to attend the party below. She'd wanted to dance and meet people and take just one sip of champagne, not enough to hurt anything, just enough to feel the bubbles on her nose.

Instead, she was locked away from life, as she had been locked away almost her entire life. Under guard and incognito, that's how Melina had lived her life.

But no more.

Melina had run away before, and they'd always found her. But this was America, a country so sprawling that a person could vanish and never be heard from again. Here, millions of people lived their lives without a lot of fanfare.

This time, she wouldn't fail. This time, there was

more at stake than Melina's own happiness. There was even more at stake than her father's happiness. Yes, leaving this way would cause him pain. But he'd left her no choice. She'd tried reasoning with him, threatening him, pleading with him.

He was adamant.

Well, now, so was she.

Forcing a smile, Melina took a halfhearted spin around the room in her evening dress, trying to recapture the pleasure she'd had a few hours earlier in the feel of the silky fabric swirling around her calves and ankles. She knew she looked pretty in the dress and she regretted no one would see her in it. She unzipped the dress. Maybe she would take it with her. Surely even average American housewives wore evening dresses sometimes.

She thought she heard little snicks of noise at the door to the adjoining bathroom, but of course there would be no one there. She would have been delighted to find someone there, to invite a little adventure into her deadly dull life, but that was never going to happen. Not as long as her father treated her like a priceless family jewel instead of a living, breathing human being with a life of her own.

She slipped off her shoes. First, she would change into street clothes. Then—

A hand covered her mouth. A strong arm pinned her arms to her side. Fear shot through her. She fought. Kicked. Flailed about as best she could. But she was small. And the arms that bound her to a hard chest were strong. She struggled, panting behind the hand that covered most of her face.

Her assailant took her to the bathroom door. Soon she would be beyond rescue. If she could manage a sound, the guards right outside her bedroom door would hear her, would save her. She kicked, aiming for the bedside lamp. Missed. The strap of her gown slipped off her shoulder.

"Hold still," he whispered into her ear, his voice a soft rasp. He slid the strap back into place on her shoulder. "They aren't on your side."

That stopped her, froze her in his grasp. He was right, of course. Who was he, that he knew that?

They entered the dark bathroom. Melina grew still and they moved quickly beyond the small room into another adjoining bedroom, also dark.

"Nobody's going to hurt you," he said. "I'll explain. But first we have to get somewhere safe."

A trick, of course. But there was something in the voice.... And there was the promise of escape. He might have something else in mind, but in her heart a notion of her own stirred to life. This stranger would help her escape from them, then she could escape from him.

The thought gave her courage. She drew the deepest breath possible, picking up the scent off his hand.

Something stirred to life in her mind. A memory, a feeling...

He shifted his grip on her. "I'm going to zip your dress. Then I have to gag you. Cover your mouth. I don't want to, but..."

He stuffed something in her mouth. Something soft and silky but still unwelcome. She growled a protest as she felt him slide the zipper snugly into place.

"Sorry."

Her nose was free now. She inhaled deeply. Recognition struck her. The soft voice. The distinctive scent of cypress on his flesh. Adrenaline gave her strength.

She burst free of his grasp and turned to face him, snatching the silk out of her mouth in the same instant. It was dark, but she could see the faint outline of his face. The square jaw, the slope of forehead, the fullness of the lower lip.

"You!"

He froze for an instant, then dragged her to the window, threw up the shade and let moonlight into the room.

He looked as stunned as she felt. "You!"

CHAPTER TWO

WHAT A NIGHTMARE.

Ash should have insisted on seeing a photo of the mysterious Melina Somerset. He should have made a point of watching TV the last few days, just to get a look at her. If he had, he would be somewhere else right this minute. A continent away.

He was almost furious enough to leave her right there in the dark second-floor room. But he heard the tone of her voice and suspected that if he didn't take her with him, she'd see to it that her father's goons were on top of him in less time than it took to finesse a home security system.

"What are you doing here?" she whispered furiously.

He'd never seen her angry before, although it was entirely possible she'd been a tad irate in London when she'd realized he wasn't coming back. "Can we talk about this later? Somewhere else? Like in the next county?"

She glared at him a moment, then nodded abruptly.

They slipped through the window, down the trellis he'd scouted earlier in the week as a possible emergency escape route. They made their way to the parking area. Ash surveyed the cars, looking for the most nondescript and inexpensive car.

"Don't you know which one is yours?" she said sharply.

"Whichever one I want, princess," he retorted.

"I see. That one, then."

He looked where she pointed. A vintage red sports car.

"No way."

She marched over to it, her stance and her tone regal. "This one."

"Too flashy. It'll draw too much attention."

"I like this one," she said, treating him to a cool smile. "And I can make a scene if I don't get what I want."

"Oh, I don't doubt that."

Grinding his teeth in frustration, Ash hot-wired the convertible in a matter of seconds. At least he didn't have to jimmy the lock on a convertible. He pulled quietly out of the parking area and eased down the long driveway without turning on the headlights.

"You have some interesting talents, Ash Thorndyke," she said when they reached the street. "Kidnapping. Car theft. You're much more fascinating than I imagined."

She kept her tone light, but he couldn't mistake the underlying bite.

"Can we keep it quiet," he said softly.

"Oh, I hardly think they can hear us now."

From the corner of his eye, he noticed that she

leaned back and took in the stars, like a young woman without a care in the world.

Like Mel Summersby, the saucy and sultry young woman he'd thought she was in London.

"I've always wanted to ride in a convertible," she said.

There it was—the soft purr of a voice that had been the second thing that drew him to her. The first had been her smile, sometimes naive and sometimes seductive, but always too big for her thin, fine-boned face, as were those sable-colored eyes of hers. She was like the girl next door wrapped up in the packaging of a temptress. He'd been seduced before. He could be again. That was the worst of it.

"Save the innocent-waif routine, princess." He pointed the car toward the middle of town, where he could drive around long enough to decide what to do next.

She rode in silence for a long while. When they neared the city center, she edged forward in the seat. "There's a McDonald's."

He spotted the famous golden arches. "So?"

"I want a hamburger." She turned in the seat and watched as they passed the arches. "I said—"

"Not this close to the caviar-and-champagne set, princess."

"My name is Melina."

"So I've discovered."

"Is that why you came back for me? You found out who I was?"

"Princess, I can assure you, if I'd known who you were, I would have stayed in Anaheim tonight."

"Not a very likely story." She pointed again. "Is that a grocery store? A supermarket? Could we—"

"No, we couldn't."

"You were never this cross in London."

"I was young and foolish in London."

"And now you're old and cranky?"

"Something like that."

In London he'd been mesmerized, hopelessly bewitched by the woman he knew as a winsome American student. Mel Summersby had shown him what it was like to be carefree and normal for the first time in his life. They ate fish and chips and rode one of those silly double-decker buses like all the other tourists, something he'd never deigned to do in all his many trips to London. They walked in the bleak drizzle of early March and didn't care if their hair was plastered to their heads or their shoes squeaked with rain. And they made love in the little attic room at the bed-and-breakfast in Parsons Green.

For two weeks, three short months ago, Ash Thorndyke had tasted everyday life. And he'd discovered that he had an unfortunate appetite for it.

"What are you going to do with me now that you have me?" she asked.

"What I'd like to do is dump you in the middle of town and be out of this mess," he said. It wouldn't take her long to find some poor sap to dupe, he supposed.

"Fine," she said. "How about that corner? They look like nice people."

He glanced at the women posturing on the corner, wearing vinyl boots that covered their knees and stretch miniskirts that barely covered their fannies. "What they look like is hookers. Women of ill repute, Your Highness."

"You know, you really should be nicer to me. I could land you in plenty of hot water, if I wanted to. My father—"

"Your father had his goons lock you up."

She laughed lightly, but he detected a hollow sound to it. "So you were rescuing me?"

"Something like that."

"I suppose the next thing you'll be telling me is that you're a man of honor."

"No. I wouldn't claim that." He couldn't after the way he'd left her in London, without a word of explanation, without a backward glance. It hadn't been his finest moment. But he'd never been that scared before. Funny how a healthy dose of fear could make a man violate every principle he'd ever believed in.

The alluring young woman he'd known as Mel Summersby had him thinking about going straight. Starting a family. Getting a... Even now, the blasphemous idea elevated his blood pressure. Getting a job.

"I think we should leave town," she said.

"I think we should have a plan before we do anything." He'd had a plan, of course. Get the heiress out of the house, meet the feds—the so-called feds—

at the Embarcadero, get a good night's rest at the Ritz-Carlton and head for the East Coast, where Bram Thorndyke would soon be the recipient of clemency in exchange for tonight's little escapade. That had been Ash's condition for participating.

"If we don't get out of town now, we may not have another chance," she said. "They'll be looking for me very soon. Every highway out of town will be covered. Plus, we have a stolen car. A very ostentatious stolen car."

She was right about the all-out search, of course. "So you've done this before."

"Well, not quite this dramatically."

"So you must have plenty of aliases. Aside from Mel Summersby."

She was silent. And he'd been feeling guilty for dumping her. What a chump. She'd probably been twenty minutes away from doing the same to him. Apparently dalliances with the working class were a way of life for the rich and famous Melina Somerset.

"The highway to Big Sur is that way," she said. "I've never been to Big Sur." There she was, an edge of girlish delight in her otherwise sultry voice. Despite everything he knew, it made him want to give her whatever she longed for. Quite a talent she had. Well, she could find another way to Big Sur.

At the last minute, he made a sharp, tire-squealing turn.

"But don't get the idea we're going to Big Sur," he said. "All we're going to do is get out of town. Then we're going to make a plan."

MELINA ALREADY HAD a plan. The trick, she realized as they left San Francisco behind, was to get Ash Thorndyke to help her implement her plan.

They sprinted along the freeway to the south and Melina sat up and took notice. The highway was lined with precisely what she longed to see. American suburbia. Neon and fast food, billboards and discount stores. Parking lots full of SUVs and minivans.

She was in America. Somewhere there was a place for her, a place where she could belong and blend in and become average.

Ash turned on the car radio, cruising the dial, pausing whenever he landed on a news report.

"It won't be on the news," she said softly.

Tom Somerset would never let the world know that his daughter was on the loose. Sometimes it felt to Melina as if she only existed in her father's imagination. Out of his sight, beyond his control, she ceased to be a real person. Deep in her heart, she knew that wasn't so. Beneath the anger she felt toward him for completely disregarding her wishes for her life, she loved him as only a child who has already lost one parent can love. But she couldn't dwell on that. She couldn't think about how much she would miss him or how much pain this would cause him. He'd left her no alternative. Time and again he'd refused to treat her like an adult.

That's what she had to remember, her anger and her frustration. Not her love or her guilt.

"Hungry?" Ash asked. "I seem to recall that you eat like a workhorse coming off a diet."

She decided not to take offense at the comparison. It was unarguably true. Besides, he must recall more than that. She certainly did. The smell and the taste and the touch of him, all of it unavoidably poignant in her memory. Of course, it had been an adventure for her, one more thing she'd never done in her life.

For him, she supposed, it was just another meaningless romp.

"I want a cheeseburger," she said. "Two all-beef patties, pickles, the works. French fries."

"I wouldn't subject a princess to fast food."

"I don't think you have a choice," she said, not allowing her longing to show. If he knew how much she wanted to go into an American hamburger joint, if he knew how many months and years she'd daydreamed about doing just that, he'd never let her out of the car. "It'll be fast. We need to keep ahead of them."

Ten minutes later, they sat in a brightly lit hamburger restaurant, sacks of food on the table in front of them. The place was packed with teenagers and families with young children. Real Americans. Melina's heart fluttered with excitement. Even when her family had lived in the U.S., they'd never visited a fast food restaurant. They'd had a French chef.

"I think we're overdressed," she said, smoothing a paper napkin over the lap of her evening dress and doing her best impression of nonchalance. "Although I do seem to have forgotten my shoes in our haste."

"Black-tie is never in bad taste."

Melina caught herself in a laugh—he was hard to

resist. But she didn't want to laugh with him, to get caught up in his easy charm again. She turned her attention to her food. She set the paper-wrapped cheeseburger in front of her, placed the little box of French fries beside it, then put a straw into her milk shake. Perfect. She relished the picture it made before she slowly unwrapped the sandwich. It looked just the way it looked on television.

"Quit staring at it as if you've never seen one like it before," Ash said. "You're the one who wanted to stop here. This is eat and run, remember."

If he only knew. The closest she'd ever been to a real American cheeseburger was a thirty-five-inch television screen. But she wasn't going to tell him that. "I savor my food."

The first bite was heaven. Ground beef and melted cheese and grilled onions and crunchy pickle slices. She closed her eyes and smiled.

"You realize you're calling attention to yourself," he said, "acting orgasmic over a cheeseburger."

She glanced around and realized the only one paying her any attention was Ash. She started to tell him the only person in the entire world who might recognize she looked orgasmic was one Ash Thorndyke. She decided against that reminder.

But for just one moment, she was sufficiently distracted from her food to notice the hands wrapped around *his* sandwich. His fingers were blunt, the nails clipped with precision. They were clearly strong hands; what was not so apparent was how sensitive those same hands were.

But Melina knew.

To head off any more disturbing memories, she smiled at him brightly. "So, what are you doing here, if you're not kidnapping me for ransom?"

"Could we have this conversation later?" His gold-flecked eyes narrowed as he darted a glance around the dining area. He looked nervous and off center.

"I'd like to have it now. Explain yourself, please." She took another rapturous bite.

"I overheard some people at the party. I thought you were in danger."

Another paranoid man? Melina's life had been so distorted by her father's obsessive fear that it was a disappointment to find out that Ash was cut from the same cloth. His fears did not concern her in the least. She swallowed and chased with vanilla shake. "What people? What were you doing at the party? What kind of danger?"

"You don't sound especially concerned."

"If I flew apart every time someone worried about me, I'd have three ulcers now. Then I would not be able to enjoy this cheeseburger."

"You won't enjoy it anyway if it gets any colder."

He was right. She ate another bite, dragged two fries through catsup, ate another bite of hamburger. Ash, she noticed, was barely touching his meal.

"What people?" she pressed, determined to ferret out what he was actually up to. "My father's security people?"

"Yes."

"You heard my father tell his security people to lock me up and that made you think I was in danger? Don't you think that's overreacting?"

"Do they routinely lock you up?"

"You don't read many fairy tales, do you? Princesses are *always* locked up." She feigned casual indifference, finishing her hamburger. Then she started on the fish fillet sandwich and the chocolate milk shake she'd also insisted on sampling. The fish was crispy and the milk shake sweet and thick. She sighed with pleasure. She couldn't wait for breakfast. Eggs and hash browns, maybe, at a greasy spoon. Then, for lunch, pizza. A meat-lover's pizza. And for dinner tomorrow, tacos and burritos. Or maybe fried chicken.

Life was good. Very good.

She finished her food. Ash had only picked at his. She'd studied him carefully. Funny what tricks the mind could play with memory in only a few short months. Before, in London, he'd always seemed so worldly, so mature, so versed in life. Tonight, he looked younger, troubled, as if he were adrift in a current he couldn't navigate. She found she liked him at this disadvantage; it made him seem vulnerable. It made her feel strong.

"There's more, isn't there?" she asked.

He looked at her intently, the way he had sometimes after they made love. Rather, after they had sex. Clearly, there had been no lovemaking. That had been her delusion.

"You're a grown woman," he said quietly. "Why

do you keep running away? Why not just leave? Permanently.''

She had noticed in looking around that average Americans cleaned up after themselves, wadding up their paper wrappers and stuffing everything back into the sacks. She busied herself doing the same.

''What kind of danger?'' she asked, to keep him from pursuing his own questions. ''What else did you hear?''

He snatched their bags from the table and stood. ''Let's get out of here.''

''I like it here.''

''Well, I don't. And I have the car keys.''

She smiled. ''No, you don't.''

His eyes grew dark and troubled. ''No. I don't. But neither do you.''

She stood and walked toward the door with him. As they exited, she looked up at him sweetly and said, ''I watched what you did when you hot-wired the car. I think I could do it, too.''

He made tiny slits of his eyes and jabbed one of his blunt fingers into her chest. ''Don't even think about it.''

She merely smiled. She liked distressing him. She liked the little sizzle of danger that pinged through her when his fingertip met her chest.

''I mean it, princess. A night in the pokey might sound like a lark, but it could be the least of your problems.''

''Oh?''

"Some people wouldn't mind shooting a car thief."

They were walking away from the restaurant, away from the sports car they'd driven up in. "I see. Like horse thieves."

"Yeah. Like horse thieves."

"We're going the wrong way," she pointed out.

"No, we're not."

They made their way to the darkest part of the parking lot, beside a massive discount store.

"Are we shopping for a new car?" she asked.

"You're sharp, princess."

"I like that one." She pointed to another convertible with sleek, sporty lines.

"This time I pick."

He chose a boring sedan with faded brown paint. It had a canvas bag of knitting in the passenger's seat and an array of straw hats in the back seat.

"We shouldn't take her knitting," Melina said.

"She'll get it back before she can count the stitches in the next row."

The car rumbled to life when he hot-wired it, and they headed out of the parking lot.

Melina reached in back for one of the straw hats, a rolled-brim number with an orange-and-lime band. It didn't fit. "I guess that's why we're leaving the other one. So its owner can get it back soon." She didn't bother to hide the sarcasm in her voice.

He said nothing.

They drove through the traffic, beyond the neon, into the darkness that soon led them to the coastal highway. Moonlight glittered off the restless Pacific. Melina rolled down the car window to let the sound of the surf break the silence.

"Why'd you have to lie?"

His question came out of nowhere, but she knew what he meant. Why had she pretended to be someone she wasn't when they'd met in London? She wished she could have seen his eyes when he asked. Was there hurt? Anger? Or just idle curiosity? Melina didn't know how to answer his question truthfully. Three months ago she would have been happy to confide in Ash. But she knew better than to trust him now.

She decided on another lie. "It was just a game."

"Who won?"

She didn't know how to answer that, either. He was the one who'd walked away, so some might call him the winner.

But she knew better. Their…liaison had been much more than a game, and in about six months, she'd have the evidence to prove that. "Why, I did."

SWEET IDA'S TEAROOM stayed open late that night, to accommodate the Hope Springs high-schoolers finishing up their prom dates. Granted, most of them ended the evening at Confederate Cove with a flask of vodka, a carton of orange juice and steamed-up windows. But Sweet Ida's was a tradition, too.

Ida Monroe had been staying open late on prom night for longer than any of these young 'uns had been alive and she expected to keep up the tradition as long as she still had anything to say about it.

Ida perched on her stool behind the counter, smiling fondly at the half-dozen youngsters attempting to look and act grown-up. She knew them all by name, remembered each and every one of them in diapers. Ida loved prom night.

There was Honey Lou Weidemann, looking like Scarlet O'Hara about to fall off her platform shoes. And Richie Holcomb, who didn't know what to do with the tails on his cutaway when he sat. Stacy Tillman, the sheriff's daughter, elegant as a model. And Winnie Wickerstaff, poured into something that ought to be illegal for underage girls. All of them sipping tea or coffee and nibbling on pastries and giggling over the night's activities.

Ida was content to sit and watch.

Finally most of the couples paid up and left. She was down to one lingering couple, and preparing to lock up after they left, when the front door of the tearoom opened to admit a couple who weren't dressed in formal wear. Maddie Sheffer and Leon Betton wore the uniforms of emergency medical technicians. They looked wrung-out.

"Thank goodness you're still open," Maddie said. She sounded as worn-out as she looked. "If we don't get some coffee, they might have to come haul *us* down to County General."

"Bad night?" Ida was already pouring the last of her coffee for them.

"Could've been worse, I suppose," Leon said, taking the cup she brought and sprinkling in some sugar. "Didn't lose anybody."

"Yet," Maddie added.

Ida stood beside the third chair at their table. "What happened?"

"Tood Grunkemeier. You know Tood?"

Ida's breathing grew shallow. "What's wrong with Tood?"

"Massive heart attack. He's lucky to be alive."

Leon shook his head. "He might not make it till morning. Seems sadder, somehow, him not having anybody."

Maddie rubbed her eyes, a weary gesture. "When we were hooking him up to the heart monitor, he said, 'Don't bother. Ain't nobody going to care one way or another.'"

"That really choked me up," Leon said.

Ida felt her own heartbeat going haywire on her. She clutched the back of the little white metal chair. The room seemed to swim around her. Tood Grunkemeier, not expected to live.

"Ida, you okay?"

She tried to reply, but the words of reassurance wouldn't come. Maddie reached for her and guided her into the seat.

"Sorry if we gave you a start."

Ida nodded, realizing there were tears in her eyes. Tood Grunkemeier lay in a hospital a few miles away, his sad old heart giving out. Thinking nobody cared. What if he died without ever knowing the secret she'd kept all these years?

It was almost more than she could bear.

CHAPTER THREE

"WHERE ARE WE going to sleep?"

Ash hadn't been thinking of sleeping. He'd been thinking of putting as much distance as possible between him and anyone who might have it in mind to harm Melina. He also had no cash to pay for sleeping anywhere and his credit cards would create a trail leading straight to him—and Melina.

"In the car," he replied.

"*This* car?"

"What's wrong with this car?"

"I get the back seat," she said.

Figures. "I could look for a van."

"Something in red, maybe? Brown isn't my color."

"Of course not. I wasn't thinking."

Now he was. Now he could see the impish quality he'd been drawn to three months earlier for what it really was. She was spoiled, that was all.

"Aren't you getting sleepy?"

"It's not even midnight."

"That's right. You're a night owl."

A spark touched off in him. She'd been a morning person. She'd laughingly suggested they compromise and spend the entire day in bed, getting up from ten at night until ten in the morning to accommodate them both. They'd spent the day in bed, all right, but they hadn't slept.

"Are we going to get different clothes? Something to sleep in? Something for tomorrow?"

"Of course," he said.

"When?"

How could a grown woman sound so guileless and so eager? She was good, no question of that. A shame she was so rich; she could be quite a success on stage.

"Soon," he said brusquely.

But the truth was, he didn't know where or when or how. He didn't know what to do with her or who to trust. Worst of all, he was damned if he even knew why any of it mattered. This was her problem, not his.

They passed through a little town that promised to be the last one for quite a few miles. Ash slowed down, studying carefully the narrow, quiet streets, the tidy little houses with their spring gardens that seemed to speak of trust and safety.

"Are we shopping for a new car again?" she whispered.

He wished she wouldn't whisper. It stirred him in spite of himself. It reminded him of other whispers, other sighs, other nights alone with her in the dark.

When he didn't reply, she asked, "Are you casing the joint?"

He was getting grumpier by the minute and he knew it. Her lack of concern for the gravity of their situation wasn't helping. "You watch too much television."

"I know." She sounded pleased with herself.

He was looking for something with legroom, as well as something old enough that it could easily be hot-wired. He found a comfortable-looking van parked in the dark corner of a lot surrounding a stucco condominium. He left the brown sedan in its place and took some satisfaction in knowing that the knitting would be returned to its owner very soon. Ash didn't like stealing cars; the last one he'd stolen was when he was fifteen, and his father had grounded him for six months. Cars were a necessity and stealing them was for emergency situations only. Bram Thorndyke had been clear on the matter of stolen cars.

Diamonds and rubies, however, were sheer extravagance and therefore fair game.

On the way out of town, Ash spotted a little boutique. He parked in a narrow alley behind the row of pastel-colored shops, hemmed in by a brick wall at the edge of a municipal golf course. "Wait here."

She was already getting out of the van. "I'm not letting you pick out my clothes."

He pinned her between the open door and the van. "Yes, you are."

She stared at him with those dark eyes and he knew he'd be undone if he didn't back off. He could almost feel her breath, sweet with chocolate milk shake but no longer cool. Warm. Hot, even. He grew warm himself in the chill northern California night air.

"What if it doesn't fit?"

"It will fit."

And that mouth. Soft. Full. Wide. Trouble any way you looked at it.

"What if I hate it?"

"You'll get over it."

She looked ready to pout. He supposed that worked a lot when a person was rich and spoiled. "I want to go with you. I've never been on a break-and-enter before."

"And you aren't coming now."

"I can help."

She was wheedling. He was dismayed to find he was susceptible to it. He had to toughen up. "You'll be in the way. I know what I'm doing. You don't. It's too dangerous."

"Are you a professional criminal?"

"In the car, princess."

She studied him carefully, but he remained unyielding. She finally relented and backed into the car. As he walked toward the dark back entrance of the shop, she hissed out the window, "Size six. Jeans. I want blue jeans. Boot cut. And sunglasses. Ash, do you hear me?"

He turned and glared at her. "I hear you. Barney Fife hears you. Every neighbor for miles around hears you. Could you please pretend you have some common sense? Just for the next twenty minutes."

She raised the window and turned away from him, nose in the air. She had the perfect nose for it, too. Narrow, straight, very aristocratic. Along with a very stubborn chin.

Accessing the shop was easy. He did harder jobs every day. But he didn't like doing it. He wasn't accustomed to stealing from people who probably couldn't afford it. He told himself the shop had insurance and the insurance company could certainly afford it. But he also saw the three snapshots taped to the side of the cash register—an attractively plump middle-aged woman and two younger women just past their teens who had to be her daughters. This was who he was robbing, for the sake of a spoiled heiress.

He didn't like himself.

He loaded two shopping bags. One for him, with a limited selection of unremarkable khakis and polo shirts. Then he started on a second shopping bag. He got jeans, size six. Underwear, cotton and serviceable, size selected by memory. Unwelcome, distracting memory. He selected a very ugly T-shirt with gold sequins in the design of a cat, a flouncy nightshirt in pink and yellow, a floppy-brimmed straw hat and a pair of gaudy sunglasses.

To heck with her if she didn't like his choices.

He made it out of the shop and back to the red van—its selection had been based purely on availability and had nothing to do with Melina's color preferences—without incident. Melina took the bags and began rummaging through them as he stuck conscientiously to the speed limit all the way out of the sleeping, unsuspecting town.

"If you're not a professional, you certainly have

an interesting hobby," Melina said, pulling clothing out of a bag.

The judgment in her tone raised his hackles. "I am not a two-bit thief," he said, aiming for a tone that wasn't defensive. He knew he'd failed.

"Aren't you?"

"No, I certainly am not."

"You're right! You're a very classy thief. This is wonderful. Blue jeans! Movie star sunglasses! A gold-sequined T-shirt! You can steal for me anytime, Ash."

"You were supposed to hate my choices."

"That's because you look at me and see a princess. I'm really just a suburban housewife in disguise." He heard the click of her seat belt and looked to see her clambering over the seat into the back of the van.

He glanced over at her. "What are you doing?"

"Changing clothes." She winked at him. "You're welcome to look, but we'll probably be better off if you keep your eye on that big truck heading this way."

He quickly focused front and center. The road ahead was as deserted as it had been moments before. But that was okay. He really had no desire whatsoever to watch her change clothes.

Well, maybe a tiny bit of interest. Idle curiosity. She wasn't exactly a *Baywatch* babe. A little on the skinny side, actually. Little-boy hips and lots of rib action. Breasts—

Okay. Eyes *and* mind on the road.

"If you aren't a two-bit thief," she said, her voice

momentarily muffled by clothing going over her head, "I don't suppose you'd like to explain how it is you know how to hot-wire cars and break into clothing stores without even turning a hair."

He thought of trying to explain his childhood, his upbringing, his family. Not possible. You see, we've been thieves and con men for generations. But we only steal from the rich. Probably direct descendants of Robin Hood, don't you see. With a slight variation. We might steal from the rich, but we definitely do not give to the poor. "No, I would not."

"Is it a compulsion? An addiction of some kind. I'll bet they have a twelve-step group for it. You could get help. Lead a normal, productive life."

"The only way I'm going to lead a normal life is to figure out what to do with you."

"I'm not your problem, Ash Thorndyke. I am perfectly capable of taking care of myself." The sound of delighted laughter floated up from the back of the van. "And I am perfectly stunning in my new wardrobe."

She climbed back into the front seat and Ash noted that she did indeed look stunning. The jeans fit like second skin—had she filled out in the last three months, or was his memory that faulty? The T-shirt looked campy and fun, the 1950s sunglasses went perfectly with her gamine-like grin.

"Mel's the name," she said, adopting a familiar midwestern twang.

It was the same voice she'd used in London.

"We've met," he said dryly.

Her enthusiasm wilted. "So we have."

She lapsed into silence. They drove along the coast until he couldn't stand the silence any longer. He saw a trail off the highway and followed it to a secluded clearing overlooking the ocean.

"Welcome to the Holiday Inn," he said gruffly.

She scrambled into the back of the van again, making a little nest of her slightly bedraggled evening gown. For a pampered heiress, she looked not the least perturbed to be preparing for a night on the hard floor of a van in the middle of nowhere. She looked as cheerful as a kid on an adventure.

She'd used that to reel him in before, too.

He yanked off his tie and pitched it onto the floor behind the driver's seat. The cummerbund followed, then his tuxedo jacket, cuff links, watch and shoes. He contemplated the gym shorts and T-shirt from the boutique and decided there was no way he was disrobing with her in the vehicle.

"Would you roll down the windows?" Her voice had a dreamy quality to it. "So we can hear the surf?"

His first impulse was to say no simply for the sake of saying no. Then he realized there was no good reason to be hard-nosed with her. After all, this had been his decision. Nobody'd said he had to bring her with him. As soon as he'd figured out that the deal he'd agreed to was not what he'd thought, he could've walked.

But no. He'd had to play hero. Rescue the woman in jeopardy.

He'd had no idea what he'd been getting himself into.

Thoroughly disgruntled with the way his day had gone, he rolled down the windows so Her Highness could hear the surf, crawled into the back, selected the corner farthest from Melina and stretched out on his back.

"Good night," she whispered.

His reluctant response was gruff.

The full moon spilled in through the front windows. The sound of the surf was mesmerizing, stirring a matching rhythm in his pulse—a little wild, a little fast. And Melina Somerset—his Mel Summersby—lay two feet away.

She was fun to kiss, he remembered that in sharpest detail. She could make him laugh right in the middle of a kiss, then keep right on going without spoiling the rhythm of their lovemaking. She liked to tickle him awake in the mornings when he still had lots of sleeping to do—little tickles, feathery tickles that made him smile.

He'd never laughed and smiled so much in his life as he had those two weeks with her.

And it had all been a lie.

THE OCEAN CALLED to Melina, its sharp scent and steady roar beckoning. She lay curled in the back of the van, head resting on her silky pillow, and thought of slipping out of the van and walking along the rocky shore she'd glimpsed through the trees. Lying here in the dark with no one to talk to wasn't very relaxing.

She kept thinking of her father and his anguish when he discovered she was gone again, and how much worse it would get when he realized he wasn't going to find her this time. She kept thinking of the new life she was going to make for herself. Her thoughts were a whirlwind of guilt and excitement. And, she had to admit, a little anxiety.

A walk along the coast, surely, would quiet those troublesome thoughts.

She doubted she could get away without waking Ash. Every time she rustled around, his deep breathing stopped and she could almost sense him tensing, waiting to see what she had in mind. He slept like a cat, with one ear alert.

What kind of man could sleep that way? What kind of man knew how to hot-wire cars and break into dress shops?

What kind of man made love to you, then took off in the night without a word of explanation?

Who was Ash Thorndyke, anyway?

That mystery had haunted her for months.

He'd been a mystery from the moment they met. But she'd been naive enough to find that intriguing, alluring, downright exciting.

They met on her first day in London. Despite the constant cold drizzle, Melina had been almost giddy with her freedom. She had managed to elude her father's people through northern France, then taken the Chunnel to England. Surely in a city the size of London, one could simply vanish.

She had next-to-no money and even less experience. All she possessed was the small valise she'd had at her side when she escaped, containing a few changes of clothes, some toiletries—and her mother's diamond wedding choker. She was standing at the entrance to the Underground, London's subway, studying the map that was a confusing maze of colored lines. She had the address of a pawnshop and no clue how to translate the map on the wall.

The voice over her shoulder was friendly and American. "You look like a damsel in distress."

The voice alone would have been enough to make her fall in love with him instantly. An American. She could barely catch her breath as she turned toward the voice.

"Yes, I guess you could say that's what I am."

"Ash Thorndyke." He'd tipped forward slightly, almost an old-fashioned bow. "At your service."

His face was kind and his dress impeccable. And his gold-on-green eyes held just a hint of the rogue in them. Oh, yes, she might just be in love. "Mr. Thorndyke, how very kind of you."

He moved a little closer then, looking over her shoulder at the address she'd written on a slip of paper. He was tall, too. An all-American hero. No doubt about it. Melina's heart tripped wildly.

"A pawnshop, Miss…?"

Melina opened her mouth, then clamped it shut. Oh, my. What now? The last thing she'd counted on was meeting someone.

Not someone.

Her all-American hero.

How could you be incognito when your all-American hero walked up?

"Mel," she said. "S-Summersby. Mel Summersby."

"Mel?"

"Mmm, yes. Melinda, actually. But I'm much more the Mel type, don't you think?"

His eyes had roamed her up and down. Melina felt the caress of his eyes clear from her toes to the roots of her hair.

"Mel suits you quite well," he said, smiling. "What doesn't suit you is a pawnshop, I'm afraid."

Melina felt herself flush. She lowered her eyes. "Oh. Well, I have this…item. And I'd very much like to be rid of it." She had to think fast. Wouldn't do to have him think of her as destitute. "Bad associations, you know."

"An…item?"

"A bauble, really. It would… It would give me satisfaction to simply be rid of it."

"Well, then, we're off to the pawnshop."

"Oh, really, I couldn't—"

"Nonsense. I wouldn't dream of sending you off to such a place on your own." He took her by the elbow. "But please, allow me to treat us to a taxi-cab."

"Oh, no, please. I'd really like to ride the tube. I've never ridden the tube, you see. It's part of the adventure, don't you think?"

"Adventure is precisely the word I might have chosen, Mel Summersby."

He'd guided her through the maze of the London underground, teaching her the etiquette of standing to the left on the long, steep escalators so those in a rush could pass on the right. He taught her how to hang on to a pole and plant her feet before the train left the station so she didn't lurch against others or land on her backside when the train screeched to a halt at the next station. He explained the map to her during the ride and signaled her when it was time to get off.

By the time they reached their destination, Melina was quite hopelessly in love with American Ash Thorndyke.

At his urging, she allowed him to guide her to a different establishment than the one whose name she had been drawn to in the telephone listings. The narrow lane, it turned out, was awash in pawnshops, and Melina felt a thrill at the slightly shabby row of businesses.

She also allowed her new American friend to handle the bartering with the gentleman who operated the place. The negotiations sounded quite civil to Melina, but she could tell that Ash was happier than the elderly shopkeeper when the bargaining was completed.

Melina, too, was quite happy with the neat stack of pound notes he pressed upon her at the end of the transaction.

"Thank you ever so much," she said. "I would have been hopeless without your help."

"My pleasure. It would also be my pleasure to have your company for dinner."

"Oh, that would be lovely. My treat." She saw him

ready to protest. "At a pub. Oh, please say yes. I've never been in a pub, you see."

They found an authentic-looking pub in the neighborhood and ducked in out of the drizzle, which was growing colder still as the sun sank out of sight behind the dingy gray buildings. The bar was dark, infused with the mingled scents of ale and damp umbrellas. They chose a table near the fireplace, where the embers glowed and flickered. He ordered two pints of dark ale and she chose their dinner—shepherd's pie.

"Tell me this, Mel Summersby," he said, touching the rim of his mug to hers when the lukewarm ale arrived. "How does it happen that a young woman who's never ridden the tube or eaten in a pub is running around London alone looking for pawnshops?"

She sniffed the ale and took a tentative sip, buying time. She had the foolish urge to confide in him. He had the face of an honest man, and he had certainly proven himself trustworthy. But she was clearheaded enough to know that she had to be careful. The wrong word from her and she could wind up back with her father, confined to a life that was nothing more than a prison.

Besides, she wanted to know if a man like Ash Thorndyke could possibly like her for herself, and not because she was heiress to one of the world's largest fortunes. She tamped down the bitter thought that her father would probably attach strings to his will, keeping his ironclad hold on her even from the grave. She would probably inherit only if she took a vow to be a lonely, celibate recluse in Siberia for the rest of her life.

No, she couldn't tell Ash the truth yet. She wanted nothing to spoil this time, however short it might be.

"I'm a student," she said. "An American graduate student. I was to visit a…a friend. But when I arrived, things had…changed."

"Ah. The friend who made the gift of the item that's financing our dinner tonight."

"That's right."

She smiled brightly, looking for some sign that he didn't believe her story. Shadows fell across his golden skin, highlighting his full lips. Raindrops glistened on his slightly rumpled hair. He sat back casually in his seat, loose-limbed and at ease. A man with the confidence to be in command of the world.

She wondered if there was a way to make a man like that fall in love with a woman who knew precious little about the world.

"So I'm on my own, you see. I should probably go home…to…Omaha."

"It seems a shame to go without seeing some of the sights."

"That's precisely what I was thinking. Do you…do you think I can manage it? On my own?"

He shook his head. "I don't think so."

"You don't?"

"I think you need a guide. Someone who knows his way around."

She longed to believe there was a hint of innuendo

in what he said. She tried her best to find an easy, flirty tone. "Where would I find someone like that?"

"I'll give it some thought while we eat," he said with a faint smile.

They sat in the soft glow from the fireplace, ate foul-tasting shepherd's pie and drank a little too much of the dark, bitter ale. He told her about his family back home in the States—a kindly grandfather and an ailing father. Without going into the boring details, he mentioned their investment business, which had brought him to London. And she made up a lovely family, in which she was the oldest of three children living in a large two-story house. Her brother, sister, mother and father looked remarkably like the family in *Father Knows Best.*

She didn't make that comparison aloud.

She told him she was studying classical literature in graduate school, the only subject she'd managed to learn much about in the years she'd flitted from one convent school to the next. She confessed that she'd never driven a car before she remembered that revelation might label her as unusual in America.

And when he learned that she didn't yet have a place to stay, he took her to the home of a friend who operated a bed-and-breakfast out of her home. Mrs. Wentwhistle was a silver-haired lady with a hitch in her walk, and her home was a narrow, three-story Victorian in Parsons Green. It was three flights up to the refurbished attic.

Ash insisted on carrying up her valise for her.

"It's a good thing you're not staying," she said as he ducked the sloping ceiling.

He placed her valise in the chair beside the narrow bed tucked beneath a dormer window. "Is it?"

He came back to stand beside her now. He seemed very close. The room was small and he was not.

"Yes," she said, her voice barely audible. "It's sized for me, not you."

"That's true."

He looked down at her, his eyes searching her face. She imagined that he knew all her secrets.

"I'll join you for breakfast, if that's okay."

"That would be lovely."

He stepped back. "Then, until morning..."

He was leaving. She thought she wouldn't be able to bear it if he left without touching her. "You really should kiss me good-night."

"I should?"

"Oh, yes."

He stepped in her direction. Their bodies brushed. She felt the heat, caught the scent of him—faintly evergreen, like the cypress trees that had dotted the landscape at her favorite convent the year she'd turned sixteen.

"What kind of kiss?" he asked softly.

"What kind?"

He touched her hair where it trickled against her cheek. "A peck-on-the-cheek kiss? A brush-of-the-lips kiss? A lingering, promise-her-anything kiss?"

She closed her eyes as he spoke, contemplated each alternative, mesmerized by his deep, velvet voice and the images he conjured. "Oh. Well. What about the blistering, ravaging, curl-her-toes kiss? You forgot about that one."

He chuckled, deep in his chest. "I think, with Mrs. Wentwhistle waiting downstairs, I'd better play it safe."

Then he drew her into his arms and brushed his lips against hers. His were soft and they tasted of ale. He didn't let her go.

"That's really quite unsatisfactory," she said.

He took her face in both his hands. He whispered against her lips. "I know."

"You could try the lingering variety."

"Maybe I should."

"Oh, yes."

He pressed his lips to hers again, gentle but insistent. She felt all of him pressed to her, as well. He was lean and hard and his hands cupped her head as he tilted her face to deepen the kiss. His tongue touched hers lightly, the promise of more, just as he had said. Had he not been holding her, Melina felt certain she would have melted right into the floor.

"Will that do until morning?" he murmured.

"Not in the least."

"Then it must have been satisfactory."

"Quite."

She hung over the railing and watched as he circled down the stairs to the attic door. "But I'm holding out for blistering."

"Let me guess. You've never done blistering."

She smiled. So did he. The air between them crackled.

"You know me too well, Ash Thorndyke."

"Let me assure you, Melinda Summersby, as your guide to London, you won't leave for Omaha without experiencing all the city has to offer..."

He had delivered on both his promises—both the spoken one and the one in his kiss. By day, he showed her everything that made London charming, unique and memorable. They toured the Tower, rode double-decker buses, marveled over an exhibit of Queen Victoria's clothing, cried over *Romeo and Juliet* at the reconstructed Globe Theatre. The changing of the guard, the tolling of Big Ben, the swarming pigeons at Trafalgar Square.

London by day was a magical adventure.

London by night was every woman's fantasy of how she should be introduced to the ways of love.

Ash became her first lover and, she had been certain at the time, would be her only lover. He was tender and passionate, considerate and thrilling. He taught her everything only guessed at or dreamed of by a girl raised in convents. Ash Thorndyke was the man she'd been hoping for all her life.

When he left her at Mrs. Wentwhistle's on their fourteenth night, she perched on her knees and watched from the dormer window as he headed for the tube. She loved his loose, easy walk. She loved everything about him.

"I love you," she whispered to his retreating figure.

The need to tell him so was becoming an impatient ache. But she knew she couldn't tell him how she felt until she told him the truth about herself. She made up her mind as he turned the corner. She would tell him tomorrow. Then there would be nothing in the way of their love.

Except that he didn't come the next day.

When she phoned his hotel, he was gone. Checked out. Only then did she realize she knew nothing about him, not the town he was from, not the name of his family business. Nothing.

Except that he was not the man she'd believed him to be.

He was, instead, a rogue. The kind of man who could cavalierly seduce an innocent woman and walk away with no explanation.

Her heart was broken. Bereft, she was almost grateful when her father's men found her a day later.

On the hard floor of the van, Melina tried not to dwell on the way she'd felt when they made love, on the way she'd trusted him, on the way he'd betrayed her. What irony that he should be her rescuer.

Rescuer he might be, but he was no hero. He'd proven that and she would do well to remember it.

But she would find a hero. America was full of them. Yes, somewhere in this country she would find the perfect all-American town, and the perfect all-American hero to help raise the baby she now carried. A father for her baby.

And no matter what the biological facts were, Ash Thorndyke would not be that man.

CHAPTER FOUR

THE TWO MEN with military-issue haircuts and non-descript charcoal-gray suits arrived at the rendezvous point forty-five minutes early.

"Thorndyke must be good," said the one who was built like a prizefighter gone to pot. "Not a peep of a problem at the party."

"He's good all right." That from the one who looked like a college professor, thin and bespectacled. "Oughta be. Runs in the blood."

"Yeah. What's his old man in for, anyway?"

The professor studied the tips of his shoes, which were marred by pinpoint specks of dirt. "Counterfeiting. Ran a big real estate flimflam in Chicago, the whole thing backed by play money. Very slick. Hell, the whole family oughta be locked up. They've handled more hot ice than the first guys to climb the North Pole."

"Didn't nobody *climb* the North Pole, dumb ass."

"Yeah, well, you catch my drift."

They waited, each contemplating how he would spend the money he would receive when the Somerset woman was handed over to the guys at the Tokyo airport. They didn't know what would happen to her then and it really didn't matter. They didn't even know the identity of the nutcase who wanted something to hold over Somerset's head.

"You still planning to invest your take?" The professor glanced at his watch.

"Gotta plan for retirement." The boxer tossed a cigarette butt onto the ground and tamped it out with his shoe.

"A waste of good dough, I say. What's the likelihood either one of us'll make it to a ripe old age?"

"Like spending it on some bimbo's a wise use of resources?"

"She ain't a bimbo," the professor said, his carefully correct speech falling away as easily as the shine on his shoes. "She's classy. A dancer."

The boxer's chuckle was gravelly. "Yeah, at Tony G's in the Bronx. Some class."

"Listen, pal—"

"Aw, never mind. You spend your way, I'll spend mine. We're gonna have too much to squabble over."

"Ain't that the truth."

At the appointed time, Thorndyke didn't show. Not a huge cause for alarm. Traffic could account for that.

Fifteen minutes passed. Then thirty. Still a no-show.

The professor and his pal exchanged uneasy glances. Neither of them relished the idea of explaining why they didn't have the woman.

They waited two hours. The professor had used up every profanity he knew and his pal had smoked every cigarette in the pack in his pocket.

The professor spit out one more string of words

that his mother would have slapped him silly for using. "He ain't coming, is he?"

"I think that's a safe bet."

"We gotta find him."

"The hell with him. We gotta find the girl."

"*Then* we gotta find him. 'Cause you're gonna ruin that pretty face of his."

"That's right, professor."

ASH AWOKE the next morning to find the van empty except for her discarded evening gown and the ravaged shopping bags.

He leaped up, head still groggy, eyes gritty, and stumbled out of the van. She'd been helpless enough in London; how could she survive on a busy California highway with unknown enemies on her trail?

She could be dead already, for God's sake.

He saw her sitting on the rocky cliff overlooking the Pacific Ocean, legs hugged to her chest, chin on her knees. Wind off the water played with her hair, tossing it around her shoulders. The sun was already high. She wore the funny sunglasses he'd stolen for her, but her feet were bare and the hat dangled from the tips of the fingers curled around her legs.

She looked like a magazine ad for the Eccentric Traveler.

At that moment, he would have followed her anywhere. She was more appealing than he remembered, more of a woman, sensuous without trying. And he was so glad to see her, he could have scooped her into his arms and covered her face in grateful kisses.

He took a moment to remember that this maddening woman was the one who'd first stirred in him the notion of going straight, of settling down and leading a normal life. The whisper of that idea had sent him scurrying for cover. He'd thought that if he ran away from the irresistibly charming American student, the crazy notion would leave him. Instead, the idea had taken hold, kept shaking him to the roots of his hair. And all the time, she'd been deceiving him.

What a joke. The con man conned.

"Do you suppose you could steal me some makeup today?" she said without turning, without moving, without any other indication that she'd been aware of his presence.

"We're not going to steal anything else today." His voice was still jagged with unfinished sleep.

"We're not? How boring. I was growing fond of a life of crime."

She was thoroughly aggravating.

"We're not keeping these cars," he said pointedly. "We're borrowing them."

"That's right. And my jeans? My sunglasses?"

"We'll let your daddy pay them back."

She stood in one fluid motion, unfolding with the lazy ease of a cat. Unbidden came the image of the way she moved beneath him, effortless, liquid, like no other woman he'd known. He hadn't been able to forget her. He hadn't wanted anyone since.

"I'm never going to see my father again," she said with quiet intensity.

"Don't be ridiculous."

She strode across the rocks as deftly as a bird on a ledge and faced him defiantly. "I'm not going back there. If that's your plan, we can part ways right now."

"I'm not letting you go off on your own." And why not? he wondered. Wouldn't that be the simplest thing? The sanest thing?

"You're not *letting* me?" He saw her emotions rising, saw her dark eyes go stormy with rage. "Mr. Thorndyke, you've got nothing to say about it!"

"You're in danger. Someone hired me to kidnap you. You think they're going to let you waltz around the country without—"

"I'm not in danger! And you don't— What did you say?"

"I said someone hired me to kidnap you."

She cocked her head to one side—as charmingly as a 1940s screen starlet—and stared at him. "Who?"

"I don't know."

Now she tossed her head in another classic starlet move. This time the fiery vixen. She couldn't have done it any better if she'd been personally trained by Bette Davis. "So when do you deliver the goods?"

Ash realized his heart was thumping, his fingertips aching with the urge to sift through her soft, thick hair. He remembered the feel of it with stark clarity. "I…" What had she said? Oh, yeah. Delivering the goods. "I'm not. I… I realized… I thought it was for your own good. That's the only reason I was in on it."

"Well, I can certainly understand why you'd think that."

"They said it was your father's idea. To keep a closer eye on you." He thought her gaze hardened at that. "Then I overheard the plan and realized you were in danger. Possibly." He hesitated. This wasn't the kind of thing you wanted to say to anybody, but it had to be said. "Your father wouldn't... You just said you don't want to go back to him. Is there a reason? Would he harm you?"

"That's so ridiculous it doesn't even deserve an answer."

"You're positive?"

She stalked off, leaving him staring for the moment at the spit and roar of the ocean. His heart raced out of control. He was on the rising edge of an adrenaline surge, the kind that he always rode through one of his capers.

He went after her.

She sat in the open side door of the van, putting on the little canvas shoes he'd brought her. They were red with big yellow silk ribbon, which she'd tied into a remarkable bow.

"You have impeccable taste," she said, holding up one narrow foot, pointing the toe and striking a pose. She had the legs of a dancer, muscular and taut.

She also had the nerves of the best burglars in the business. He'd just informed her that her life was in danger and that her father might be behind the plan to get rid of her, and she was striking poses and taking playful jabs at his taste. Amazing.

"I used to think I had good taste," he said. "Sometimes I wonder, princess. Come on. Let's get another car. We're too close to home to hang on to this one much longer."

"And breakfast? I woke up this morning with a hankering—that's an Americanism, isn't it—for ham and eggs. With pancakes and syrup. And maybe toast and grape jelly."

They ditched the van in a wooded area just past a collection of shops, then walked back there for breakfast. Ash ordered a bagel. Melina ordered everything she'd mentioned earlier, along with a large orange juice. She probably weighed all of a hundred and five pounds. Yet she'd outeaten him the night before and now again this morning. She'd done the same thing in London. She ate the same way she soaked up life, like a starving person invited to a banquet.

Why was this happening to him? he wondered. He'd managed, using every bit of willpower he possessed, to walk away from her once. Could he manage it again?

"We need a plan," he said. That's it. Focus on logic, on reason. "If you're sure we can trust him, I suggest we call your father and—"

"Please." She held up her hand to stop him. "I'd really rather not walk out on my food."

"Why won't you at least—"

"Besides, *I* have a plan."

"I can hardly wait."

She smiled. Her lips were sticky with maple syrup.

She licked them with obvious relish. The tip of her tongue caught his eye and sent his pulse galloping.

"You're not paying attention," she said.

He tried to forget about her sweet lips, her teasing tongue. "Yes, I am."

She grunted her disbelief. "I was saying I want us to tour the countryside."

"Tour the— Melina, people want to kidnap you."

"My father has been telling me that all my life. Maybe it's even true. But I don't care." She dunked a forkful of pancake in syrup, drowning it. "I want to see Hollywood—the big sign, you know. And the desert. Las Vegas—maybe I could be a showgirl, do you think? I'm thin and I have long legs."

"You're five-two. You don't have long legs." He really didn't need a conversation about her legs. He remembered them too well as it was.

"I don't?" She popped the bite of pancake into her mouth and glanced down at her legs. "I always thought I did. Maybe it was being around Mother Aloysius. She was very short, I suppose. Under five feet. I always felt statuesque around Mother Aloysius."

"Well, you aren't. You're petite. You're no match for the kind of men who—"

"Okay, forget Las Vegas. But there's the Grand Canyon. And Texas. Do you suppose I could get a pair of hand-tooled boots? Now, if I had a pair of cowboy boots and a Stetson hat I would certainly be tall enough to—"

"Are you crazy? Look me straight in the eyes and

tell me you're not crazy." If not, she was at the very least making him crazy. Because he was falling for it—for *her*, God forbid—all over again.

She paused, put her sweetly pointed chin in her palm and looked at him with dark-fringed eyes. She didn't need makeup, stolen or otherwise.

"I'm not crazy," she said. "I'm just making up for lost time."

"Making up for lost time. You've had more advantages than ninety-nine point nine percent of the world and you want more. You are crazy...and spoiled!"

She tossed her fork into her syrup-logged plate with a dull splat. She stood and snatched her sunglasses and hat off the table. "You don't know the first thing about me."

"That's for sure! It's hard to get to know a mirage, *Mel*."

Her dark eyes snapped. "If I'm a mirage, what are you? Showing up in my life, disappearing, showing up again and snatching me right out from under the best security money can buy. Traipsing me down the California coast in stolen cars and pilfered—"

He slapped a twenty-dollar bill on the table, took her by the arm and directed her toward the door. "If you're trying to attract the highway patrol, you're doing a very good job," he said between clenched teeth as they exited the restaurant.

She kept silent but snatched her arm out of his grasp. When they were almost out of the parking lot, her gait slowed, and then she came to a complete halt as she stared into the woods.

"Oh, my," she said.

He followed her gaze. A black-and-silver Harley-Davidson was parked off the path, near a shed.

"Don't even think about it," he said.

"Oh, Ash." She turned her best coaxing gaze on him.

"I know. You've never been on a motorcycle before."

She smiled, all sign of her temper gone. Her emotions were as quick as summer lightning. "What fun."

The way she said it held all kinds of promise. Not knowing what visions she had in her mind, Ash suddenly had plenty of his own. Her thighs pressed to his hips, her small, pointed breasts nudging his back, her excited breath in his ear.

He heaved an exasperated sigh.

"Just for a few miles," she said.

"Mel, you don't understand. People and their Harleys—this is asking for trouble."

She pushed her sunglasses up and propped them on her head. "Ten miles. Five. Then we can trade it in for the most boring tan sedan you've ever seen. And we can make a plan. Whatever kind of plan you want."

"Then you'll call your father?"

"Not *that* plan. But any other plan."

Ash knew when he was being had. But he simply couldn't resist her.

He had to push the bike through the woods to another trail that led to the highway to avoid starting its engine close enough to attract the attention of the owner. And he was doing it, he reminded himself and her, on half a bagel and two cups of black coffee.

But when the Harley-Davidson roared to life and Melina curved her lithe body to his and linked her arms around his chest, Ash knew he would have done it a dozen times over, with an army of enraged Hells Angels behind him. They rode for twenty miles before his arousal subsided.

TOM SOMERSET STARED out the window of the room his daughter had vanished from sometime during the night. Mid-morning sun was burning the mist off the Golden Gate Bridge. The bay glistened a glorious blue. It was going to be a beautiful day in the city by the bay.

Tom fought dry heaves.

His daughter was gone. The only thing left in the world that mattered to him had vanished. He'd been through this before. He wasn't sure he could survive it again. That's why he'd insisted on bringing her to the United States with him. She hadn't been out of his sight since his men picked her up in London three months ago. He'd been in hell the entire time they'd searched for her. Because each time she disappeared—and it had happened three times before this—Tom was convinced it was a replay of that day fourteen years ago.

No, he told himself. *Not that. She's run away. That's all. You know that's all.*

He knew that was all because she'd warned him. The day before, in no uncertain terms, she'd told him he had to allow her to lead a normal life or she would find a way to escape.

This was his fault. The result of his excessive fear. He knew it. And he hated himself for what he'd done to her. But he didn't know what else to do.

Yes, she'd run away again. That was all.

He turned and looked around the room. Tom didn't know anything about decor, but he knew it was the kind of room that should have delighted any young woman. The high iron bed was covered with a fluffy rose-colored comforter and ruffled pillows. He could almost see his daughter at the dressing table, her long, dark hair shining in the sunlight that streamed through the bank of wall-to-wall windows. To him, the room looked like something from a fairy tale.

It's just another prison! Another in a long line of prisons!

Tom closed his eyes against the memory of Melina's angry accusation the afternoon before. She hadn't wanted to be here. She'd wanted to go to some museum, had wanted to wander around Haight-Ashbury, for God's sake. Her eyes had communicated her frustration.

And, as he had done for half her life, Tom Somerset had insisted that he knew what she needed far better than she knew herself.

And now she was gone.

And he had no one to blame but himself.

He couldn't help thinking about the camera crews

her arrival had attracted the day before. The whole world knew Melina Somerset was in San Francisco. And she was too naive to know how dangerous that could be.

But Tom wasn't. He remembered. He broke out in a cold sweat.

His men were combing the room, looking for clues, trying to piece together what had happened. His security chief, Poseti, looked as ashen-faced as Tom felt. Poseti was behaving like a pro, cool and detached, but Tom knew the man was distraught. And not just because Melina's disappearance was an affront to his professionalism. Poseti was loyal to a fault and he adored Melina. He would protect her with his life.

Poseti joined Tom at the window. "I think we can rule out kidnapping."

Tom let himself hope. "Can we?"

"There's no sign of a struggle. And neither of the men posted outside the door heard a sound all night."

Tom glanced at the half-filled valise on the bed. "But she didn't take her things. When she runs away, she always takes her things."

"I know. That's a concern. That, and the fact that she managed to get out of the house without detection."

"A professional could pull it off."

Poseti nodded grimly.

Tom closed his eyes.

"We'll find her, sir."

Poseti hadn't been with him fourteen years ago.

Maybe things would have been different if he'd had Poseti. That time, Tom had come home to a ransacked house, a place turned upside down and screaming to him of the horror his beloved wife and older daughter must have felt. He'd seen their torn clothes. He'd almost been able to feel their terror.

Thalia and Justine had never come home. Thank God Melina had been away for the day with schoolmates.

"Find her," Tom said. "Bring her home."

"I will, sir."

"And whoever did this…"

Poseti nodded. "I'll take care of it, sir."

Tom Somerset stood by the window for a long time, the memories of his long-dead wife and daughter eventually mingling with the fresher visions of the frustrated anger of the daughter he'd foolishly believed he could protect.

MELINA WAS DISAPPOINTED when she learned they were heading in the wrong direction to take in the wine country. But even she had to admit that they couldn't see everything in America in a few days, or even a few weeks.

"I can do without the wine country," she said, settling back in the seat of the old Chevrolet with which they'd replaced the Harley-Davidson. "Getting to Wichita, Kansas, is the most important thing."

"Wichita? What's in Wichita?"

The rusting Chevrolet smelled of tobacco and dogs. Melina liked that. She could almost picture the owner smoking a hand-carved pipe, his mutt hanging out the window, ears blowing in the wind.

"That's where I'm going to live." She pitched forward as the car almost came to a stop.

"You're going to live in Kansas?"

"I told you I had a plan."

"Okay. Tell me the plan."

"Oh, look! Seals! Stop, Ash! You have to stop."

"We don't have time to stop, Melina. People are after us."

"Ten minutes. Ten minutes to watch the seals. And I can tell you about my plan without your getting worked up and driving off the road."

They stopped. Ash cautioned her about the slippery rocks and the restless, crashing surf. But Melina ignored him, climbing out onto an overhanging boulder, as close as she could come to the water's edge. Ash followed, to protect her, she presumed.

The seals sunned themselves on the rocks in the bay, their slick bodies lit by the sunshine. They barked at one another and slithered off into the water from time to time. Just watching them in their freedom made her heart sing. For surely that same freedom was now within her grasp. The price, she knew, was high. She would miss her father every day. And she knew this was breaking his heart. She understood that now more than ever. As she grew accustomed to the idea of a new life growing inside her, she was filled with a need to keep the child safe and give him or her the best of everything.

Her father's way of doing that had been to keep

her a prisoner, to try to protect her from life. Melina understood the fear that had driven his decisions. She could only pray that she would make better decisions herself.

She swallowed the tears that threatened to clog her throat and concentrated on the seals and their song.

"What do you suppose they're saying?" she asked, fascinated by the haunting melody they made.

"They're saying, 'Why in the world would anyone want to go to Wichita, Kansas, Maudie?' That's what they're saying."

She laughed. "Precisely because nobody in the world would ever think of looking there."

"Ah. So you're going to hide out in Kansas."

She looked at him. He was alluring with the damp ocean wind ruffling his sandy hair. His eyes looked almost gray at the moment, with no sign of green or gold.

"Yes," she said. "I'll hide out in the suburbs. In a brick bungalow. They do have suburbs in Wichita, don't they?"

"I'm sure they do. Listen, Mel, this is nuts. How will you live? How will you support yourself? What'll you do when someone recognizes you and the media shows up on your doorstep and plasters your picture in every newspaper and on every TV newscast?"

Discomforted by his words, Melina was nevertheless not about to let him see her vulnerability. She had thought of all those possibilities and they all terrified her. "I'll get a job. Nobody will ever suspect that I'm in Wichita. You said so yourself."

"What kind of job?" he demanded, thrusting his face into her line of vision.

She smelled cypress again, and told herself it was the nearby trees. "America is the land of opportunity," she told him.

"America is the land of the minimum wage."

He towered over her. His chest was at eye level. She shoved her vamp sunglasses on, just in case he could see the thrill that crept into her eyes with his nearness. There. He wouldn't be able to see a thing. She pretended to glare at him.

"Maybe I'll meet a handsome, successful doctor."

He grunted impatiently.

"I could work at an art gallery. I know a lot about art. Or I could…" She hesitated. It was true her repertoire of marketable skills was limited. "I'm very resourceful. I would find a way."

"A twelve-year-old would have a better chance of survival."

She couldn't honestly argue with him, but deep in her soul she knew she would make it simply because she had no choice. She would sling burgers or ring up groceries or scrub people's floors all day long if she had to, because her baby and its happiness meant more to her than anything. She might sound flippant, but she was far from it. She knew how important this move was. Because living the rest of her life the way she had always lived it would be a slow death—and not just for her.

She knew what a life of isolation and paranoia did to a child. It had robbed her of her childhood. But her baby would have a life. A real life, with friends and school and teachers and a bicycle and playing quarterback on a baseball team.

Or was that football?

Never mind. She knew what she wanted for her baby and she would make it happen. One way or another.

"Maybe you should just take me to the next town and let me catch the bus for Wichita."

"Using what for money?"

Darn. Did he always have to be so practical?

"That's not your problem."

"Okay," he said. "Here's a plan. We'll take what cash I have to Las Vegas and—"

"Oh, Ash, Las Vegas! Can I play the slot machines? You know, I've never—"

His withering gaze stopped her. His eyes held not one iota of warmth, yet they still had the power to incite emotions she couldn't afford to reveal.

He continued. "And when we've turned our limited resources into something a little more substantial—"

"You can do that? I mean, you can beat the house? I saw that on a TV detective show once. You know, the house always wins."

"Not always."

The mystery of this man to whom she'd once surrendered herself silenced her for a moment. At the time, she thought she knew him. He was noble and kind and sensitive. Then he'd left her in a way that was none of those things. And now she was discovering that the traits he actually possessed were not the traits of the good guys—the heroes—in the entertainment that had been her only training for the real world.

"Ash Thorndyke," she said softly, "who are you?"

His lips narrowed to a thin line. "Right now, princess, I'm all you've got."

CHAPTER FIVE

STOMP HAD HER EYES peeled for a mark.

She knew exactly the kind of mark she was looking for. A couple would be best. Some ordinary-looking couple freaked out by the glitz and glitter of Las Vegas. Folks who wouldn't ask any questions if she pointed a gun in their faces.

A couple with a car, of course.

Stomp huddled at the mouth of the alley behind the big casino. It didn't smell so hot back here and there sure wasn't any neon to spiff things up. But a fourteen-year-old street kid didn't get hassled nearly so much if she stuck to the shadows. It hadn't taken Stomp long to learn that.

Besides, from here she had a view of the comings and goings in the casino's big parking deck. She saw the rich fat cats and the gaggles of pudgy, blue-haired ladies from Arizona and the wide-eyed families from Nebraska. She would know the right people when she saw them, and she could reach them before they locked the trunk on their Touristers.

Something clattered behind her, and Stomp put a hand on the pistol stuffed underneath her T-shirt. It was only a cat, a raggedy-looking orange cat rooting around in one of the cans in the alley. Stomp squatted and reached out a hand.

"Hey, mange-monster," she crooned.

The big tabby looked at her warily. Stomp respected that.

"Yeah, me, too."

The cat edged up on her, lured by the extended hand and the potential for a handout.

"You can hang around if you want to. But me, I'm gonna blow this taco stand."

The cat drew close enough to sniff her fingertips. Discovering nothing of interest, the cat settled back on its haunches and leveled an amber gaze on the teenage girl.

Stomp ignored the cat and thought about Hope Springs, Virginia, a place where people had been so nice to her that she didn't even want to utter the name of the place in this alley with its smells of rot and filth and drugs.

The cat raised a paw and began to groom its scruffy orange coat, clearly disdainful of Stomp's plan.

Stomp dropped down to her haunches, too, and let her mind drift. Hope Springs, Virginia. She'd visited there with her parents before her mother died and her old man's brain was fried on drugs. She had an uncle there. She'd never forgotten the little town in the mountains. It was like paradise, so green and pretty. She'd ridden a horse and dipped her bare feet in a stream with a waterfall. Yep, it had been just like she supposed heaven would be.

Nobody in Hope Springs had even seemed to mind

that her mother was black and her father wasn't. They'd been nice to her anyway and that had hardly ever happened anywhere in Stomp's entire life.

Stomp had thought about that place a lot over the years. She'd thought about it at times when kids of both races shunned her for her mixed heritage, at times when her old man took it out on her that her mother had died. And now, she thought about it again when the cops and everybody on the street thought she knew more than she ought to about a couple of dealers who'd offed a cop.

The cat slithered forward and rubbed against her knees. Tears stung Stomp's eyes, surprising her. It was the first gentle physical contact she'd had with a living thing in years.

"Beat it," she said harshly. "I don't need a partner. You'll just slow me down."

She watched with regret as the tabby meandered back to the cans of garbage in the darker parts of the alley. Stomp was tired and hungry and it occurred to her that the cat would soon have a full stomach and a place to sleep. Stomp dragged herself back to her feet and trained her eyes on the parking deck.

Her ticket to Hope Springs, Virginia, was out there somewhere.

Melina wanted to wait in the hotel room while Ash tested his luck in the casino. She wanted a hot bath, a soft bed, room service, cable TV.

"Princess, we're joined at the hip." Ash took her

by the wrist. "Until I'm convinced you're safe, where I go, you go."

"I'm not afraid," she protested, his touch arousing sensations better left dormant.

"That's what makes you dangerous," he said.

So she sat beside him while he played blackjack. They were dressed like a couple in an appliance store commercial. A denim jumper swallowed Melina's slight frame. Ash managed to look far from sophisticated in his khaki slacks, garish sweater and geeky eyeglasses. He squinted a lot.

"You are rather dashing tonight," she said as the dealer slapped cards around the table.

"You're seeing me through the eyes of love, my precious," he said, tipping the edges of his cards and peeking at them. The words—delivered only as part of their little game—nevertheless brought heat to her cheeks. Certainly she had looked at him that way once. But never again. Melina Somerset may not have oodles of experience, but she was nobody's fool, either. Ignoring the jolt his playful words had caused, she peered over his shoulder, but she had no idea whether his hand was good or bad. She moved too close to him and caught the whiff of fresh outdoors that always seemed to cling to him. She shivered.

To distract herself, she sat back on the high stool and studied the casino.

The room was raucously noisy, enormous and teeming with people. The crowds made her nervous, despite what she'd said to Ash about not being afraid. Some of her father's constant worry had rubbed off on her, and her uneasiness reminded her that he was alone somewhere, worrying about her. She couldn't help feeling guilty.

Anytime someone laughed too loudly, her skin prickled. The clang of the slot machines kept her on edge. The waitresses with their skimpy costumes and abundant bosoms made her feel inadequate. She glanced down at her meager bosom, which didn't yet show any sign of being enhanced by impending motherhood, and wondered if every other woman in America had indulged in implant surgery. She hadn't noticed that on *I Love Lucy*.

A lush blonde with dark roots and a deep cleavage delivered a martini to Ash. Ash paid her more attention than he was paying to Melina.

When the flashy blonde took her come-hither smile to the next table, Melina poked him in the shin with her red canvas shoes. "Married men aren't supposed to ogle pretty waitresses."

"You've got a lot to learn, princess," he muttered.

The dealer shoved a stack of chips in Ash's direction. Melina noticed that the pile in front of Ash was sizable.

"You're winning."

"You doubted me?" His voice was like silk.

Hers was like barbed wire. "I'm supposed to *trust* you?"

He signaled the dealer to hit him with another card. He seemed not even to notice her comment. She pretended it didn't matter. It *didn't* matter. She sniffed his martini and nearly gagged. She occupied her mind with plotting her second escape—this one from Ash Thorndyke. First, she thought, she'd let him win a lot more money. After all, this time around she would have nothing to hock and no one to commit petty larceny on her behalf.

They cashed in their chips and moved to another blackjack table at another casino. Then another. Everywhere they went, Ash won. The roll of bills in the pocket of his khakis was growing.

"If you buy me a purse, I could carry the money," she offered with a sweet smile.

He ignored her. *It doesn't matter.* Why couldn't she remember that?

When they went back to the hotel that night, to their two double beds, Melina figured they must be rich.

"How much did we win?" she said, sitting on the side of the bed feeling a little self-conscious in the nightshirt he'd selected for her.

"*I* won about half what we need."

He pulled his sweater over his head. Beneath it was the smattering of sandy hair she remembered on a chest that was not thin, not overmuscled. It was...perfect, that's what it was. Perfect. His sandy hair stood up in soft tufts that made her long to smooth them. He took the money out of his slacks and studied the room. Melina studied the money in his fist. Was it enough, she wondered, to buy a house in the suburbs? She had no idea how much money it took to buy a simple two-bedroom house with a yard fenced in for kids and dogs. A million dollars? Two?

Just in case her face revealed her thoughts, she asked, "Enough to buy me breasts like the waitresses downstairs?"

He looked disconcerted. He opened his mouth to reply, then seemed to reconsider. He stuffed the money back into his pockets. "Go to sleep, princess."

She thought about the new escape plan she'd dreamed up. "Aren't you going to hide the money?"

"Not while you're watching, princess."

"You don't trust me."

He didn't even bother to deny it before he went into the bathroom to prepare for bed. Melina turned the covers back on her bed, turned off the light and lay there in the dark, thinking.

She thought about the baby growing inside her. She thought about the ways her body would change in the months to come, and realized her education by various nuns had left her woefully naive about many things a woman—*a mother*—needed to know. She'd been sixteen before another schoolgirl had explained what her monthly cycles were all about. Melina sighed into the darkness. How was she going to make a normal life for herself and her child when she knew nothing about normal life?

She sighed and tried to change the direction of her thoughts. She would just concentrate on the little human being developing within her, a baby who would have soft skin and chubby fists and a smile just for her. She thought about the miracle of it all because that was better than dwelling on the fears.

She also thought about the man who helped create

that miracle, who was still in the dark about the possibility of soft skin and chubby fists. Under other circumstances, they would be sharing the miracle. They would be talking about whose eyes the baby would have and whether to name the child after her grandmother or his. But that wasn't possible. It had become impossible the minute Ash Thorndyke walked away from her one night in Parsons Green and never returned. At that moment, he ceased to be the man she'd thought he was.

And the longer she was with him now, the more apparent it became. This Ash Thorndyke was a man who could make heiresses vanish under the watchful eyes of trained security people, who knew how to steal cars and win small fortunes at blackjack tables.

He wasn't a man she could love. He especially wasn't a man with whom she wanted to raise her son or daughter.

No matter whose eyes the child had.

He came out of the bathroom. He walked softly, maneuvering in the darkness deftly. She heard him slide into the bed beside hers, heard the rustling of the sheets, the creak of mattress springs.

The little bed in Parsons Green had creaked and sagged with their weight. But she hadn't noticed. Not then.

He held her face and kissed her as if she were the most treasured thing in his life. Melina supposed she was being naive, but she wanted to believe it, so she did.

His lips were soft, coaxing and intoxicating. Hers were hungry, desperate, eager.

"Slow down," he whispered.

"Hurry up," she whispered back.

He chuckled softly, his lips never leaving hers. "We have all the time in the world."

But Melina knew how quickly her freedom could vanish. She wanted this moment, refused to be robbed of it. His patience only fueled her impatience.

He undressed. She watched in the faintest of starlight drifting in through the dormer window over the bed. His shoulders were broader than she had imagined, his chest deeper and lightly furred with golden curls. He was fully erect.

Tremulous, she touched the tip of him. His flesh was hot silk.

His big fingers manipulated her buttons and zippers and hooks like a man accustomed to handling things precious and delicate. His hands on her skin were at once soothing and electrifying. He explored her flat belly, her narrow hips, her slender thighs, her breasts that had always mortified her with their unwillingness to fill out.

But he groaned over her tight, blushing nipples and Melina felt the first promise of womanhood.

He caressed the soft, hot place between her thighs and Melina raised herself to his touch. A quiet rain had started, pattering on the roof. He raised himself over her and she drew him to her, encircling his waist with her legs.

He encountered her body's resistance and he hesitated.

"Don't stop," she pleaded.

"Mel. Oh, Mel." He trembled, poised above her. His eyes searched her face. "Don't tell me you've never done this before, either."

"Please don't stop."

"This isn't like your first ride on the subway, Mel." She brushed her lips over his ear, felt him shudder. "I hope it's much better than that."

"This should be special. Something you're sure about."

His voice was hoarse, his body still touching hers, so close to being one with hers. She wanted to tell him that it was special, that he was the one she'd been waiting for all her life.

"I'm sure," was all she said.

Then he had pressed, slowly. She moved into his thrust and felt the sweet ache of becoming a woman in his arms.

The bittersweet memory drew tears, surprising Melina. She would never have believed that a man who could love her so gently, with such sweet passion, could ever betray her. She had been wrong.

Despite it all, she still trusted him with her life.

Hers, but not her baby's. Her baby's life was too precious to her for taking chances. She knew without question that Ash would protect her and keep her safe if it was in his power. But she couldn't trust him to be a force in her baby's life. She had seen things that couldn't be easily explained and she wouldn't expose her child to those things.

Her baby would have a normal life. That was her commitment, her only goal. And Ash Thorndyke didn't fit that goal.

A few feet away, his breathing was deep and even. He slept. She fought with the urge to sleep herself, knowing she had to get away from him while she could. While her secret was still safe.

She glanced at the clock. Long past midnight. He would sleep for many hours, the deep sleep that she knew so well. He hadn't moved that morning when she left the van. He wouldn't know now, when she slipped out of the room and out of his life.

Stealthily, she got out of bed and dressed. She wanted to take the clothes he'd gotten for her, but the shopping bags would make too much noise. Foolishly, she wanted to leave him a note.

He never left one for you, did he?

She made her way to the foot of his bed, to the pair of khaki slacks draped carefully there. She lifted them. Half the money, that's all she would take. Enough to catch a bus to somewhere she'd never heard of before. She slipped her hand into the pocket, felt the fat roll of bills.

"You'd make a pretty decent thief, if that's the route you decide to go," he said.

Melina jumped, dropping the trousers, the roll of bills unfurling in her hands and spilling onto the foot of the bed.

"Of course, your nerves need a little work."

He flicked on the light between their beds. He lay there, hands behind his head, chest bare above crisp, white linens. He was smiling. A wickedly self-satisfied smile.

"You can't keep me here," she said, struggling to cover her embarrassment with self-righteous indignation.

"And you can't take my money." He made no move to gather up the money. He simply stared at her.

"Part of it," she said. "I wouldn't have taken all of it."

"Just enough to get to Wichita?"

"Something like that."

He tossed back the sheet and got out of bed. He was wearing burgundy silk boxer shorts. His legs were sharply muscled. The room grew suddenly warm.

Ash gathered the money, stacked it neatly and laid it on the bedside table in the halo of the lamp. "You're not clever enough to pull a fast one on Ash Thorndyke, princess. You might want to remember that."

"That's not what I want." She became aware that her voice trembled, that her eyes stung with fresh tears. "I just want to be free to live my life. I'm entitled to that."

He studied her.

"I'm tired of being somebody's prisoner."

He took her hand and drew her to sit on the edge of the bed. "I won't hurt you. But somebody out there wants to. I only want to make sure you're safe. And as long as you're with me, you're safe. On your own, you're at their mercy. I know you don't like the idea, but until we figure out who wants to get their hands on you and why, you're safer with me.''

She'd lived under that shadow all her life. Only this time, someone apparently *had* tried to kidnap her. So what Ash said could be true. It didn't make the prospect any more bearable. ''But—''

''Unless you want to go home to daddy.''

She shook her head. ''Never.''

''Then I'm your white knight, princess.''

She struggled to accept him in that role. To accept help from the man who had betrayed her once already.

''All I want is to settle down somewhere. Somewhere nobody can find me.''

''It won't be easy.''

''But you know how to do it, don't you? To help somebody disappear and start over?''

The crease in his forehead deepened. ''Yes, I know how to do that.''

Once again, she wanted to know who Ash Thorndyke was. But she didn't ask. Instead she went back to bed. So did he. Ash Thorndyke might be no hero, but for now anyway, he was the best she could do.

TWO DAYS LATER, Ash was pleased with the amount of money he'd managed to win off a dozen different casinos in Vegas. He'd been careful to spread out his winnings, moving around, never calling attention to himself. Those three years watching Grandfather Thorndyke dealing blackjack in Monaco had paid off.

The only problem he still had was figuring out what precisely to do with Melina Somerset.

Logic told him she needed to go home to her father. But she opposed that idea so vehemently that something told him it would be the wrong thing to do to her.

And he'd already done the wrong thing to her once.

So he figured he owed her. Maybe he could help her do what she wanted, find a place somewhere in the States where she could simply disappear. His brother, Forbes, was a pro at creating new identities. And now Ash had enough of a stake to get her started. He couldn't contact his brother right away. The men who wanted Melina would be expecting that. But soon.

"How long will it take to get to the Grand Canyon?" she asked as they settled into the front seat of the wood-paneled station wagon that she'd fancied so much he bought it from a used-car lot. The car was theirs. No more grand theft auto for Ash.

"We're not going to the Grand Canyon."

"Of course we are." She waved the map at him. He should never have bought her the damn map. "Look how close we are."

He pulled out of the parking deck behind the casino. "I thought we were going to Kansas."

"Maybe. How about Arkansas? Have you ever been to Arkansas? Look, there's a little town called

Birdsong. Wouldn't that be a wonderful place to live? Either way, the Grand Canyon is on the way.''

Her bright enthusiasm cheered him, reminding him of the young woman in London who had wanted to experience everything. The memory of that woman still called to him despite the fact that Melina had had her hair cut and lightened at the salon in the hotel the afternoon before, a sedate bob that barely grazed her chin. With every strand of long, dark wave that had landed on the salon floor, he'd watched the impish young woman he'd known in London vanish completely.

Just as well. She'd been a fraud, anyway.

And you aren't? he chastised himself.

Nevertheless, that young woman with her untempered enthusiasm for life had been hard to resist.

The new woman at his side, all sleek sophistication, pointed to the right. ''There's the highway.''

He started to sail right past it, changing his mind only at the last minute. Tires squealed on the asphalt as he made the turn.

''Maybe *I* should learn to drive,'' she said.

''Over my dead body.''

''That seems like a reasonable bargain to me.''

He turned on the radio. The only station he could pick up was country music. He was about to turn it off when Melina flashed to life.

''Oh! I love country music. We didn't get much country music at convent schools, you know. Oh, this is wonderful.'' She turned up the volume.

She might have changed her looks, but she was still

working the same routine. At least the music would save them from conversation.

Maybe it would even save him from looking too closely, too honestly, at his presence in Melina Somerset's life. He was wondering what Grandfather Thorndyke would do under similar circumstances, when he felt something hard and cold pressed against the back of his skull. Alarm shot through him.

"Keep driving," said a voice from the back seat. "We're not going to Kansas or Arkansas. We're going to Virginia."

CHAPTER SIX

AMERICA WAS TURNING OUT to be much more of an adventure than Melina had imagined. It was a good thing she'd included a few TV detective shows with her steady fare of sitcoms.

It was even possible she should be frightened, but the smudged face behind Ash looked frightened enough for all three of them.

The person holding the gun to Ash's head also looked young. Very young. It was hard to be sure, beneath the enormous plaid shirt, baggy jeans and the tan-and-green splotched hat covering her—his? its?—shaved head, but the thug in the back seat looked remarkably like an adolescent girl.

Ash apparently reached the same conclusion, for he said, "Listen, kid," he began.

Listen Kid gave the gun a jab. Ash's head jerked forward. "I'm not a kid. On the street they call me Stomp. And you don't even want to know why. Got it?"

Fascinated, but still not frightened, Melina took in the grim set of Ash's mouth and the high pitch of Stomp's voice.

Stomp poked the back of Ash's head again. "Got it?"

Melina poked his arm with her finger. "It looks like a real gun to me. I'd answer if I were you."

Stomp didn't wait for an answer. "Virginia. Due east. You got that?"

"You'll have to clear it with the tour director," Ash said, gesturing toward Melina. "She's in charge."

Melina smiled. "I knew you'd see it my way."

Stomp sank back in the seat. "No, I'm in charge."

Melina unhooked her seat belt and got onto her knees to look over the seat at their uninvited passenger. "What's in Virginia?"

"Are you guys crazy, or what? I've got a gun, okay?"

"Well, there's no point in shooting us, is there? Who'd drive if you shot Ash?"

"I would," Stomp said with an admirable degree of belligerent self-confidence.

"You can drive?"

"Can't you?"

Melina noticed that the girl's finger had eased off the trigger. Keep her talking. She'd heard that on one of her shows, she was sure of it. "Me? Drive? Heavens, no. He won't let me."

"Lady, you need a new husband."

"Oh, he's not my husband. He's… What are you, Ash, exactly?"

He delivered a disgruntled look across the front seat. "I'm ready to bail out on both of you, that's what I am."

"Fine. Stomp can drive. Why is it we're going to Virginia, Stomp?"

"Getting away from the drug dealers."

"See, Ash. You can rescue Stomp, as well."

He didn't seem to appreciate her efforts to defuse the situation. "Swell."

Stomp yawned, a big, weary yawn. "And the police."

"See, Ash. Lots of people are looking for Stomp, also."

"Who's looking for you?" Stomp asked.

"My father."

Stomp grunted. "'Nuff said."

"I was going to Kansas, but I'm sure Virginia would work just as well."

"It's pretty cool, actually." Stomp's eyelids appeared to be growing heavy.

"Is it?" The girl didn't look tough at all. She looked as if she was in desperate need of a mother. And then Melina had the most disconcerting feeling that she herself knew precisely how to fill that need in a motherless girl. She smiled softly. How utterly amazing, to discover that she could feel maternal about a total stranger. Pregnancy was resulting in some amazing changes. "She says it's pretty cool, Ash."

"Horses and waterfalls. Apples growing right on trees…" Her voice was drifting. Melina tried to picture the scene, but what she saw instead was the girl's fingers growing lax around the gun handle. "Really?"

Stomp's next words were barely audible. "Uncle's farm." Her eyes closed.

Melina smiled and dropped her chin to the hands she clasped across the back of the car seat. "She's worn-out."

"Get the gun."

"Oh, Ash, she's not exactly a desperado."

"Let's not give her a chance to turn into one. Get the gun, Melina."

Melina raised on her knees. She leaned into the back. The gun had slipped out of Stomp's grasp and onto the seat. Melina would have no trouble reaching it. She hesitated. What if it went off? What if she dropped the weapon and it exploded? "Actually, I've never touched a gun before."

"Pick it up by the butt."

"The butt?"

"The handle. Not the trigger, the handle."

"I see. The handle." She inched her fingers toward it. The metal was cool against the tips of her fingers. She flinched. "It's cold."

"That's good. That means it hasn't gone off in the last few minutes."

Stomp sighed and shifted, moving to lie down in the seat. Melina snatched the gun just as Stomp would have rolled right on top of it.

"I have it." She held it gingerly by the handle.

"Give it to me."

"You're driving."

"I know what I'm doing."

Apparently he did. When she handed him the gun he managed not only to keep the car on the correct side of the double yellow lines with one hand, but also to use his other hand to remove a metal box from the handle of the gun. He then dropped the metal box into his lap and examined the gun before slipping it into his pocket.

"What's in the box?" she asked.

"Box? Oh, the clip. The clip holds the bullets."

"She had real bullets?"

"This isn't TV, Melina. Most carjackers use real bullets."

"Carjacker?"

Melina glanced over the back seat at the sleeping girl. She had curled one dirty hand up under her cheek. "Oh, Ash, you make her sound like a criminal. She's just a child."

"Do you have any idea how many teenagers in this country kill every year? Every day?"

Melina shook her head. "I never watch the news shows. Besides, she's not going to kill us."

"Not now, she's not. I've got her gun."

"Is Virginia nice? The way she says it is?"

"Don't even think about it."

"Well, we have to go somewhere. Virginia is as good as any place, I suppose."

"Melina, for heaven's sake—"

"She should be with her uncle. On his farm. You know, I've never—"

"Let me guess. You've never ridden a horse."

His irritation made her smile. Too many people had

treated her like royalty for too long. It was nice being around someone who didn't, even if he did call her princess. "Or picked an apple right off a tree."

"Or been on a farm."

"That's right." She closed her eyes and tried to picture it. "I should at least see a farm, before I settle down in the suburbs. Don't you think?"

"Melina, it will take us days to get to Virginia."

"Then one extra day to visit the Grand Canyon won't matter much, will it?"

She heard him sigh and mutter something about out-of-control females. She liked the tenor of his voice when he talked to himself; it was rough, almost gravelly. She smiled for a moment, then realized why she liked the sound of it. It was the voice he used when he made love.

She hated it when she started going soft again. She gritted her teeth and decided to push him a little closer to his limit. "Do we have enough money for hiking boots?"

"I suppose you'll be wanting three pairs."

"Whatever. We really don't care if you join us or not."

"We don't need *any* hiking boots," he said. "Because we don't have time to go to the Grand Canyon."

"Of course not," she said.

"Of course not," he reiterated, very firmly.

She decided to keep quiet and started placing bets with herself. Ten to one he would turn off at Kingman, Arizona, and head for the Grand Canyon. No, five to one. The longer the chilly silence, the better the odds became.

When they reached Kingman, Arizona, a big green sign said it was two hundred and forty-three miles to the Grand Canyon National Park. Ash drove in the direction the sign indicated.

IDA MONROE KNEW that everybody in Hope Springs wondered why she kept such a steady vigil outside the coronary care unit at the county hospital.

Of course, she'd been Tood Grunkemeier's wife's best friend all their lives. But Edith Grunkemeier had been dead for almost ten years now, and nobody, she was certain, could imagine why Ida sat here, day after day, waiting for Tood to regain consciousness. The coronary care unit waiting room was full of people from Hope Springs, day and night. There was no shortage of people stopping in, waiting for word, praying for a miracle.

"Four days now," said Fudgie, who came by every morning before the barbershop opened. "Hanging on like that, he always was a stubborn old cuss."

Ida could have added a hearty amen to that, for she'd heard every detail of Edith's married life over the years. But she said nothing. She sat and knit and watched the clock.

"I heard it on good authority they lost him twice on the way over in the ambulance," added Lavinia Holt, who never missed an opportunity to repeat tales that no one was able to confirm. "Brain damage is highly likely."

Ida felt her insides shrivel. She wanted to tell Lavinia to shut her big trap, which is exactly what Tood would have said. She kept knitting and purling.

Eben Monk, one of the barbershop gang, said, "Reckon it's gonna take a miracle."

"We should never lose sight of the fact that miracles happen every day." That was the Reverend Haigler, whose presence was the only one that gave Ida the least bit of comfort.

"I suppose you'll be going home today." Lavinia looked straight at Ida when she said it.

Ida was disinclined to reply to the town's busiest body, but she was loath to be rude in the presence of Reverend Haigler. "Not yet."

"Land's sakes," Lavinia said. "I don't see why not." She paused for a reply, but none was forthcoming. "Why, that piece you're knitting is already big enough to cover the football field at the high school stadium."

Ida knew Lavinia never had been fond of her. Younger folks in town never guessed that the two had graduated high school the same year. Because, although Ida was pleasantly plump, she walked enough to keep her moving parts toned up, she visited the Sheer Delight regularly to maintain her silvery blond hair and she considered a smile God's natural facelift. Lavinia, on the other hand, was built like the engine parked in front of the volunteer fire station, sort of chunky and square. Her hair was the color of a dull dime and the most exercise she ever got was her jowls flapping when she talked—although, everyone conceded, that was considerable exercise.

Ida knew that with a minimum of thought, she could come up with something to say that would offend Lavinia Holt enough to send her straight home and keep her away for at least two full days until curiosity got the better of her.

But Ida didn't have the brainpower to waste.

Right now, she was so wrung-out she didn't have a sharp word for anyone, which she supposed was one more reason everybody in Hope Springs was baffled by her behavior.

Eventually the morning visitors left, and Ida was alone for a while. She was nursing a tension headache when Faith Davenport showed up right before lunchtime.

Ida smiled; the muscles that worked that part of her face felt rusty. "Oh, dolly, it's so good to see you."

Faith hugged her, then sat beside her in one of the uncomfortable waiting-room chairs. Faith took one of Ida's hands in hers. "Ida, why are you wearing yourself out like this?"

Faith was pregnant again, less than two years after her first baby. She was barely showing yet, but her face glowed. Faith had lived next door to Ida all her life, a motherless little girl whom Ida had taken under her wing to compensate for her own childlessness.

"You don't need to be here," Ida said, "in your condition."

Faith had had trouble the first go-around. Little Patrick had been early—dangerously early—and it had been touch-and-go the first three months of his life. Today, the little scoundrel was all boy, his dark eyes brimming with mischief and his pudgy fists making a grab for everything within reach. He'd walked early and talked early and he already called her "G'amma Ita."

"I'm fine. Doc Sarah says I may have to go to bed with this one, too. But not yet."

"Maybe this time you'll follow orders."

"That's what Sean says."

Ida nodded. "He'll see to it."

"Maybe I ought to send Sean down here to get you home."

For the first time since the night of Tood's heart attack, Ida's eyes filled with tears. "Oh, dolly, you just don't know."

Faith clasped her hand. "What is it, Ida?"

"He was my best friend's husband."

"I know. But… There's nothing you can do, you know."

"I love him." Ida saw by the expression on her young friend's face that Faith didn't quite understand the import of what Ida had said. "I always have. Do you know what I'm saying? I was in love with my best friend's husband."

"Oh, Ida. You poor old sweetheart, you."

"She never knew. Nobody ever knew."

"Not even Mr. Grunkemeier?"

Ida shook her head. "Not even after Edith died."

"Why not?"

Ida squeezed back unshed tears. "I thought about

it, once or twice. Then I'd think about Edith and what a good and loyal friend she'd always been and... It just didn't seem right.''

Ida stabbed her knitting needles into her dwindling ball of yarn. ''I kept the secret all these years. Because of friendship. What if I was wrong? What if Edith wouldn't have minded after all? What if Tood didn't like being out there all by himself?''

She looked at Faith and realized tears now streamed down her seventy-year-old cheeks. ''What if we've both been alone all this time and it didn't have to be that way?''

HIKING THE GRAND CANYON, Ash had discovered, used an entirely different set of muscles than those used climbing in and out of second-story windows. He was sore and he was tired and he was troubled.

Especially troubled.

He'd spent a small fortune on hiking and camping gear, but that didn't bother him. Ash had learned long ago that a little creativity could always generate another pile of cash. No, what troubled him were the two females lying a few feet away on the floor of the Grand Canyon in their state-of-the-art tent, nestled in top-of-the-line sleeping bags.

They didn't know it, but he could hear every whispered confidence they shared. He was hearing things he didn't want to hear because he didn't want to care. And Ash already cared way too much. Way more than he wanted to, or was safe to.

He remembered vividly Stomp's refusal to ride a burro down the path.

"I can make it on my own two feet," she'd insisted. "I don't have to depend on any stupid donkey."

In fact, she had refused help all day long. Although she looked as if she barely tipped the scales at one hundred pounds, the teenager had insisted on carrying all her own supplies, had refused to take his hand when navigating a particularly steep part of the trail, had adamantly refused assistance in setting up the tent.

It hadn't taken an expert in child psychology to figure out that Stomp didn't trust anybody to take care of her. And she didn't trust herself to have fun. She hadn't cracked a smile all day, even when Melina almost slid off the backside of the burro she rode. Stomp had gone through the entire episode with a sullen, bored expression.

Melina had been an entirely different story.

Melina had thrown herself into the day like a child determined to wring every bit of fun possible from the experience. Once they actually arrived at the Grand Canyon, Ash had discovered that viewing the grandeur would not suffice.

"We have to hike down," she'd said, staring up at him with awestruck eyes. "We can't just look down and leave. We have to go down."

Ash had peered into the rugged canyon. "All the way?"

"Well, of course all the way. Did you know they have burros you can ride down?"

"Let me guess. You've never ridden a burro."

Melina had winked at Stomp, who continued to stare at them impassively, taking only surreptitious glances into the yawning chasm of the earth's belly.

"I've never ridden a raft down a river, either," Melina had said.

"Now, wait a minute."

"Of course, if you're afraid, you don't have to join us."

Reaching the canyon floor had taken most of the day and rafting the wild Colorado River would take the better part of a day tomorrow. None of it was easy going for a guy who practically grew up in tuxedos and had never owned a pair of jeans until this very day. Museums and cocktail parties were familiar terrain for Ash; the great outdoors was foreign territory.

But as he lay in the dark and stared into the star-sprinkled sky, Ash realized he wouldn't have missed this day for anything. And it wasn't just the smell of the fresh air, the sightings of deer, porcupines and beavers or the raw beauty of this corner of the earth.

It was Melina.

At her first sight of the canyon, she'd touched her fingertips to her lips. Tears had gathered in her eyes.

"Oh, my," she'd breathed. "Oh, my, have you ever seen anything so magnificent?"

Her unbridled delight, her enthusiasm had spilled over into Ash. Being in her presence was making him experience life on an entirely different level, just as it had in London.

He flopped over on his side, suddenly disgruntled.

Okay, so her attitude about life had been genuine. That didn't mitigate the fact that she'd lied to him. Given him a phony name and made up a phony life for herself, had fooled him completely.

The familiar question popped into his mind. *And what you did was so different?*

He closed his eyes tightly. He needed his sleep.

Stomp's brusque whisper came to him in the darkness as she addressed Melina. "What'd your old man do to you?"

There was a long silence. Ash thought Melina might not answer. "Kept me prisoner."

A gross exaggeration, Ash was certain, although he did remember with sharp clarity Tom Somerset's order to his men. *Lock her up.*

"Yeah? In a dungeon or something?"

"In convent schools."

Stomp groaned. "Oh, yuck."

"I went to a different one every year, all over Europe, from the time I was twelve. Always under an assumed name, with a life story he made up so no one would know who I was."

Ash winced. Okay, so hers was learned behavior. Did that make it excusable?

He thought about his own happy, if unorthodox, childhood. He remembered bedtime stories from Grandfather Thorndyke, his mother's insistence that he learn piano because she couldn't play a lick herself, summer camp with his brother, Forbes. He remembered distinctly the way his father always put a hand on his shoulder when they took a walk to talk about the mysteries of life. The hand was warm and welcome, a visible symbol of the emotional guidance his father always gave so readily.

He tried to imagine growing up without all the trappings of a nurturing family. Heck, he couldn't imagine being without it now. These last years, with his father serving time, had been painful, and never more so than when he'd learned about Bram Thorndyke's failing health. The bond between father and child was powerful.

He ached for these two, who didn't know that bond.

"Are you really a princess, the way he says?"

Melina's response came on a soft sigh that tore at Ash's peace of mind. "No. Just too rich."

"How can you be too rich?"

"You can be too rich if it means you can't have a life. Or friends."

"Friends are overrated."

"I had a friend once, actually. She was the daughter of the cook the year I was fifteen. She helped me sneak out so we could go into town for a movie."

Ash didn't miss the implication in Melina's statement that she'd had a friend once. He began to resent Tom Somerset for what he'd put his daughter through, no matter how well intentioned he might have been. Melina Somerset's childhood had been emotionally bankrupt, that was clear.

"A movie? That's the best you could think of to do after you went to all the trouble of sneaking out?"

"It was the first movie I'd been to in three years. The first time I was out in public without a bodyguard in three years."

"Wow. At least my old man never did that to me. I guess you could say he let me run wild."

"That sounds like heaven to me." Through the darkness, Ash heard the wistfulness in Melina's comment. "But I don't suppose it was."

"Nah. It just meant whatever I did, he could say it was wrong and stupid and I was never going to amount to anything."

"So you ran away."

"Not until Mom died."

Ash longed for an extra pillow to pull over his head. Both their lives had been scripted like bad soap operas. Compared to them, he had lived the privileged life.

"My mother died, too," Melina said.

"Yeah?"

Ash listened to them discuss Stomp's mother's illness and Melina's mother's kidnapping. They both sounded so matter-of-fact. In fact, their very detachment spoke volumes to him of their pain, pain too sharp to acknowledge aloud.

"So that's why he kept you like a prisoner. So the same thing wouldn't happen to you."

"That's why. But it isn't much consolation."

The woman and the girl talked late into the night. Ash tried to tune them out, but their voices, one pensive, one determinedly tough, latched on to his heart. They were like lost children, dreaming of a normal life.

He considered the irony of the fact that Melina had inspired the same longing in him, when they'd met in London. At least he was realistic enough to realize some dreams never came true. And the idea of a normal, average life for either of them—much less for the two of them together—was one of those.

CHAPTER SEVEN

THE COUNTRYSIDE UNFOLDED before them mile after mile. Mountains, mesas, scrub brush and dust.

Stomp sat in the back seat, staring at nothing and discerning everything. When Ash caught her gaze in the rearview mirror, he shuddered. The thousand-yard stare, he'd heard it called. The look of someone who missed not a single thing while simultaneously being wrapped up in her own fears, lost in the terrors of the heart and mind.

Then there was Melina, who also didn't miss a single detail and could not be dissuaded from chasing heart-first after everything she encountered. A flea market. A roadside vegetable stand. The hand-painted wooden sign that directed them twenty miles off the highway to view the World's Largest Ball of Twine, a side trip that also made it necessary to purchase a camera to record their adventure.

Through Melina's eyes, the entire world was fresh.

Ash felt the strain of alternately viewing the world first through Stomp's jaded eyes, then through Melina's enthusiastic ones. Sometimes he could actually absorb Melina's delight. Other times, he knew the truth that lay behind Stomp's stare.

He should have been able to relax, but he couldn't.

Their trek ran into no snags. No sign they were being followed, no indications that anyone recognized the young woman who had been splashed all over the news broadcasts days before, with no follow-up news concerning her disappearance. He derived no comfort from any of it.

At day's end, Ash slumped in the armchair in the Cowboy Corral Motel somewhere in the panhandle of Texas—after all, Melina could hardly be expected to pass within a few hundred miles of the great state of Texas without getting a look at a few steers, could she?—and glared at the grainy TV screen. He'd decided she was right about stopping at the Cowboy Corral. After several days of camping out, they could use a shower and a good night's sleep.

Especially Melina, who didn't seem to feel well. She was tired all the time. And she'd been sick to her stomach this morning, not for the first time. She wouldn't see a doctor, but he could make sure she had a comfortable place to rest.

He punched the remote impatiently, searching for some hint that the world was still concerned that Melina Somerset had vanished.

"You're missing some good reruns," Melina said from the double bed she would share tonight with Stomp.

Stock reports and presidential scandals and mud slides in southern California, but not a word on the vanishing act by one of the world's most-loved heiresses. Amazing.

"I like the one about the small-town sheriff with

the little boy and the maiden aunt. It's always sweet.'' Her voice was gentle, when she forgot herself and lapsed out of her royal-command mode.

She was lying stretched out on the bed. From the corner of his eye he caught a glimpse of her bare toes. They wiggled. She had painted them red, white and blue, alternating toes. Stomp thought it was a scream. Melina was delighted with the patriotic effect.

"There's always a moral to the story," she concluded her review of the old sitcom.

"Life doesn't come with morals at the end," he said.

"It might. Maybe you just haven't noticed."

She was naive. Too naive for her own good. He had noticed that in London.

"Maybe that's your problem," she said. "You aren't paying attention when life gives you the moral to the story."

"That's not my problem."

"I wouldn't be too sure."

He was sure all right—because *she* was his problem.

He thought—for the umpteenth time—of dumping both of them, the princess and the teenage hooligan, in the lap of the local authorities and chartering the closest private jet to the Mediterranean. That's what Grandfather Thorndyke would tell him. He was sure of it.

Her mattress creaked. She was standing. Stretching. Slipping her royal feet into the ridiculous high-heeled sandals she'd insisted on acquiring at the flea market she'd insisted on stopping at right before they crossed the Texas state line. They matched her gold-trimmed T-shirt, she said. Indeed they did. And they made her hips sway provocatively when she walked.

He wondered when she'd developed hips. In London, she'd been skinny. Girlish. Hadn't she? But sometime during the three months since he'd seen her, she'd begun to develop curves, sweet, gentle curves.

He thought of the slow, sweet roll of those hips cradled in his hands, surrounding him with softness and heat. She crossed in front of him on the way to the door. Her hair was tousled from an afternoon nap. The same as it had been when they spent afternoons in bed together, even though it was shorter and lighter now.

Wanting her made no sense. He told himself that a million times a day. Tomorrow he would believe it.

"Where are you going?"

She had her hand on the doorknob. "Looking for Stomp. She's been gone too long."

Anxiety uncurled in him. He was surprised to realize he would worry if the girl disappeared. She didn't even have her gun anymore, although he supposed she could put her hands on one quickly enough. He hated to think how a girl her age survived on the streets. What he said was, "Good. Maybe she decided to run out on us."

Despite his words he was up and at the window, peering between the drawn curtains. Stomp had gone in search of a soft-drink machine. She was nowhere in sight.

A police cruiser, its blue lights flashing, sat in the motel parking lot.

"Oh, no," Ash said.

Melina peered out and gasped. "She's been hurt."

Before he could tell her to stay out of sight, she was gone from the room, ridiculous high-heeled sandals clicking across the parking lot.

Swearing softly, Ash started after her. He would remind her what could happen if the cops realized who she was. They could take her into custody. Contact her father. Charge Ash with kidnapping.

And what would happen to Melina? The men who had hired him were surely waiting in the wings somewhere. Even the man who was supposed to love and protect her was no doubt waiting somewhere to redouble his security measures and rob her of even more years of her life.

What a mess.

"Melina!" He called her name softly, but she didn't slow down. She turned the corner on the sidewalk leading to the motel office. Ash followed, despite the little voice of self-preservation that urged him to get in the car and slip away before the heat was on.

If Melina chose to walk into trouble for the sake of a bad-tempered runaway, that was her problem. It didn't have to be his, too.

So why was he still following her in his bare feet?

When he turned the corner, it was as bad as he had

imagined. Melina, Stomp, the potbellied Cowboy Corral manager in his elastic-waist jeans and pointy-toed boots, two police officers wearing uniforms, firearms and deep frowns, and a soft-drink machine with a jimmied door. A small pile of cans lay scattered on the sidewalk. Everyone was talking. Yelling, perhaps, was a better way to describe it. Throbbing broke out behind Ash's eyes, in a band around his temples.

"Oh, look, Officers!" Melina's voice broke through the commotion. "It's my brother. Hubert. Hubert can explain everything."

Everyone turned to look at Hubert. The band tightened around Ash's head. He would have to explain to her that it wasn't a good idea to give the police a name unless you had the identification to back it up. Especially a name that didn't match the one you'd given to the pudgy cowboy when you registered for the night at the Corral.

Ash smiled his most trustworthy smile. "Is there a problem, Gladys?"

Melina beamed sweetly. "These nice gentlemen believe your daughter broke into the soft-drink machine. I told them my niece would never do a thing like that. Would she?"

Ash looked at Stomp, who was still outfitted like an L.A. gang member. Her gun, which could probably be traced to whatever crimes she was running from, was locked in the glove compartment of the car. And Ash's present ID documents claimed him to be Carlton Ward, a computer software salesman from Lima,

Ohio. Hubert didn't even match the middle initial on his driver's license-of-the-day.

And Stomp was giving him an evil eye that said she knew better than to expect him to back her up. The jig was up, that was clearly her assessment of the situation. Melina, however, looked at him with complete trust that he could fix things.

"Of course not, Gladys. Now why don't you run back to the room and lie down?" He gave the officers an apologetic look. "My sister hasn't been feeling well, Officers. Our little trip hasn't been easy on her."

One of them tipped his hat and drawled, "Certainly, ma'am. We oughta be talking to the…" He glanced uncertainly at Stomp. "The girl's father, that's who we oughta be talking to anyway."

"Oh, but I'm far too upset to lie down."

Ash reached for her wrist and nudged her out of the circle. "Do it anyway, Gladys." In her ear, he whispered, "This is not Andy of Mayberry, and the only moral to this story is likely to be 'crime never pays.' Would you kindly go back to the room and give me one less thing to worry about?"

She gave him a bright smile and a peck on the cheek. "Horace is such a fussbudget. Always worrying about me. Aren't you, Horace?"

Horace. Hubert. He wondered if she was making a concerted effort to raise the suspicions of the local constables. Well, it just so happened that Ash Thorndyke had never been fingerprinted, and he didn't intend to start today in a wide spot on a Texas highway.

"The women in my life cause me a lot of grief," he said to the two middle-aged patrolmen. "That ever happen to you gentlemen?"

The two men exchanged a glance. The one with the handlebar mustache said, "I've seen that happen before, yessir."

"You want to tell us about it, Hiram? It was Hiram, wasn't it?" said the other.

"Actually, it's Carlton. Carlton Ward. Lima, Ohio. I believe the manager here can confirm that. My sister likes to horse around. It's sort of a family joke."

Mustache gestured at the vandalized machine. "This really isn't a joke, Mr. Ward."

"No, of course not. I understand that. My sister understands that. My daughter understands that, don't you?"

Stomp's sullen expression softened somewhat. "It was an accident."

"An accident!" The manager sounded outraged.

"It stole my money. A whole dollar." Stomp apparently knew a little bit about how to run a scam herself. Ash would have sworn she was about to cry. Real tears. "It was the dollar Grandma gave me. I didn't mean to spend it and I realized it too late and I pushed the lever to get it back and the machine took it anyway."

Melina moved in to encircle the girl's narrow shoulders. "Oh, sweetheart, you poor thing. Carlton, Mother gave her that money." She brushed the corner of one wide, completely convincing eye. "Right before she died."

Another con artist. The three of them were quite a trio. He glanced at the officers to see if it was working. Even the manager looked mollified. There might not be a hanging in Texas this week after all.

"Still, she should have asked for help," Ash said, the soul of fatherly sternness.

Melina hugged the girl closer and matched Ash's no-nonsense glare. "Now, Carlton, she has no reason to turn to you for help and you know it." She turned limpid, beseeching eyes on the officers. "Carlton has not been a reliable father. He disappears."

"Now, wait a minute—"

"He's abandoned her before, you see. It's no wonder she's troubled."

Mustache and his sidekick now turned their suspicious eyes on Ash.

"There are extenuating circumstances here, Officers." Ash heard a very unprincess-like snort from his sister, Gladys. "The matter at hand is this. My daughter has destroyed some property. She and I may have a difficult relationship, but she has to accept responsibility for her actions."

"I'll pay for it," Stomp said, backhanding one of her real tears. "I'll baby-sit the Holden triplets every week until I pay back every penny."

Mustache looked skeptical that anyone would hire a teenager who looked like this one to care for three precious babies. But the manager looked sufficiently appeased and Ash could only pray that no charges would be filed against a teenage baby-sitting entrepreneur whose beloved grandmother had recently passed away.

They finally settled it with a fistful of crisp Las Vegas twenties to the manager and a stiff warning from both the officers. Nobody even asked to see Ash's ID or threatened to search his car for weapons being sought in connection with felonies, or questioned whether Melina's name was really Gladys or if that was a family joke, too. And Stomp got a dollar back.

"See," he said to Melina as they walked back to their room. "There isn't always a moral to the story."

He watched Stomp's back as she preceded them to their room. She walked with her usual slouching swagger, the gait of the street, meant to demonstrate her unconcern. But he'd caught the piercing gaze she'd trained on him as he peeled off bills for the Cowboy Corral manager. A gaze that said she'd called his bluff and couldn't figure out why he hadn't folded his hand.

Melina almost had a skip in her step. "But it was kind of fun. You have to admit that."

He remembered how readily she'd fallen in with the scamming that came so easily to him and the teenager. "It's never fun when the police show up."

"I guess you know."

He was silent. Melina paused, blocking the door to their room. She searched his face with her dark eyes. There was no delight in them now, only a hurt she hadn't allowed him to see until this moment. He remembered her contribution to their little scam. She'd accused him of being prone to abandon the people he loved.

And of course, he had done precisely that.

"Who are you, Ash Thorndyke? You're not who I think you are. Who are you?"

She had asked the same question before. He owed her an answer, if not an explanation. "I am exactly who you think I am."

A frown creased her perfect forehead. "But—"

"A con man. A thief. Someone you're better off not knowing."

He watched the reactions cross her face. The skepticism, the confusion, the inevitable moment of belief. "But—"

"That's all you need to know, princess. That ought to explain everything."

He brushed past her into the bedroom, wishing he could explain why her knowing the truth about him filled him with such emptiness.

POSETI SLIPPED his credit card across the counter of the Cowboy Corral and wrote a name and address in the ledger. He could hardly believe that Melina's trail had led him here, but what he'd heard from the garrulous hotel manager confirmed it. She'd been here the night before, accompanied by a smooth-talking man she called her brother and a rough-looking teenager she'd said was her niece.

The boss would have a coronary. Of all the places Tom Somerset's daughter had stayed at on her little escapades, this was the worst. And in such company. Poor Tom.

And poor Melina, Poseti thought as he crossed the parking lot. He understood what she wanted. A normal life. Unlike Melina, however, Poseti also understood what Tom Somerset understood: It wasn't possible. Not for one of the world's richest young women. Of course, things could have been a bit more normal, if Tom permitted it. Tom was obsessive about his daughter, no question about that. And who could blame him? Poseti figured he'd be the same way, if he'd lost family the way Tom had.

Poseti understood both the father and the daughter. He sympathized with them both. But he was being paid to do what Tom told him to do.

He opened the room, the same one Melina and her traveling companions had been in. Maybe he would find something, some detail the cleaning crew had missed. At least he knew he was closing in. Less than twenty-four hours behind them. He would have her in hand soon. He would search the room thoroughly, then head out again before the trail grew any colder. Tom would be relieved to hear the news.

He picked up the phone.

Before he could punch the first number, he felt the knife blade at his neck. He heard the harsh whisper in his left ear. "Tell us who you are and what you know about the woman and you don't have to die here in a grungy little stinkhole in Texas."

Poseti had no intention of drawing his last breath anytime soon. But he also knew that was exactly what he'd do if it meant keeping this man away from Melina Somerset.

MELINA PICKED the restaurant at the Tennessee freeway exit because it had a video arcade. She didn't even have to explain to Ash why that was important. She saw his comprehension before she even opened her mouth to repeat her familiar refrain. She didn't need to tell him that she'd never played a video game before. He seemed to see it in her eyes and he pulled into the parking lot.

It bothered her that he found her so transparent.

It made her wonder what else he could see. She knew her body was changing, even if only slightly. Would he notice that, too? She would have to think about that from now on, dress to disguise her condition until they went their separate ways. She couldn't risk his finding out the truth because she knew now that he was the kind of man who would want to do the right thing.

But he wasn't the kind of man she wanted around her baby. A con man. A thief. The father of her baby. She shivered.

He ordered their pizza and sat at one of the tables outside the arcade while she tried to play the video game. It was too fast, too loud, too out of control for her.

"I can't do this," she said to Stomp, who slouched against the machine and viewed the arcade with nonchalance.

"It's dumb anyway. Say, there's a cigarette machine. I could cop a smoke while you watch out for the warden.''

"Cop a smoke?" Melina wrinkled her nose. "That's so smelly."

Stomp rolled her eyes. "You're hopeless."

"And you'll get addicted."

"So?"

Something clutched at Melina's heart. She knew her own losses intimately, but she couldn't imagine how it felt to have no one who cared what you did or what happened to you. What was it like to be so lacking in people who cared about you that you learned not to care yourself? She didn't want to find out.

"Teach me the video game."

She watched as Stomp turned her eyes to the game. Melina caught a flash of hunger in the girl's usually carefully noncommittal eyes before she shrugged and looked away from the flashing screen.

A faint smile flickered across Stomp's face. "You'll get addicted."

Melina grinned. "At least it's not smelly."

A snort of derisive laughter was Stomp's only reply, but she moved in to take over the controls. Melina learned quickly, but just as quickly she realized that Stomp had let down her guard long enough to wholeheartedly enjoy the game. Soon the girl was laughing and hooting and completely caught up in her attempts to slay the aliens invading the planet.

Smiling, Melina backed off and left the game, and the pile of quarters, to the teenager. She glanced back at the table and saw Ash's steady gaze on them. Sometimes she thought he never took his eyes off them. That should have bothered her. But it didn't.

She returned to the table.

She sat across from him. A television hung from the wall over his shoulder. Old-fashioned rock and roll drifted from the jukebox. Three tall glasses had already been delivered to the table. She peered into one of them. "What did you get me this time?"

"Dr Pepper. You haven't had that yet."

She reined in her pleased smile. He always tried to order something she'd never tried. She sipped cautiously. So far she'd loved everything he'd ordered. "It's wonderful. Not peppery at all."

"You think everything's wonderful."

"That's because everything is wonderful," she said with a satisfied sigh. "The world is full of wonderful stuff."

"And you want your share."

"I want to experience my share," she clarified. "I don't care a fig about owning any of it."

"Americans don't care a fig," he corrected her.

"Oh. Then I don't care a hoot."

"*Give* a hoot."

The pizza came. Neither of them reached for it.

"Is that so wrong?" she asked. "To want to live life completely."

"Of course not."

He transferred a slice to her plate, then one to his. Melina tried to analyze his tone of voice but found she couldn't. He was too good at hiding what was really going on with him. "A professional skill, I suppose."

"What?"

"Nothing." She stared at her steaming pizza. "Do I seem silly to you? Childish? I'm more of a kid than she is. That's not right, is it?"

He reached across the table, hesitated, then touched the tips of her fingers only long enough to get her to look into his eyes. "It's exactly right, Melina."

Oh, but looking into his eyes was so dangerous. Feeling the brush of his fingertips wasn't safe, either. "Why?"

"Because you never got to be a kid. It's okay to do it now."

"She never had a childhood, either."

"No."

"Then—"

"Be a good example for her."

Melina felt a stinging behind her eyes and had to look away. "Can I do that?"

"Look at her."

Melina glanced into the arcade. Stomp was high-fiving a little boy. She had a broad smile on her face. She looked so young. So heartbreakingly young to have been through so much.

"It's not too late for her, is it?" She looked at him with hope in her eyes, searched his face once again, this time for some sign that he shared her hope. "She can have a normal life, can't she? Once we get her to Hope Springs? We can all have a normal life."

His jaw worked. He looked as if he needed to say

something or burst. She waited. Hoping he would talk about whatever was gnawing at him. She needed to understand what he'd told her two days earlier in Texas. She needed to hear from him why the man she'd once believed to be her all-American hero called himself a con man and a thief.

But before he spoke, she saw a face flash onto the television screen over his shoulder. Her father's security chief stared down at her from the TV screen. Mouth open, she watched the report, straining to hear over the restaurant noise. Poseti was dead. Murdered in the Cowboy Corral Motel.

And in that moment, she had the answer to her question. The answer was no. Maybe they could manage a normal life for Stomp. But not for all of them. Not for Melina.

CHAPTER EIGHT

THE VIEW of the little valley that cradled the town of
Hope Springs, Virginia, gave Melina her first spark
of enthusiasm since learning of Poseti's death. Green
and lush and serene, the picture-postcard town re-
stored her hope that America offered refuge for someone with a bruised spirit.

"It's like paradise," she murmured.

The three of them were gathered beside the hood
of the car Ash had bought with his Las Vegas earn-
ings. At Melina's insistence, Ash had pulled over at
the scenic overlook on the mountain road. Woodlands
and rolling meadows reached down toward the town,
which was made up of meandering, tree-lined streets,
a rainbow of Victorian houses mixed with sturdy
stone cottages, a handful of pristine church steeples
and a breathtaking, century-old inn sprawled across
the hillside on the opposite boundary of the valley.

"I told you," Stomp said. "Come on. Let's get
going."

The girl sounded bored, an attitude she seemed to
work hard to cultivate. But Melina detected the un-
dercurrent of excitement in her voice. Stomp might
not be able to admit it—might not even realize it—
but she was eager to reach their destination.

Eager to get home.

Melina smiled softly and looked down on Hope Springs. Could this be the home she longed for, too? Or would it present another disappointment, another dashed hope? Would it bring her one step closer to the harsh truth that there could be no safe haven for her and her baby? Poseti's death had filled her heart and soul with dread and anguish, the pain all the sharper because he had died trying to find her.

And that meant the danger to her was real. Horrifyingly real.

Every night since Poseti was killed, she had cried herself to sleep, grieving for the man who had always been kind to her. Then, in the early hours of the morning, terror had awakened her. She wanted her father. And yet, she wanted to take her baby as far away from her old life as it was possible to get.

Her only consolation in the days since learning of Poseti's death had been Ash. He'd been a rock, a gentle rock. More than once, sitting beside the bed she shared with Stomp, he'd held her hand until she slept. Without Ash, she would have drowned in her fear and sorrow.

Maybe things would be different, now that they were in Hope Springs. A part of her wanted to push ahead and find out. A part of her wanted to stay right here on the side of the highway overlooking the valley and enjoy the dream from afar, without the risk of disappointment.

Ash put a hand on her shoulder. "She's right," he

said in the tender voice he'd used since Poseti's death. "It's been a long trip. Let's get it over with."

She felt the sting of tears behind her eyes. Tears brought on by the promise of Hope Springs, by the comfort in his voice and by the warmth of his touch. She felt the emotional tug of that contact—both physical and emotional—clear to her belly.

Hadn't he earned the right to know about their baby these past few days?

She reminded herself that gaining the trust of others was his stock-in-trade. She had to be careful that her grief didn't make her more susceptible to him. She swept away from Ash, away from the view. "You're right. Let's go."

Halfway down the valley, in the midst of the rolling meadows they'd seen from the highway, Stomp pointed out a slightly battered metal mailbox. The name Edgar Grunkemeier was clumsily painted on the side.

"That's it!" she cried.

Ash slowed the car. The mailbox was stuffed, full to overflowing. Stomp strained forward in the back seat. No house was visible from the highway. They turned onto a dirt driveway.

"Is that your name?" Melina asked. "Grunke-meier?"

"Pretty bad, huh?"

"It's different, that's all."

"Yeah, right."

The house at the end of the driveway was neither a Victorian beauty nor one of the imposing stone houses common in the mountains. It was a simple clapboard farmhouse, white with peeling green shutters, brick chimneys at both ends, a porch stretched across the front. The flower beds along the front of the house contained mostly weeds and the aging pickup truck parked alongside the house listed to one side. A barn to the rear of the house needed paint and the calico cat in the front-porch rocker looked in need of a meal. The cat scurried toward them, welcoming them with a demanding yowl.

Melina had never seen a place so utterly ordinary. Momentarily, her guilt and her grief eased. She fell in love.

She hopped out of the car. The cat immediately wound itself around her ankles, clamoring for attention.

"Oh, Stomp, it's beautiful! It's perfect!"

"It is?" Stomp was exiting the car warily.

"Of course it is. It's so…so…all-American."

"And I thought it was just run-down," the teenager said dryly. "Sometimes, Mel, you are just too weird."

"But look at it," Melina protested. "It's…it's got rocking chairs. And shutters. And flower beds."

She leaned over and picked up the cat, hugging it to her chest. "And a cat."

Stomp advanced on the quiet house. "Yeah. Probably fleas, too."

The cat continued to offer the only welcome. She struggled free of Melina's grasp but remained close as they approached the house. No one answered their knocks at the front door. Stomp insisted her uncle must be home because of the truck, so they went to the back of the house to check the barn. The barn door stood open, but there was no sign of anyone there, either.

"Let's go in," Stomp said, heading for the back door. "He always left the back door unlocked. He said anytime I came I was to treat it like home."

Melina picked up the calico again and held the cat close to her cheek as they entered through the back door into a small, untidy kitchen. The room smelled stale. The cat purred. On the plain wooden kitchen table sat most of a meal, unfinished.

Melina could tell that the food clinging to the plate had been there longer than a few hours.

"Let's get out of here," Ash said briskly.

"It's okay," Stomp said. "Really it is. Uncle Tood said—"

"Uncle Tood hasn't been here for a while," Ash said. "And it looks like he left in a hurry."

Ash was right. The evidence was all there. A starving cat, a full mailbox, an unfinished meal. Melina's fingers tightened around the scrawny cat, who wriggled and complained.

"You don't think—"

Ash put hands on both their shoulders and moved toward the back door. "We're not going to think. We're just going to leave."

"Not until I feed the cat."

"Not now."

His voice was beyond firm, and the gravity of his

concerns communicated itself to her. But she refused
to give in to fear. Wasn't it fear that had ruined her
life?

"She'll starve," she said stubbornly.

"Then bring her with you. Now."

Urgency sharpened Ash's voice. Nodding, Melina
followed him and Stomp back out to the car. By the
time they reached the front of the house, she heard
another vehicle approaching.

"In the car," Ash ordered in a voice that brooked
no argument.

Before they could get into the car, however, the
other vehicle pulled in behind them. It was driven by
a pleasingly rounded blond woman with a face grown
long with weariness.

"Well, hello," she said, her soft, breathy voice
touched by a Virginia drawl. "Are you—" Her eyes
landed on Stomp and her eyes grew wide. *"Emily!"*
She rushed forward and threw her arms around the
teenager. "Emily, I'd know you anywhere! Oh, I'm
so glad you made it."

Melina watched as Stomp submitted uncomfortably
to the older woman's embrace and muttered, "Hi,
Miss...um..."

"Ida, dear. It's Ida Monroe. From the tearoom.
Your aunt's best friend."

"Yeah. Miss Ida."

"Oh, Emily, now that you're here, everything is
going to turn out just right. I know it is!"

STOMP FIGURED, as they all headed for the county
hospital in Miss Ida Monroe's little car, that it wasn't

too late. She could get away.

A hospital. They were going to a hospital. Stomp's heart pumped faster and faster as Miss Ida's car chugged along the highway. Stomp hated hospitals. She hated sick people. She'd sworn, when her mother died, that she'd never hang around another goddamn hospital in her life. She'd had her fill of sickness and death.

She thought she might throw up.

In a matter of instants, her mountain paradise had turned into her very worst nightmare.

Her uncle was sick. He would probably die. But not right away. Stomp knew that routine. And she was his only living relative. Miss Ida had said so, between all her rattling on about how she hadn't had a chance to see after the house and the mail because she'd been staying at the hospital day and night and how Tood's fool friends from the barbershop had seen to milking the cows and not another blessed thing. Stomp barely registered any of that. She heard only the important parts. The parts about the hospital and the heart attack.

She could run again. She wouldn't even think about missing Mel and Ash. She wouldn't think about anything but saving herself.

She should have seen it coming. It was her own stupid fault for thinking anything in life could ever turn out the way it was supposed to. Uncle Tood had been her only hope and here he was dying. Except that, with her luck, he'd live and she'd end up playing

Cinderella, cooking and cleaning and quite possibly milking cows or doing something equally gross.

Damn.

No wonder her old man did drugs. Life was too damn hard. Whenever you thought you just about had it licked, something came along and yanked the rug out from under you again.

She brooded all the way to the hospital. She didn't pay one bit of attention to Melina, who went gaga over every single stupid thing they saw along the way, like Uncle Tood's apple orchards or the stupid old horses in his meadows, or the falling-down wooden stand on the side of the road where somebody had blackberries and muscadine jelly for sale.

"Oh, look!"

Melina put one hand on Stomp's arm and pointed with the other.

"What now? The eight millionth wonder of the world?"

In the front seat, Ash chuckled.

"No," Melina said, unfazed. "The town sign. Look what it says."

Stomp rolled her eyes. Welcome to Hope Springs. You'll Need No Other Medicine but Hope. "Ten on the barf-o-meter."

Stomp knew she was acting like a real jerk, but it beat crying, which seemed to be the alternative.

Melina just laughed. "Well, I think it's—"

"Beautiful," Stomp finished for her.

"Actually, Emily, I was going to say wonderful."

"And it's Stomp. Not…" She wrinkled her nose. "Not Emily."

"But Emily's such a pretty—"

"No, it's not."

Then she lapsed into silence. Nobody called her Emily. Nobody. Not anymore. Not since she was 11.

"Emily?"

Her mom's voice was weak, so tiny and lost amid the sounds of the machines in her hospital room that Emily could only hear her by scooting up so close to the bed that she could smell death. But she didn't let that stop her because she didn't want to miss a single word her mom said.

"Emily, I want you to promise me…"

Emily had touched her mom's skin. It was rough now, not soft the way it used to be. Her dark, crinkly hair had no more life in it. Even her lips had grown thin and tight. Emily pictured her own face, part Caucasian, part African-American, and wished with all her might she had more of her mother to keep with her.

"Sure, Mom. Anything. You name it."

"Take care…take care of your dad."

Oh, man. The one thing Emily knew she couldn't do, the one promise she knew she'd never be able to keep. Her old man didn't even show up at the hospital anymore, just left it all to Emily. But what could she do but promise?

"Sure, Mom."

"Take him home. Back to Hope Springs."

Emily didn't know how she was supposed to do that

when nobody could even get him to come back to their house anymore, unless it was to lift something else he could hock for drugs. But she didn't ask. Emily was a good daughter.

"Sure, Mom."

"That's my girl. My Emily."

They got to the hospital too soon to suit Stomp. She felt kind of broken inside. Smelling the hospital smells, hearing the hospital sounds didn't help. She kept thinking of the hours and hours she'd spent at her mother's side in a hospital just like this, hours so endless they ran together.

Except for the hour when her mother died. That one stood out.

Her heart hurt.

It took every ounce of courage she had not to run away. Turn and run and run and run until...

Until what?

There was nowhere else to go.

"You're going to be fine." That was Melina, close by her shoulder, touching her elbow and whispering softly so nobody else even noticed.

Stomp wanted to grunt out something flippant, but she couldn't find enough breath for words. She looked at the woman who had made possible the trip all the way across the country and wished she had a big sister just like Melina Somerset. Somebody strong and pretty and full of life, so Stomp wouldn't feel so scared and ugly and dead inside.

Melina spoke again. "I'm right here. You're not by yourself anymore, you know."

Stomp felt some of those broken pieces inside her begin to fall apart. She couldn't remember the last friend she'd had. "Yeah, well..."

"Come on. I'll go with you. Just us two. Then it won't matter what happens."

If Melina said one more word, Stomp knew she'd be crying right here in front of the whole world. She didn't do that even when her mother died.

So, to avoid a scene, she took the hand Melina offered and marched off toward the intensive care unit, bracing herself to see the uncle who might just turn her into Cinderella.

Triple damn.

THE ROCKING CHAIR on the front porch creaked in the dark. To Ash's ears, the sound was louder here in the country than any noise pollution he'd ever encountered in the major cities of the world.

He kept the rocker moving. It wasn't a restful, contented rocking. It was the constant motion of a man who didn't know whether to run or run faster.

The screen door of the old farmhouse creaked, too, when it opened behind him. The crack of a gunshot would have startled him less. He'd begun to feel very much alone, the last man alive in the world, or at least between here and that bump in the road called Hope Springs.

Melina dropped into the rocker beside him. "She's asleep."

Stomp. Emily. After crossing the country to get here, the teenager was now agitated and afraid. After the neighbor woman, Ida Monroe, dropped them off at the farm following the visit with Edgar Grunkemeier, Stomp—Emily—had huddled in a threadbare chair in the living room for hours.

"I don't want to be with a sick old man," she'd insisted over and over. "Nobody can make me, can they?"

Melina had been patient and soothing. He knew from the look in her eyes that she'd been afraid the girl would take off in the night.

"Nobody's going to make us stay here if we don't want to," Melina had said. "We're just here for now, because it's safe and pretty and we want to be. Whenever we want to leave—"

"*You* can leave." Stomp had looked from one to the other of them accusingly. "Both of you. Just walk away. Ride off into the sunset. Nothing holding you here."

"*You* hold us here," Melina had insisted. "We're here for you."

That's when Ash had escaped to the porch, leaving them to talk. Melina had a bond with the girl that he didn't, he rationalized.

But the truth was, he wanted to do exactly what Stomp had accused him of. He wanted out of here, before his feelings for both the girl and the woman closed in on him.

Melina's foot reached out to tap the porch banister and set her rocker in motion. "I didn't lie to her, did I?"

"What do you mean?"

"When I said we aren't going to run off and leave her alone."

Ash hesitated. He thought of driving away. In one day, he could be in Washington D.C., New York City, Boston. He could already feel the ease of being responsible for no one, owing allegiance or honesty to no one. He could take deep breaths of the freedom of knowing he would disappoint no one if he couldn't cut it in the real world, as a real person.

"This could be the perfect place for you," he said. "Off the beaten path. Norman Rockwell American. Just what you're looking for, isn't it?"

"So *you'll* be leaving? Is that it?"

She had to put it that way, put such a bald face on what he wanted to hide as subtext.

He tried on another picture—the two of them, Emily and Melina, here alone, helpless. Neither of them could cook or drive or earn a living. They needed him. Damn! He didn't want to be needed.

"I've never seen a night so dark," he said, not knowing how to answer her. His code of honor told him one thing; his sense of being on unsure footing told him another.

Help them, said the voice of decency.

Get out of their lives, argued the voice of common sense. *That's the best way to help them.*

"It always seems darker in the country," she said. Her voice was as soft and light as the night air, barely a breath of sound against the backdrop of swaying tree branches and the occasional ominous hoot Ash presumed was an owl. "No city lights. Is that it, Ash? You need the excitement that much?"

That wasn't it at all. But maybe it would be just as well if it looked that simple to her.

"I don't know a tractor from a tree frog, princess."

"How about a teenager? Do you know a teenager from a tree frog, Ash?"

He heard the disdainful accusation in her voice.

"How about a teenager who's never known anything but abandonment? A teenager who needs to know she can count on somebody in this wretched world she didn't ask for? Maybe you'd recognize that if you saw it."

"You're a better one for her to count on than me," he said, hating the weak-sounding words.

"Yes, I am."

She stood and disappeared into the house, leaving him alone in the darkest night he'd ever known.

HE WAS LEAVING this morning. Melina knew it in her bones. She knew it deep in her belly, where the life they'd made together felt more vulnerable than it had felt the day before.

Her heart said she should tell him about the baby. He'd been so kind since Poseti died. She owed him her honesty.

Then she thought about the way he'd left her in London, the way he'd all but admitted he was going to leave her and Emily, and told herself she would be better off if he did go. He clearly couldn't be counted on, that's what her head told her. He was dishonest and unreliable.

Except lately.

Her heart kept chiming in. But Melina knew it was time to listen to her head. She made up her mind to pretend it didn't matter, to show him that she and Emily would be just fine—better off, really—without him.

She made bacon and eggs for breakfast. She'd never cracked an egg before and the first two became a puddle of broken yolks and crushed eggshell. The bacon was extra-crispy, made up for by the fact that the eggs were extra-runny.

"Just the way I like them," Emily said, her sarcasm a shade less biting than usual.

Ash said he wasn't hungry.

"That's okay," Emily said, giving Melina a shrewd look. "She always eats enough for two."

Melina almost spewed coffee onto her plate of runny eggs, glancing at the girl to see if she could possibly know what she was saying. Emily smiled, but Melina couldn't figure out what was behind the smile. She switched to her best cowboy-actor imitation. "Ranching's hungry work."

"It's a farm," Emily pointed out. "Not a ranch."

"It's the same thing."

"We have apples. Ranches have millions of cows. We have only seven or eight."

"Good. Apples should be much easier to manage than cows."

Emily snapped a piece of bacon in two. "Why do

we have to manage anything? Why can't we just leave? All three of us?''

Melina resisted looking at Ash. "Because it's nice here. You said yourself, we can ride horses and eat apples right off the tree and nobody's going to bother us.''

Emily looked skeptical. "If we're going to stay, we should learn to drive the tractor.''

"Oh, no," Ash began.

"We have a tractor?''

"Get that gleam right out of your eyes," Ash said.

Melina ignored him. "You're right," she said to Emily. "That should be our first order of business.''

Ash poured himself another cup of coffee. He made a sour face as he swallowed. "That'll make it handy for visiting Mr. Grunkemeier.''

They looked at him quizzically.

"You'll *all* be in the hospital then.''

"We'll be fine," Melina said.

"You don't even know how to drive a car.''

"I don't see what one has to do with the other.''

"Judas!''

"I can drive a car," Emily said.

"See.''

Melina looked at him smugly. He looked back at her grimly. She really liked setting him off this way. It felt like payback. Maybe, in time, little bits and pieces of payback would add up to the gigantic payback he deserved. She jumped up from the table and gestured to Emily. "Come on. Ash can clean up this mess. We'll go play with the tractor.''

With a whoop, Emily started after her.

They were halfway across the dusty backyard when she heard Ash call after them. "It's not a toy, damn it!"

Melina linked her arm through Emily's. "He thinks we're children."

"Maybe he's right."

"We most certainly are not!"

"About the tractor, I mean."

"Oh, he's a fussbudget."

"They're awfully big."

"We'll be careful. Besides, there are two of us and only one of it."

Emily almost giggled. "You're a real trip, you know that, Mel?"

The barn door was heavy, but between the two of them they managed to prop it open to allow the morning sunshine to pour into the musty interior of the building. Instruments of torture made of rusty-looking metal, rough-hewn wood and aging leather hung from the hooks or leaned against the bare walls. Enormous, foul-smelling bags were stacked beside the door.

"What are those things?" Melina asked, pointing to the variously round, pointed and pronged objects on the wall.

"UFOs."

"What?"

"Unidentified Farming Objects." Emily pointed to the back of the barn. "There it is."

Emily was right. Tractors were awfully big. Melina approached it cautiously, almost afraid the machine would chug to life and launch an attack. She might have seen that once, on an old horror-movie rerun. Beneath a coating of dust, cobwebs and caked-on mud, the tractor was green. The deep tread of its tires snarled at her like snaggly teeth, waiting to take a bite out of her. Mounting the seat would require a ladder.

In her effort to thumb her nose at Ash and distract herself from his leaving, she might have bitten off more than she could chew, as they said here in America.

She began to hedge. "Actually, I've never done this before."

Emily's enthusiasm for self-destruction was clearly kicking in. She had already climbed onto the filthy monster and gripped its steering wheel in her small hands.

"I know," Emily said. "Isn't it cool?"

"Maybe I'd better go first."

"It's *my* farm."

"I'm the oldest."

"Big whoop."

"Besides, your feet don't reach the pedal things."

Emily looked down at her feet, which dangled in front of her. They were a good foot from the operating pedals. She wriggled around and adjusted her position a dozen different ways, but it was no use.

"Well, it's not like you're a giant yourself," she said, ill-naturedly relinquishing the seat of honor to Melina. "What if you can't reach them, either?"

"I've got four inches on you," Melina said, ignoring the fact that Emily had needed twelve extra inches. "I'll reach them."

She did, too. By standing more than sitting, her fanny resting on the edge of the seat, she could manage to reach the foot controls.

It took only five minutes to figure out how to start the engine.

It roared and vibrated like a horror-movie monster.

Melina was on the verge of suggesting they'd learned enough for one day when she noticed Ash standing in the doorway, backlit by the glaring sun. He was glaring, too. His arms were crossed tightly over his chest. His lips were compressed into a hard, disapproving line.

Spurred by a fit of pique, she stomped the pedal beneath her right foot as hard as she could. After all, women drove everyday. Even pregnant women. What could it possibly hurt? She would show Mr. Ash Thorndyke that she was not as helpless as he liked to believe. Who needed a man if you could drive a tractor?

The monster tractor chugged, then roared forward. She heard Emily squeal. She might have squealed herself. The front of the barn was getting closer.

Her first instinct was to wrap her arms around her midsection to protect her baby. But she needed both hands to maneuver between the open barn door. She tried to figure out how to slow down, but the door just kept getting closer.

She heard them both calling her name.

She sent up a prayer for her baby's safety.

She felt the thrum of the big machine beneath her.

Then she heard splintering wood, felt her bones rattle as the tractor chewed through half the barn door and part of the side wall. She should have slowed down, she thought as she felt herself flying through the air into the path of the lurching, growling tractor.

CHAPTER NINE

THE TRACTOR STOPPED before Melina did.

The tractor stopped in a gravel-spitting little spin. Its right rear tire hung up on the splintered barn door; its engine chugged out a protest before whining to silence.

Melina stopped when she hit the dusty ground with a thud that Ash felt clear to his bones. Then she lay there, as silent as the tractor. He tried to call her name, but all that came out was a strangled cry. He was kneeling beside her in moments, afraid to touch her. Emily skidded to a halt beside them.

"Is she dead?"

"No!"

He said it because he refused for it to be so, not because he had any confidence it wasn't. Her eyes were closed, her skin was pale.

"Want me to call the hospital?"

"No!"

That even more emphatic reply came from Melina. She still hadn't moved, her eyes were still closed. But her voice sounded far too strong to belong to a dead woman. Ash's knees began to tremble.

He croaked out, "Where does it hurt?"

She opened one eye and stared up at him with a wry smile. "My backside, what do you think?"

Emily leaned over and wiggled one of her feet. "Can you feel that?"

"Ow! I most certainly can. And I'll kick you with the other one if you try it again."

Emily giggled.

Ash still couldn't get over the rush of fear. Even as Melina was sitting up, dusting herself off, preparing to stand, he wasn't sure he could move.

"You could've killed yourself," he said, his voice hushed with anxiety.

"Well, I didn't," she said. "But I did a pretty good job on the barn door."

"You might have a concussion," Emily said.

"My head is just fine."

She stood then, but Ash saw her sway slightly. He was instantly on his feet, one arm around her waist.

"And I don't need the two of you fussing. I've been smothered all my life by people who thought I needed protecting." She jerked away from Ash. "I don't need any more of that."

She got two steps away, then stopped. She seemed to lean to one side, like the old truck beside the house. "Well, I might be a little…"

Ash grabbed her. She sagged against him and smiled up at him sheepishly.

"…woozy."

Then she began to dissolve into a puddle in his arms, her eyes drifting shut and her bones going slack.

He picked her up and cradled her to his chest, where his heart surged with fear.

"I'll get the car keys," Emily said, heading for the house in a dead run.

Ash stood there, holding Melina's slight body in his arms, praying she would be okay, cursing himself for being unable to protect her from herself or anyone else. He realized, as he walked with her to the car, that he loved her and no amount of running from it would solve the problem. He loved Melina Somerset for her innocence and her exuberance and her boldness.

He settled her in the back seat of the car.

"Hang in there, princess," he whispered.

Her eyelids flickered. A half smile lingered on her lips. "I'm Sleeping Beauty," she murmured.

"Yeah, that's right."

"Wake me up."

It took him a moment to realize what her foggy murmurs were getting at, how the prince in the story woke the sleeping princess.

"No can do, princess," he said. "I'm not Prince Charming, remember?"

She nodded slightly, still smiling. He couldn't help himself. He touched his lips to one of her closed eyelids. He heard her sigh. He kissed the other. She whispered something unintelligible. He glanced at her lips. They still smiled.

He brushed his lips over hers.

The passenger door opened and Emily climbed

noisily into the front seat. "Come on, Prince Charming. Let's get to the doc."

TOM SOMERSET STAGED a quiet memorial service for his security chief—an employee who also happened to have been his best friend. He took Poseti home to his family—a widowed mother, a sister and her four kids—and made all the arrangements without a lot of interference from the news media.

Poseti would have wanted it that way, too.

Besides, he needed to keep it that way for Melina's sake. He'd used every bit of influence he had to see that the media didn't get wind of the fact that the traveler murdered in Texas worked for Tom Somerset. And he'd already hired a team of the best missing persons trackers money could buy. They did everything short of guarantee that they'd find his daughter. But if word got out in the meantime that she was missing...

He stood by the graveside, behind the small group of family and other mourners, most of whom were other Somerset employees. A minister droned on about life everlasting. There were sniffles, but no sobs. Tom received no comfort from the minister's words of hope.

It was a sunny Pennsylvania morning, bright and beautiful with promise. That promise hung over Tom's head and heart, mocking him.

Frank Poseti was dead, gone without ever hearing that Tom's feelings for him went deeper than professional admiration.

And Melina. Where was she? News of Poseti's death hadn't brought her home. She had run before, of course, but he couldn't believe that this death wouldn't draw her back. In her nearly nonexistent family, Poseti was like an uncle to her. Her absence today meant one of two things.

Either Tom's worst fears had been realized and Melina had been kidnapped. That made sense considering Poseti's violent death, but it didn't explain why there'd been no ransom demands.

There was a second choice. Tom remembered the conversation with his daughter the day she disappeared, her tearful pleas that she be allowed to live her life the way she imagined normal people did. Tom knew it was entirely possible that he had driven her away for good.

And he had to live with the knowledge that his attempts to keep his beloved daughter safe had merely made her miserable.

The minister closed with a prayer. Tom closed his eyes and lowered his head and placed his daughter in her maker's hands and wondered why he hadn't known she was better off there all along.

ASH SAT in a vinyl chair in the office of Dr. Sarah Biggers. He was barely able to restrain himself from storming through the door that separated the waiting room from the examining room.

He managed to keep his seat only because he told himself he didn't want to worry Emily, who paced from one window overlooking Ridge Lane to another.

And also because of the forbidding-looking receptionist, who had put a hand on his chest and pushed
him into the chair when he'd tried to bully his way
into the examining room with Melina. She glared at
him periodically, and he knew that no amount of
charm would work.

"She could be dead by now," Emily said.

"She's not dead."

"You don't know that."

Emily sounded sullen as she marched to another
window like a caged animal looking for the way out.
As she passed, Ash noted the stark terror in her wide,
wild eyes and suddenly remembered Melina's words
about a teenager who had seen too much of death and
abandonment. He knew that, as the adult, he should
comfort her, offer her some solace. It suddenly struck
him that he was better equipped than either Emily or
Melina to know how real family rallied at times like
these. Putting aside his own fears, Ash walked over
to the window and stood beside her.

"It's going to be okay," he said softly. "This is
just a precaution."

Emily shrugged, her favorite gesture for demon-
strating just how little she cared. "Sure."

What would his father do? His grandfather? He
looked at the girl's narrow shoulders, down at his
hands, helpless at the moment to do a thing for Melina. Drawing a breath for courage, he lifted one arm
and draped it lightly across Emily's shoulders. He
braced for her rejection.

"She's not going anywhere," he said.

She grew stiff beneath his embrace, but she didn't shrug it off. That was something, wasn't it?

"Anybody can die," she said in a small voice he'd never heard her use before, the voice of the frightened girl she hid beneath her tough exterior. "God just lets people die all the time. People who oughta live. He doesn't care who it hurts."

Ash thought of his own father, dying in a prison. He thought of his mother, dead now five years. The hurt in both cases was sharp, but not as sharp as it would have been if he were a child. He knew that. He wished for some words to soften Emily's pain. Everything that came to mind was a cliché, sure to provoke a cynical smirk from the girl. He had nothing to offer, other than a promise he knew he couldn't keep. The promise of his own steadfastness. The words formed in his heart and leaped to his lips, but he refused to do that to her.

"I don't know why things happen the way they do, Emily. I wish—"

They both jumped when a phone rang and the door from the examining room opened at the same time. The receptionist answered the phone. At the door, a reassuring smile softened the doctor's motherly face.

"She's going to be fine," Doc Biggers said. "A few bumps and bruises, that's all. No sign of a concussion, but—"

The receptionist interrupted. "Dr. Biggers, excuse me, but this is the hospital. Mr. Grunkemeier is awake. And he's asking for someone named Emily."

Emily slumped into a chair. "Swell."

THERE WERE TUBES in his nose and needles in his arms and geegaws stuck to his chest. Tood lay there on the board they called a bed in this dad-blamed hospital and decided it must be time to get to heaven and look around for Edith.

Not much to hang around here for, he thought. Pill bottles and loneliness. Hell, the old barn cat probably already ran off for Eubank's farm, him being gone so long and her being too lazy to catch a mouse if she was starving to death.

He listened to the aggravating beep of his machines and the ones attached to the rest of the old fogies. He listened to the squish of nurses' shoes. Cardiac care unit. Must be. He vaguely remembered feeling something like an anvil fall on his chest and reaching for the phone.

Must've gotten the call through, worse luck.

He remembered babbling, when he first woke up this morning, about Emily, his nephew's girl. Must've dreamed about her, he had it in his head he'd been talking to her. Rather, she'd been talking to him. Telling him to wake up and come home, that she was gonna stay with him on the farm.

Tood frowned.

He'd never see Emily again. And he'd live out his days a dried-up old invalid.

"Helluva sense of humor you got," he growled, directing his complaint heavenward.

The curtain that served to give him what little privacy was possible in the cardiac care unit fluttered. He didn't bother to look up. A nurse or a doctor or somebody with a needle wanting to suck him dry of a little more blood, he supposed.

"Uncle Tood?"

He felt his heart jump around. Dad-blame if it didn't sound like the girl. Maybe he was still out of it, just thought he was awake. He glanced toward the curtain.

His heart did another jack-in-the-box number.

"Emily?"

She took three tentative steps in his direction. He always had thought she was the prettiest little thing in three states. Skin the color of light coffee, her eyes so big and dark. She had a lot of her mama in her, which he knew some folks might not cotton to, her mama being African-American and all. Edith, who last saw Emily when she was barely a baby, always said God must not mind much if he made the combination so pretty.

"Can't disagree with that," Tood said now, the way he'd always answered Edith.

"What?"

Tood realized he'd confused her. "I didn't dream you up after all?"

"No, sir."

"Right nice of you to come and visit a sick old man."

Her eyes were wide, all right. Looked downright scared, come to think of it. Tood supposed he looked a fright.

"I didn't know you were sick. Me and my friends

just stopped by to visit. You told me I could stay at the farm whenever I wanted to.''

Tood realized the Man Upstairs hadn't been playing games with him after all. He had a plan for old Tood Grunkemeier.

''Well, then, I reckon I better be getting well right quick so I can get home before you all leave. Right?''

She looked so solemn and lost, and hearing him mention coming home didn't seem to help at all.

''Yes, sir.''

''We'll make us some buttermilk biscuits when I get there. How'd that be?''

A light came into her eyes but it was gone just as quickly. She shrugged. ''Whatever,'' she said.

MELINA PULLED her knees to her chest and curled against the trunk of the big tree. Emily and the barn cat had settled into bed for the night. The horses were sleeping. Ash was lost in the late-night news. And Melina was enjoying her freedom.

The early-summer night was awash in stars. A symphony of music from crickets and frogs rose up from the ground. And Melina hung between sky and earth, safe in the bow of a giant oak behind the barn. She'd spotted the enormous tree, with its three forking branches, and decided from the ground that the fork looked like a perfect retreat.

It had taken her all afternoon to figure out how to get from the ground to the fork. She had a skinned knee and three broken fingernails, but she could make the climb now in two minutes flat. And when she was up here, she never wanted to come down.

Even her father would have to agree she was safe here.

She was safe and her baby was safe. She smiled. It had felt so good to finally tell someone about the baby. After only a few minutes with Doc Sarah, she'd felt comfortable enough to confide in the doctor. Following a thorough exam, Doc Sarah said everything appeared normal. Then they'd had a nice, long talk about what Melina should expect as her pregnancy advanced. The changes Doc Sarah described had both thrilled and terrified her.

She was going to be a mother. It felt so real now.

And somehow, that made the jumble her emotions were in—her guilt about her father, her grief over Poseti, her anxieties about the future—that much more intense. She wanted, more than ever, to have someone with whom she could share the months ahead. And the person her heart wanted was Ash.

Her head wouldn't hear of it.

"You've never climbed a tree before, either, I suppose."

Ash's voice didn't startle her. It didn't even seem an invasion of her peace and quiet.

"Of course I have," she said. "Twice earlier today."

"That makes you a master tree climber."

"Yes. I believe it does."

"What's it like up there?"

"Up here, it's like there's no down there."

"A place to get away from it all."

It didn't seem fair, somehow, that he always seemed to understand what she said and felt. "That's right."

"Including me."

"Especially you."

She heard a scrape and a grunt and knew he was seeking a way up the tree. She could have told him the best route, but she didn't. He found it himself in less than two minutes.

"You must be an accomplished second-story man," she said, faintly disturbed both by his presence and by the reminder that he seemed adept at anything he tackled. He'd even figured out how to milk the cows with a minimum of muss and fuss. She wondered how long it would be before he figured out she was pregnant.

She tugged on the shirttail of the old flannel shirt she'd taken off a hook at the back door, hugging it more protectively around the belly that had barely expanded more than an inch or two.

Ash swung a long leg over the V formed by two of the trunks and sat face-to-face with her, his silence and his closed expression saying he had no intention of following that particular train of conversation. She wasn't easily dissuaded.

"Have you ever been caught?"

He didn't answer right away. Then, "Never." He dared her with his eyes to keep going.

She took the dare. "Have you stolen millions?"

"At least."

"Why?"

"It's what my family does."

She thought about that. She thought about the innocent baby growing inside her. "You mean your father taught you?"

"And my grandfather and my mother."

She shuddered.

"I know," he said. "But I never questioned it."

"Our parents are supposed to know best," she said, finding a thread of empathy that she hadn't expected.

"For years, it seemed exciting and glamorous."

"Like a movie rogue." The perfect role for him.

In the shadows, his smile looked bittersweet. "Exactly like a movie rogue."

"Tell me stories."

He surprised her then. Hesitantly at first, with a growing hint of regret as he continued, he told her stories. He painted word pictures of elegant parties and baubles that could support a dozen families for a lifetime. He told about moving in that world, looking like part of it but holding himself above it, convinced he was untouched by the greed and the shallowness he saw daily. He told about cover-ups and con jobs, slick escapes and close calls. It was as exciting as any old Cary Grant movie she'd ever seen on television.

"Then the luck ran out," he said. "Mother died and Dad lost his heart for it. That's when..."

"When what?"

"When he got caught."

"He was caught?"

"He's in prison now."

Melina heard the grief in Ash's voice and knew his father's imprisonment had taken a toll on him. "Oh, how awful."

"It's a minimum-security institution. Lots of white-collar criminals. Still, he's sick now and…" He shrugged. "That's why I came after you."

"Me? What did I have to do with it?"

"The guys who asked me to…to snatch you…they said they were feds. They said if I cooperated, they could arrange early parole for my father." He frowned. "Then I heard them talking and I realized they weren't exactly feds."

She hated all these warm feelings she was beginning to have for Ash Thorndyke, sympathy and empathy and even a touch of admiration that he felt responsibility for a woman he'd never met. *Thought* he'd never met. "So you decided to save me."

"That makes it sound a lot more noble than it was. Don't forget, it was nothing but a kidnapping scheme. And I was part of it."

She couldn't help herself. Maybe Ash was a hero, after all. "Thank you for saving me."

"It was the least I could do, wouldn't you say?"

She smiled at his reluctance to take credit for his good deed. "Is that why you left before? In London. Because of who you are? Because you didn't want me to know the truth?"

"That sounds a lot more noble than it was."

"Why, then?"

"Why don't we leave it at that, princess?"

That was a sound suggestion. She knew it. Even in

the face of everything she now knew about him, Melina felt an overwhelming urge to dust off his motives and find something lofty about them.

"But you did like me." She needed him to say it, even if it made no real difference. She needed to know that her child's father had liked—maybe loved?—her.

She thought for a moment he wasn't going to answer.

"I guess I'm a sucker for mysterious women using assumed names."

At least he didn't deny it. She told herself he was still protecting her, keeping her from falling into his personal sticky business.

"I think you have a Sir Gallahad complex," she said. "That's why you're still here, isn't it?"

"I'll be leaving soon."

"When Mr. Grunkemeier gets home?" She was surprised at the rate of her heartbeat as she waited for his answer.

"Soon."

She thought of saying she would miss him. She tried not to think of the fact that her baby would miss him every day of its life. She reminded herself that her baby would grow up normally. Not in hiding, not shut off from the world, and definitely not one of a gang of thieves, no matter how glamorous and intriguing that existence might sound in theory.

She felt his touch on her skinned knee.

"That is why princesses shouldn't climb trees," he said.

"I'm not a princess."

He raised the hand that had touched her knee and brought it to her face.

"Aren't you?"

His fingertips were gentle, but the effect of his touch was powerful.

She shook her head, ignoring her response to him. "I don't even want to be."

"It's not bad duty."

"Yes, it is."

"He loves you, you know. Your father, I mean."

She knew it only too well. "That doesn't make it bearable."

"Most people think enough money makes anything bearable."

"They're wrong."

"Yes, they are." His reply, delivered with a solemn expression, surprised her. He looked at her such a long time she began to think he wanted to kiss her, to touch her. Surely that was what she saw in his eyes. Then he spoke again. "Will you be happy here?"

"Yes."

"I wish—"

"What?" She wanted to know if he wished for the same thing she longed for. She coaxed a confession out of him with her eyes.

"I'd better go."

She'd run away from her old, safe life. From living only in her dreams. Now was the time to take a chance. "You owe me a goodbye kiss."

His eyes went dark; she imagined she could see the

pulse at his throat quicken. He leaned closer. "I always pay my debts."

He brushed his lips over hers. Softly, the way he had the first time. As it had then, the gentle meeting of lips stoked a fire in her, stirred to life a heat and intensity that took her over. It had stunned her before. Now it almost broke her heart.

She'd prayed to be free of him and what she felt for him. She wasn't.

She let herself sigh against his lips. He answered her with a muted groan.

She sought the tip of his tongue with hers. Found it. Retreated. Waited and hoped and was rewarded. He covered her mouth with his.

"I'm going to fall out of the tree," she murmured.

"I'll catch you," he promised.

"You'll land on top of me," she predicted.

"Good."

He drew her close, his embrace warm and tight and safe. Her breasts ached against his chest. Her legs began to part, to give him access. He touched her.

"I've never reached climax in a tree before," she whispered on a soft gasp.

She felt him tense, then retreat. "Neither have I, princess. And I'm not so sure it's such a good idea to try it."

She nodded, disappointed.

He went down first. She saw him waiting for her on the ground, and knew if she simply allowed herself to fall into his arms the inevitable would happen.

Then he might stay.

Then he would find out he was going to be a father.

She moved down, reciting Latin under her breath to bring herself under control. He put his hands on her waist as she reached the ground. Could he tell the difference in her? She backed away.

"I think I'd better go in," she said.

"Melina—"

"Not that it wasn't a nice goodbye kiss."

His lips parted. If she waited, he might say just what she wanted to hear, the magic words that would make it possible for her to let him into her heart again.

She ran.

CHAPTER TEN

THE HOUSE WAS CLEAN, the cows were milked—Melina had to admit she'd had nothing to do with that—and the barn door and wall patched. Everything was ready for Edgar Grunkemeier's homecoming the next afternoon.

"I'm going into town," Melina announced shortly after lunch.

Emily suddenly appeared from her room. "Me, too."

Ash leveled a stern look at Melina. "I don't think that's a good idea."

She smiled at him brightly and prayed he would come no closer. "Thank you for your input, Father. But I don't need your permission."

She returned to her room to put a few dollars in her pocket and to change into her walking shoes. The truth was, this farm—all umpteen acres of it—wasn't big enough for the both of them, as they used to say in old TV westerns. Everywhere she went, he seemed to be there. If he wasn't there, his scent was, the aura of him, lingering in the air, clinging to everything. Melina's body, her heart, her mind were beginning to feel the strain of working so hard to resist his presence.

She was beginning to be tempted by the notion of telling him about his baby, simply because he might then feel guilty enough to stay. She refused to be that desperate.

So she had to get away, even if only for a few hours. Because telling Ash about the baby was a bad plan on more levels than she could count. He would be a terrible father. He would be a terrible role model. He might think he was entitled to a part of her baby's life.

He might feel obligated to stay and pretend he loved her.

When she returned to the kitchen, he was standing there with the car keys in his hand. "You should stay out of sight," he said. "You shouldn't be parading around town where anybody might recognize you."

She plopped a wide-brimmed hat on her head, then the pair of sunglasses he'd gotten for her the first day. "Nobody's going to recognize me. We've been from one end of this country to the other and nobody's recognized me."

"It's just a matter of time."

Poseti's face flashed into her thoughts, but she refused to give it space there. She would not be ruled by fear. "I didn't leave my father to become your prisoner."

He threw up his hands. "Fine. Let's go."

"I don't need a bodyguard. Emily will keep an eye on me."

"It's miles to town."

"Only if you take the highway. Through the apple orchards, you can walk there in half an hour."

She and Emily started out the back door, through the yard, along the dirt road running between the fences that separated two small meadows.

From behind them, he called out, "You have the phone number here? In case you need me?"

The worry in his voice made her uneasy. She was so accustomed to her father sending people after her that she felt the suffocating anxiety that Ash wouldn't let her go, either.

"Got it," she called without looking back.

"And money? You've got plenty of money?"

"All we need." Melina's heart raced. What if he came after her? What if it was no different even being away from her father? What if she was never free?

"We could always use more money," Emily pointed out.

Ash's voice was faint now as he called, "Well, then, be careful."

Melina wanted to turn and look at him. He wasn't following her. He was letting her go, the way one adult would let another walk off. She smiled at Emily. "We can have plenty of fun without money."

"That means we're poor."

"Maybe. I don't know."

"Will we have to get jobs? After Ash is gone, I mean."

"I might. You'll have to go to school."

"Oh, no. I've been to school. I'm not going back."

"What was so bad about school?" She remembered school as the best part of her own life. At least there had been other girls, the possibility of friends and fun.

"Other kids."

"That's bad?"

"It is when you're different."

Melina looked at the girl who worked so hard at looking outrageous. "Different how?"

Emily's eyes flashed. "Look at my skin. Look at my mouth and my nose and my hair. Well, if I had any hair."

"You're beautiful." She smiled encouragingly but Emily didn't smile back. "Even bald."

"Yeah, well, we all know you don't know jack about being normal, don't we?" Emily ran a hand over her head, where soft brown curls were beginning to grow back. "I'm not black and I'm not white. I'm nothing. I don't belong anywhere."

She kicked fiercely at a stump on the path, then marched ahead, shoulders hunched, hands shoved deep into her baggy jeans. Melina looked after her, feeling helpless.

She allowed Emily to march off, making no attempt to catch up until the girl slowed down. Melina understood that Emily had a right to her anger—life had dealt her a lot of tough blows.

When Emily finally slowed down and allowed Melina to reach her, the teenager looked at her wryly and said, "Now you're gonna tell me how everything's going to work out swell. Right?"

Melina shook her head. "No, I think I was just

going to say thanks for telling me about it. And that if it helps to have a friend, you can count on me.''

Emily studied her, warily, Melina thought. ''Not for long.''

''Why do you say that?''

''Because you'll leave soon. When Ash leaves.''

''That's not true.''

''Sure it is. You two have the hots for each other. Anybody can see that.''

Melina studied the challenge in Emily's eyes and knew her claim of friendship was being tested. Friends don't lie to friends. She made a slight concession to the truth. ''Being attracted to somebody and wanting to make a life with them are two different things.''

''Well, he'd marry you. I saw the way he acted at the doctor's office.''

Melina longed to know how he'd acted, but she wouldn't give herself away by asking.

''He'll take care of you. You wouldn't have to get a job.''

''He isn't right for me.'' Why was that so easy to believe, but so hard to accept? ''Besides, I don't mind getting a job.''

''Have you ever had a job before?''

''No. But I'm looking forward to it,'' she said, hoping it was true.

''What kind of job?''

''Well…I have an excellent palate for judging wines.''

Emily looked thoroughly exasperated. ''Great.

There's probably a whole long list of jobs for wine tasters in the paper every week.''

The talk about her marketability was definitely making Melina nervous. Real life. Was she ready for it? She raised her face to the summer sunshine and told herself she would be fine. ''And...I know all about etiquette. Maybe I could start an etiquette school for young girls. And boys.''

Emily laughed. ''That'll work, as long as nobody gets a load of me first. They'll figure right away you don't have such a good track record.''

Melina began to laugh, too, and soon they were laughing so hard they had to stop and lean against one of the sturdy wooden fence posts.

They spent the rest of their walk into town talking about jobs Melina would be good at, settling on tutoring conversational French, German and Italian for travelers and international businesspeople as a reasonable possibility. By the time they arrived at the outskirts of Hope Springs, they had developed an entire marketing plan for luring people from all over the country to the mountains of Virginia for her private, intensive classes.

''You might have to have a nose job or something,'' Emily was saying as they spotted the spire of a local church.

Melina touched the tip of her nose. ''What's wrong with the one I have?''

''Nothing. But you'll want to look different when all the magazines come to interview you. So nobody'll recognize you.''

"Oh. Of course." Despite the lighthearted nature of their conversation, this wasn't a game. She couldn't keep being Melina Somerset forever. She told herself not to worry, being Melina Somerset had never been so great, anyway.

Now she could be anyone she wanted.

The streets of Hope Springs were lined with wonderful old houses with wide front porches and bird feeders hanging from the shade trees and trellises for roses. Some had picket fences or stone walkways or vine-covered arbors. Children played in yards, laughing, chasing each other, squirting one another with water hoses or drawing games of hopscotch on the sidewalk with fat, colored chalk. When they found a game of hopscotch that had been abandoned, Emily taught Melina the game. She wouldn't join in herself—far too cool for that—but she stood by and giggled while Melina wore herself out.

"Maybe you shouldn't be doing that," Emily said after a few minutes.

"Why ever not?"

"Well, because..." Emily focused on her feet, seemed slightly embarrassed. "You know."

Melina stared at her, filling with anxiety. Surely the teenager hadn't guessed her secret. She'd barely gained ten pounds, and Emily hadn't known her before anyway. So she couldn't possibly have guessed.

"Because of your head, I guess. When you fell off the tractor."

Relieved, she said, "My head is fine. Doc Sarah said so."

Emily's frown didn't go away, but she didn't say any more. Melina was tired anyway. She tired easily these days and hiding it was growing harder.

They walked a little farther, past the elementary school and the church they'd spotted from a distance. At that corner, the street had been built around a giant old oak tree in the middle of the intersection. Melina made up her mind to bring the camera to town next time they came so they could have their picture taken under the tree.

They stopped at an ice-cream parlor and a hardware store, which had wonders Melina had never dreamed of—nails and eye hooks and fishing line and pressure cookers for pickling cucumbers.

"You mean I could grow plain old cucumbers in a garden and turn them into dill pickles?" she pressed the man in the store—Chuck, according to the name on his shirt—when he volunteered an explanation for the pressure cooker's use.

"That's right, miss. Folks do it every summer in these parts." He looked at her quizzically.

When they left the store, Emily said, "I think he liked you."

"I think he thought I was from Mars."

They laughed about that, too.

They spent an hour in the video store and ten minutes mourning the fact that the Bijou Theater was locked up tight. They ended up at the garage at the corner of Loblolly and Ridge Lane, where a grease-stained young woman explained that she was rebuilding a carburetor. The name on her shirt was Clem.

Melina watched her work. Her hands were rough and grimy, the nails cut back to the quick. But they were strong, capable hands and Melina envied them. "How did you learn to do that?"

Clem didn't look up from her labor. "From old man Hoover. He had the place before I did."

"Could anybody learn?"

"Sure, I suppose. If they were interested enough." Clem gave her a long look. "Say, I know who you are."

Melina's heart lurched. "You do?"

"Sure. You're Tood Grunkemeier's folks, aren't you? Just got to town from the Midwest this week. Right?"

"That's right. This is his niece, Emily. And I'm... Mel. I'm...ah...Emily's...aunt. On her mother's side."

Emily was seized by a violent fit of coughing.

TOOD GRUNKEMEIER CAME HOME the next morning, accompanied by Ida Monroe and what seemed to Melina to be half the town. All the old man's friends from the barber shop in town turned out for the home-coming, hanging a big red banner and passing out cigars and urging him to celebrate his freedom with various forms of unhealthy behavior. Ida shooed them all away as quickly as possible and settled a disgruntled looking Tood into a rocker on the front porch.

Emily made herself scarce. She barely spoke to her uncle before taking off for the barn or the orchards or who knew where.

But Melina, encouraged by her foray into town the day before and by the lack of interest her presence created in Tood's friends, found her spirits brightened by rubbing elbows with all these people. She even liked Tood, whom she quickly realized only appeared crochety; beneath the surface, he was a softy. So for the rest of the week, Melina spent every minute she could manage either visiting with her host or wandering around Hope Springs.

She visited the shoe-repair store and learned how to replace the sole of a shoe. She met the owner of the bookstore and newsstand and decided that Neesa Weatherly might have as many secrets as Melina herself had. She made friends with a nurse and her nine-year-old stepson, who took Emily under his wing and showed her the town from a kid's perspective—the pool, the rec center, the video games at the Mexican restaurant. She made friends with the three women who ran Times Square Crafts, especially when she learned that they all had young children and one of the women was now expecting her second child.

One day soon, Melina thought, she would share her secret with them. And with Neesa, who was quickly becoming her best friend in town. Imagine that, Melina Somerset with a best friend.

But first, Ash had to leave. And he was showing no sign at all of leaving, despite the fact that Edgar Grunkemeier was now home and there was no reason for him to stay. She needed him to leave, because every day he stayed made it more difficult for her to wish him gone.

"Neesa is teaching me to drive," she told him one night, thinking that might be one of the things holding him back.

They were washing dishes. Tonight, he washed, she dried and put away. She was better at putting away. Even after all this time, he couldn't seem to remember that the casserole dishes didn't go in the same cabinet with the mixing bowls. They looked the same to him, he said.

"Neesa?"

"From the bookstore. She says I'm so knowledge-able I could work for her during the summer tourist season."

"She does?"

Melina nodded. She could tell he was irritated. He didn't like her hanging around townspeople. He didn't trust them, she knew. He couldn't seem to understand this was going to be her home and if she couldn't trust her new neighbors, where would she be.

She stretched to reach the stack of chipped and mismatched cups in Edgar Grunkemeier's cupboard. She liked the mismatched china. It seemed homey and real. "And Clem said she knows a car I can buy real cheap."

"I could teach you to drive." He turned away from the sink, soapy water dripping from the sponge he held. "And you don't need a cheap car. We've got a good car."

"You're dripping."

"I'll mop it up," he said tersely, turning back to the sink.

"Anyway, *you've* got a good car. *I* don't."

"I'll put it in your name."

Melina picked up another cup, her favorite, a thick-lipped, ugly mug with a fading picture of the Blue Ridge Mountains ringing it. Tood had told her it was a souvenir of his honeymoon. She thought for a moment about building up a lifetime of simple memories. "I don't even have a name yet."

Ash's sigh sounded impatient to Melina's ears.

"You're right. I'll talk to my brother. He can get new IDs to us in a matter of days. I guess you'll want to be Melissa or Melinda or something. Since everybody here already calls you Mel."

"Sure. Or Melanie."

"Melody. That's a possibility."

Somehow the phoniness of a new name depressed her. She placed the Blue Ridge Mountains mug carefully on the shelf. "Sure. Melody is good."

"You'll need a last name, too. And a place of birth. You let me know tomorrow and I'll call my brother."

"The sooner we do that, I suppose, the sooner you can go."

"You're eager for me to go, aren't you?"

She didn't look at him. "Oh, it's just time we got on with things. Don't you think?"

He tossed the sponge into the water. "Absolutely."

He marched out without another word.

As she picked up the last plate to put it away, Melina noticed that her hands were red and dry. Her first case of dishpan hands. It should have been a moment of triumph, a signpost of normalcy.

Instead, she felt lonely.

She placed a hand on her belly. She wouldn't be lonely for long. Her baby would be with her.

Her fatherless baby.

CHAPTER ELEVEN

THE OLD GEEZER was back at the farm. Emily felt the weight of his presence, like something hanging around her neck. She didn't want to take care of him. She'd had enough of sick and dying people. She damn sure didn't need another one. Let that Ida Monroe woman take care of him. She seemed to like that role fine. Well, she could have it.

Emily steered clear of him the day he came home. And the next. For days, she hung out in the barn. She found the path through the woods that led into town and let that kid, Kyle, show her around. She made friends with the horse that had a new baby. She found the creek she used to wade in, the other time she was here. Wading in a creek was different when you were fourteen, she learned. But there was still something about mud squishing between your toes that made you feel good, at least for a few minutes.

She was walking back from the creek, barefoot, when she ran out of luck. The old geezer was hanging on to the fence around the horse pasture. She wondered if he was dying and tried to figure out a way to skirt around him so she didn't have to find out. He turned and saw her before she could get away. She sighed and made her way toward him.

"You okay?"

"Oh, sure. Just resting a spell. I'm supposed to walk, you know. Twice a day."

She thought he sounded out of breath. He could just be *saying* he was okay when he was really ready to keel over. She wasn't convinced. Why did this have to happen to her?

"Been down to the creek?"

She looked down at her muddy feet and was embarrassed at having been caught at something so childish. "Well, uh, yeah. I guess."

"Water's nice and cool, ain't it? Don't tell Doc Sarah, but I still like rolling up my britches legs and letting a little of that creek mud ooze up between the toes. That's probably bad for a guy my age, too, like everything else worth doing."

Emily almost giggled as she imagined him in the creek, but she held it back. She didn't want him getting any ideas. She didn't want him thinking she liked talking to him or anything like that.

"Yeah, well, I guess I better—"

"Got something I need to say, girl."

She didn't want to hear it. "Maybe later."

"Better do it now. Get it over with."

She sighed. She was still six feet away from him and she refused to get any closer.

"I was looking for you, you know. You and your dad, that is. Hoping to find you before I went on to glory."

Emily felt herself stiffen. Yep, she knew it. This was not a conversation she wanted to have. She didn't want to talk about going on to glory or her dad or any of it.

"Got word a few weeks back. About your dad, that is."

She started feeling nervous. She didn't like the way the old geezer glanced up at her, then down at his feet. She wanted to tell him to keep his news to himself. But she couldn't open her mouth.

"Just wanted to say I'm real sorry about your dad. He was my nephew, you know. The only blood I had left. Aside from you, I mean."

Emily's mouth went dry. "Sorry?"

The old man's eyes grew a little wide, as if he'd just realized something. "Lord-a-mercy, girl. Don't tell me you didn't...you don't know."

She couldn't move, couldn't speak. She didn't want to hear this.

"Emily, girl, your dad died. About six months ago."

She wouldn't feel it. She wouldn't let it touch her, wouldn't let it crash through her the way it had when her mother died. Her old man was nothing but a worthless druggie, anyway. She refused to let it matter.

Uncle Tood walked toward her with his tired old walk and put out a hand to take her in his arms. "I'm real sorry, Emily."

She backed away. If he touched her, she wasn't sure what she'd do. But she knew she would lose control some way or another. And she refused to do that.

"We've gotta stick together now, Emily. You and me. We—"

"My name's not Emily." She backed farther from the sick old man who wanted to worm his way into her life. "It's Stomp. And I don't need you, old man! Just leave me alone!"

Then she walked away, as calm as could be, tuning out whatever it was the old man called out after her. He was sick and he was dying and Emily had no place for that in her life.

THE SOUND of his brother's voice on the phone intensified the hollow feeling in Ash. He missed Forbes, with the same deep longing that he missed his father. And he saw no way around it. If Ash was really going to change his life, he was probably going to have to distance himself from all the Thorndykes.

He was acutely aware that Melina stood by watching as he and his brother caught up on the last few months. She looked tense.

He smiled to reassure her. It didn't seem to work.

"I need your help, Forbes," he said when the appropriate amount of chitchat had been covered. "I have a...friend. She needs some papers."

Melina turned away, walked to the mantel in Tood Grunkemeier's faded living room and picked up a framed family picture. She stared down at it, her back rigid.

Ash waited out a long silence from Chicago, wishing he were close enough to touch Melina even though he knew his touch wouldn't be welcome.

"Ash, I don't know how to say this. I'm…getting out of the business."

Ash was thunderstruck. "You're what?"

"It's Stacy. She's pregnant."

Another bombshell. Ash sat in one of the lumpy old chairs. His brother's wife was pregnant. His brother and his wife were starting a family. Another reminder of his loneliness. "Forbes, that's wonderful. I can't wait. When's she due?"

Melina faced him abruptly, clutching the frame to her midsection.

"You see, Ash, she doesn't want… It's nothing personal…but Stacy doesn't want the baby to be around family."

Ash's mood sank lower. "Sure. Sure, I understand." He wanted to tell his brother that the reason he understood so well was he'd been thinking of going straight himself. But he couldn't say that it front of Melina. And it wasn't right to say it to Forbes, either, not unless he could be sure of himself. Not unless he had confidence he could leave the old life behind. And the truth was, he had no idea how to start. "What are your plans?"

"Well, I'm…I'm not sure yet. Got a few irons in the fire. You know."

Floundering. That's what Forbes meant. Ash heard it in his voice and recognized the uncertainty. "You'll be great. A great family man."

Melina was staring at him intently, unfathomable things reflected in her big, dark eyes.

"You think so?"

He couldn't hold her gaze. He looked away.

"Sure," he said. "Absolutely." But he still needed help for Melina and he hated himself for what he was about to do. "But I need this one. Badly. Think of it as a send-off."

Once again, the silence crackled between Hope Springs and Chicago. He realized he was holding his breath, but he didn't let it out until Forbes said, "Just because it's you, brother. But if you tell Stacy—"

"It's our secret, pal."

He filled his brother in, caught Melina's eye and waited for her nod before giving him the name Melina had settled on. They reviewed the need for high school and college records, a social security number and a driver's license she could trade in for a Virginia license, once Neesa whoever from the bookstore worked her magic.

"What about family?" Forbes asked.

"Family?" Ash looked at Melina. "Parents? Siblings?"

Her face settled into a bleak expression. She shook her head. His heart went out to her. He'd been around before as people confronted the reality of starting life with a new identity.

"Deceased," he said softly. "No siblings."

She glanced down at the picture she still held, pursed her lips and returned it to the mantel. She murmured, "You decide about the rest. Whatever you think is fine."

Then she walked out. He ached to go after her. He stayed and finished the business at hand.

By the time he hung up, Ash realized how much he'd hated making the call. For one thing, it brought Melina one step closer to moving out of his life. For another, he hadn't liked dabbling on that side of the fine line between the world he was living in today and the one he'd lived in before.

He still ached to go after Melina. But he knew it was better if he didn't. He remembered his brother's final request as they hung up.

"I hate to ask this, Ash. But it might be better if you make yourself scarce for a while."

Ash did his best to hide his bruised feelings. "I understand," he said, for the second time.

Feeling glum, he joined Tood on the porch and dropped into a rocker. Con men and thieves didn't sit in rockers on front porches on farms in Virginia. Ash was finding the rocker a good fit.

"Taking a rest?" Tood asked.

Ash nodded. The old guy seemed gruff, but he'd made no secret of his delight in having them all here with him. "Yeah. You?"

Tood was supposed to rest. He was also supposed to walk every day, seven minutes a day the first week, nine minutes a day the second week and so forth, until he was up to thirty minutes a day. Tood, by his own admission, liked the resting part better than the walking part. He also liked the foods on the "Avoid" list better than he liked the foods on the "Recommended" list.

"Waitin' for that meddling woman," Tood replied.

"That would be Ida," Ash said.

"The good Lord help me if there's another one. The woman's going to kill me."

Ash decided to stay out of the debate. Ida came every day, sometimes twice a day. She came to make sure Tood walked. She came to bring green, leafy vegetables and tubs of no-fat margarine and cookies she'd made herself with no butter or shortening.

"Say, young feller, about that niece of mine."

"Emily."

"Havin' an ugly old handle, that's fine for an old coot like me—they've been calling me Tood longer'n I can recollect. Since I was a young 'un, I reckon, learning to count. One, tood, free, that's what they tell me I said. Anyway, about Emily, says 'er name's Stomp. What kind of name is that for a girl, I want to know. I had to tell her about her father. My nephew. He died a while back. I guess she didn't know about that."

Ash pondered for a moment the damage done by men who had no business being fathers. He also pondered the fact that he was about to become an uncle. This old man's devotion to his great-niece struck a chord within him. He wanted to try to be the kind of family man Tood Grunkemeier was striving to be. But there were so many obstacles.

"She seemed pretty tore up about it." The old man linked hands over his belly. "Might be she'd rather be back where she was. Where'd you say it was you met up with her?"

"In Las Vegas."

Tood shook his head. "Helluva place for a kid to be. All by herself, you said."

Ash nodded.

"Guess you had to drag her kicking and screaming."

"It was her idea."

One of Tood's bushy eyebrows raised in surprise. "You don't say?"

"She had good memories here. I take it there aren't a lot of other places where the memories are good."

"Be better for her if Edith was still here. Edith was a good one for fussing over young 'uns." Tood patted the front pocket on his plaid work shirt. "No more cigarettes, either. Blamed woman took 'em yesterday. Reckon she's doing it for Edith, now I think about it. They were best friends, you know. Guess she figures if Edith's not here to nag me right out of my gourd, she'll step in and do it for her."

The sounds of a car rumbling over the rutted driveway reached the porch.

"Speak of the devil," Tood said.

Actually, there were two cars rumbling down the driveway. Ida's car pulled up first, followed by one Ash didn't recognize. He stood, instantly alert. A tall, sturdily built woman got out of the car. She and Ida greeted each other. Ash tried to relax.

"That's Neesa," Tood said.

Ash felt his face settling into a frown. "Oh. Mel's driving instructor."

The porch that had been a restful haven just moments earlier transformed into Grand Central Station in a matter of moments. Ida swept in with a covered plate—"No-fat brownies. You can't tell them from the real thing."—which Tood studied skeptically. Driving coach Neesa marched up as if she lived here and started hashing out the details of Tood's double bypass surgery with him. Emily appeared from no-where, demanding a ride into town because someone named Libby Travers had asked if she could baby-sit for Kyle, her stepson, and Emily thought it would be cool if she could baby-sit him at the municipal pool, which would be infinitely better than hanging around this falling-down farm. Ida grilled Emily about Tood's breakfast. And Tood announced to Ida that he wasn't ready for a walk yet, an announcement she seemed unwilling to accept.

Melina slipped quietly out of the house and viewed the scene.

For the first time, Ash realized how different she looked from the woman he had met three months ear-lier. Granted, her hair was different now and she hardly ever bothered with makeup here on the farm. But there was something else, something calmer about her. She seemed more mature, maybe. Despite her momentary distress when he'd been talking to Forbes, Melina seemed to be gaining confidence, without giving up her sense of wonder over the de-lights of everyday life.

Maybe she really did belong here. Maybe Hope Springs was exactly what she needed, to heal.

The hubbub on the porch cranked up a notch when Ida noticed Melina.

"Oh, dolly, try these brownies. I can't get the old coot to take a bite. They're delicious, I promise you, or I'm not Sweet Ida."

Tood grunted.

Melina took a brownie.

"Isn't it okay if I take Kyle swimming, Mel? Please, Mel?"

Melina opened her mouth, whether to reply to Emily or taste the brownie, Ash wasn't sure.

"That's not a bad idea, Mel." That was Neesa. "They have swim lessons on Tuesday and the coach is not hard on the eyes. You should go along."

Ash told himself there was no reason to bristle.

"Really," Melina said, "I'm not looking for a man." She then touched her fingertips to Emily's cheek and smiled as she okayed the swimming, contingent upon the approval of Kyle's stepmother. It struck Ash that she had the soft grace of a natural mother. The idea rattled around in the emptiness that filled his soul.

"Oh, Neesa, that coach is divorced," Ida protested. "Go ahead, dolly, take a big bite. You're going to love it."

"I said—" Melina tried to protest, but Neesa cut her off.

"Ida, half the single men in the free world are divorced. He volunteers to work with children. That should count for something."

"Maybe he's strange. You know what I mean?"

Neesa rolled her eyes. Melina bit into the brownie, having given up her objections awfully easily, Ash thought. Emily announced she was going upstairs for a swimsuit.

"What about Chuck Hurd?" Tood asked. "Good, solid young feller. Family business, all that."

"He's sweet on Faith Davenport, you know that."

"She's married two years now."

"He's right," Neesa pointed out.

Ida shook her head. "That's a can of worms, I'm telling you. Ralph Strong, now, he's a nice young man. No ex-wives. No baggage."

"He's got no ex-wives because he's gay," Neesa said.

Ida's eyes grew wide. "Is he really?"

"But John Wesley is available. Very available."

They debated the merits of John Wesley, then the pluses and minuses of an administrator at the county hospital, a teacher at the high school who was recently widowed and the new bank manager who was a recent import from somewhere in Maine. Melina ate the brownie.

"So what's your preference?" Ash asked her, telling himself he had no right to be irritated by the inventory of eligible bachelors.

She swallowed a bite, licked her lips and said, "I prefer mine with walnuts."

"I meant, the hospital administrator, the widowed teacher, the import from Maine or the hunk who teaches kids to swim when he isn't carrying his baggage around?"

Melina laughed. "Oh, that." She shrugged.

Ignoring him, that's what she was doing. Refusing

to answer on the grounds that it might tend to incriminate her. Ash debated telling her he didn't like the sound of any of them. He took a brownie instead.

Then they all loaded up in cars and headed for Hope Springs. It grew quiet again. Pastoral. Irritatingly idyllic. Melina would have a wonderful day, plenty of fun. And there'd be plenty of people to befriend her and care for her long after he was gone. Good. That would make it easier for him to leave. She was in good hands.

"Strike you as odd?" Tood asked.

"What's that?"

"How they all pretend nobody knows who she is?"

Ash turned to look at the old man, who was tearing a brownie into bites for the cat. The cat turned up its nose, too.

"I mean, ain't a soul in this country don't know Melina Somerset after all that ruckus when she landed in San Francisco." Tood gave Ash a shrewd look. "So why you reckon they're all playing so coy?"

It was a good question. One Ash couldn't answer. Could an entire town have ulterior motives?

Maybe it wasn't yet safe for him to leave after all.

CHAPTER TWELVE

"THIS IS DUMB."

Emily sat on the cold earthen floor of the crumbling building in the woods near Heritage Manor, the big old resort hotel that drew lots of tourists to this one-horse town, even though it didn't have gambling or neon or half-naked showgirls like they had in Las Vegas. She poked one of her toes at her companion. Actually, the Civil War–era ruins were kind of cool, but she wouldn't want her nine-year-old companion to know she thought so.

Kyle squinted one eye shut and peered through a sizable crack between two of the stones in the chapel wall. "No, it's not. They'll be here any minute and we're the only ones who can save the town."

Emily grinned. "If they make it all the way up here, the town's probably already bought it before you can fire off a shot."

Kyle turned and made a face at her. "You sound like a grown-up," he said, giving the word all the contempt a kid could muster. "It's better than swimming at the dumb old pool in town with everybody else, isn't it?"

"No." Hiding in the woods waiting for imaginary murdering marauders was just plain stupid. Emily knew what it was like to really have to hide from people. It wasn't a game. "You're just a kid. You ought to be playing with other kids."

"I don't like kids."

Emily was startled by a moment of identification. She wondered if there were things she didn't know about her young friend. "Why not?"

He ignored her.

"What'd other kids do to you?"

Kyle rolled over and lay on his back, crossing his chest with the high-powered, semi-automatic tree branch he was using to protect Hope Springs. His bangs flopped back off his face. He had more freckles every day, it seemed to Emily. He said he'd gotten his freckles from his mother—the mother who was in the cemetery in town, not the mother who was the nurse.

"I dunno."

She jabbed him with her toe again. "You dunno? What's that supposed to mean? Why don't you want to be with the other kids in town?"

Kyle jabbed her back. "They're jerks, that's all. They give me a hard time."

Emily knew about that. But she couldn't imagine what other kids could find to put down in a cute, blond, freckle-faced kid like Kyle. "Why?"

"You wouldn't understand."

"Bet I would."

He gave her a skeptical look. She remembered the night she and Melina lay in their tents at the Grand Canyon, discovering all the things they had in com-

mon. She'd never imagined someone else could feel
the way she felt, especially someone who looked as
different from her on the outside as Melina did. Finding out how many feelings they shared had made her
feel lighter, somehow. She looked at Kyle, at the
crabby little scowl on his face, and made a decision.

"Kids made fun of me, too," she said.

"No way."

She nodded. "'Cause I'm half-black."

"You are?"

Emily grinned at his astonishment. "Why'd you
think I look this way, you little dope?"

Kyle sat up and studied her carefully. "Cool."

"Yeah, right."

"Mine's better than that."

"No way," she retorted, turning his words back on
him.

"Sure. My dad was a jailbird."

That revelation did amaze her. A jailbird, in a place
like Hope Springs? "Yeah?"

He told her a pretty sad story then, about how his
father was accused of practically killing some old
schoolteacher and went to jail for it until the jury let
him go. But the whole town, just about, still believed
he was a stone killer and hated him and Kyle, too. A
year ago, everybody in town found out who really
attacked the old lady, but Kyle couldn't forgive the
other kids and didn't trust them to be his real friends.

Emily listened sympathetically. At least she was
old enough to know how to handle her problems. But
Kyle was just a kid. And she knew what he was do-

ing. Pulling away. Cutting the other kids in town out of his life so he wouldn't get hurt again. He couldn't see that it was all over and done with.

"Grow up, Kyle. You're just acting like a jerk because you're afraid they won't like you. That other stuff was a long time ago."

"How do you know that?"

She opened her mouth and realized she didn't know it. For all she knew, the kids in town would keep giving Kyle a hard time until he was old enough to blow this taco stand and make his way to Las Vegas and hang out on the streets and get mixed up with drug dealers and have his entire life in a humongous mess.

She looked at his sweet, trusting face and hated to think of him doing that. It was fine for her, but for a nice kid like Kyle... Well, it just didn't seem right.

"You want to belong somewhere, don't you?" she asked the little boy.

"Sure, but—"

"Then get over it."

"What do you mean?"

"I mean all that stuff they did to you was before. They're trying to be nice to you now, aren't they?"

"Yeah, but—"

"So let 'em. I know what I'm talking about, okay?"

He thought about that for a few minutes. So did Emily. It was good advice for Kyle. But there were reasons it didn't make sense for Emily. Still, it was getting way too heavy-duty. To distract her young friend, she gestured toward the clearing, where a squirrel rustled in the leaves.

"There's one sneaking up on you now."

Kyle rolled over and blasted the terrorist squirrel to kingdom come with his semi-automatic branch.

Maybe she ought to leave him to his imaginary world as long as possible. Stuff was probably easier there, she thought as she stared through the overhead trees into a bank of rolling white clouds. Surely, stuff was easier somewhere. She'd thought it would be in Hope Springs. Look where that had gotten her.

HOPE SPRINGS SEEMED to be populated by mother hens. In the two weeks they'd been in town, Melina had learned that much. She could think of a handful without trying hard. There was Ida, of course. And Neesa. Faith, Donna and Kelsy at Times Square Crafts took turns outdoing one another for the mother-hen-of-the-week award.

The most unlikely but persistent mother hen was Edgar, who hovered around Emily. She refused his offers to look through the family photo albums or name the new colt herself. Whatever he offered, she rejected. Instead, she lavished her attention on young Kyle Travers, whom she coddled and protected even when he didn't seem to need it. Melina thought it was sweet—and sad—the way Emily gave the boy all the loving and attention she refused to accept for herself.

Coming late to the competition for the mother hen award, but gaining on the inside track, was Ash. Like tonight, when he'd shown up at the skating rink for the express purpose, in her opinion, of keeping an eye on her.

Melina had almost lost her balance and had to grab on to the arm of her date when she'd spotted Ash lounging casually against the railing of the skating rink.

"What's he doing here?" she asked when she and John Wesley finally finished flailing about and were steady on their roller skates once again.

"Who?"

Melina turned to look over her shoulder as they glided past Ash. "Him. Ash Thorndyke."

"The fellow staying out at Tood's with you?" John jerked around so quickly they both landed on their fannies this time.

Melina could barely stay on her feet the rest of the evening. She had assumed that, as an accomplished ice skater, she would have no problem roller skating. She blamed her awkwardness on Ash's presence. She also noticed that John Wesley's arm was disturbingly scrawny. And he had an aggravating habit of tweaking her earlobe when he thought he'd said something terribly cute.

"I don't think he's the one," she said later to Neesa. They sat on benches around the rink waiting for John and Neesa's date to return with soft drinks.

"John's awfully dependable," Neesa pointed out.

"He pulls my ear."

"That's sweet."

"It is?"

"Well, it could be. Who are you staring at?"

"I'm not staring."

"You certainly are. You're— Oh. Him." Neesa snapped her fingers in front of Melina's eyes. "Are you sure you don't have a case on him?"

"Absolutely not."

"Uh-huh."

Melina stood up, still unsteady on the unfamiliar roller skates. "I'm going to tell him to go home."

"Just remember," Neesa said, "he doesn't have a steady job. Or his own riding lawn mower."

Melina held on to the railing and guided herself to the opposite side of the rink, where Ash was pretending not to notice her. His jeans, she noted, were no longer new and stiff. He wore them every day at the farm and they were now soft and weathered, fitting him well enough to remind her of certain attributes she was better off not remembering. She rolled to a stop in front of him, bumping her knees against his before she got stopped. He grabbed her by the waist to steady her; she gripped his arms automatically. Ash Thorndyke's arms were not thin. She released her grip.

"Who invited you?"

He looked up at her, his eyes all innocent confusion. "Did I misunderstand? Is this public skating rink by invitation only?"

"This is *my* date. You have no right to show up and spoil it."

He smiled. "I didn't know my presence would have such a profound effect."

"You're spying on me."

"He's a little bowlegged, you know."

"He is not." She tried to picture John Wesley when he'd walked up onto the front porch. Was he?

"Not that there's anything wrong with being a little bowlegged. Cowboys are, you know."

"When do you plan to leave town?"

"Not right away."

"Why not?"

"Maybe I like it here, too."

"You're casing the town, aren't you? Thinking about all those rich tourists who show up every summer at the Heritage Manor. Is that it?"

He looked angry now. When he spoke, it was between clenched teeth. "Maybe you'd better keep an eye on me, make sure I'm not up to anything illegal."

"Maybe I should."

She skated off with as much dignity as she could muster. Keep an eye on him, indeed. As if she wanted a thing to do with him.

Nevertheless, he made it easy for her. Over the next few days, as Melina became a social butterfly thanks to Neesa's efforts, Ash turned up everywhere she and her various clean-cut dates showed up. He landed in the car next to them at the drive-in movie seven miles down the highway, offering to bring back popcorn for them when he went to the concession stand. He do-si-doed past her at an old-fashioned barn dance sponsored by the local merchants, smiling broadly, apparently very happy to be ruining her good time. He craved an ice cream soda on the precise night she and the swim coach went for banana splits—it was her very first banana split, too, and she didn't taste a single bite for glaring at Ash over the mound of whipped cream and crushed nuts.

"He's not going to let you out of his sight," Emily said while helping Melina decide what to wear for the first band concert of the summer, a special event on the rolling green lawn at Heritage Manor. "I think he's jealous."

"Don't be silly." Melina held up a red-white-and-blue-striped tank top.

"Save that for Independence Day."

Melina cast aside the striped top and selected a sunny-yellow one. "There's no reason for him to be jealous."

"Are you sure?"

"Positive." She pulled on her new white capri pants and was mortified to realize they wouldn't zip. She'd gained too much weight. She tried to slink out of them without calling attention to it. She would have to wear the denim skirt with the elastic waist and the tunic that covered her to the hips.

How soon, she worried, before she could no longer disguise her condition?

"Country cooking getting to you?" Emily asked.

"No more banana splits for me."

Two hours later, she lay on a blanket on the lawn at Heritage Manor and stared into the sky, which was darkening as dusk approached. This was her second date with John Wesley and she couldn't remember a thing he'd said all evening. She wondered if every all-American hero would be so boring.

Maybe they wouldn't seem quite so boring when Ash was gone for good.

Tears sprang to her eyes at the thought.

"You okay?" John asked, concern and tenderness in his voice.

He was a dear. And his arms weren't thin at all. He particularly wasn't bowlegged. She'd let Ash Thorndyke sway her thinking when it came to John Wesley. She nodded, blinking back the tears. "The music."

His smile struck her as sappy. "Not many people react that way to a Sousa march."

He even knew composers. Kind *and* cultured. Perfect father material.

He leaned over to kiss her on the forehead. She had to battle her instinct to flinch. If he was so perfect, why didn't she want him to kiss her the way Ash Thorndyke had kissed her? Why didn't she like holding his hand? Why didn't his every word interest and intrigue her?

Maybe it was simply nature's way of protecting women who were already pregnant with another man's baby.

She breathed a sigh of relief when John drove her home after the concert and walked her toward the Grunkemeier front porch without attempting to inflict any unwanted kisses, touches or verbal intimacies on her. She stopped on the bottom step, hoping to keep him off the porch, which was in deep darkness.

When he asked when he could see her again, she tried in vain to remember how TV heroines turned down men who weren't the TV heroes. Her mind was blank.

"I'll call," she said.

"You will?" He looked astonished and alarmed.

She remembered TV shows in which the heroine sat waiting for the calls that never came. To promise and never call would make her a cad. "Maybe."

"Maybe?"

"I'm…"

"It's Chuck Hurd, isn't it? I know he's got family money and—"

Chuck Hurd was thin on top; Neesa had pointed that out. "That's not it."

"Even if you're used to having money—"

Melina felt a shiver of alarm. "What makes you think I'm used to having money?"

John Wesley stared at his shoes for a moment. "You've got a way about you, that's all. But money isn't everything, you know."

As if she didn't know that better than anyone else. She couldn't help it. She laughed. John backed away.

"Fine. I can take a hint."

"Oh, John…"

He was already halfway to the car. He cast a forlorn glance in her direction, climbing in when she didn't react. As he swung his reliable sedan around and pointed it toward the highway, a voice came to Melina in the darkness.

"Let him think it's the money. It's kinder that way."

She whirled. It was so dark on the porch she hadn't

seen a soul, but she knew whose voice she heard. "You. You... You're no thief. You're a spy."

He chuckled. Her eyes adjusted to the darkness and she saw his silhouette. He was draped along the side banister, leaning against the house. She approached him. He offered not a word in his defense.

"Emily says you're jealous."

"Of them?" He sounded incredulous.

She drew closer. She wanted the satisfaction of hearing him admit it. She was close enough now to feel the energy he exuded, the power of his presence—a power that the nice, all-American men she'd been dating couldn't match.

"They're decent men," she pointed out. "Clean-cut, reliable."

"What more could a woman want?"

Indeed. She remembered his lips, his touch, his taste. She remembered the excitement and the mystery of him. She remembered the deep, unassailable conviction that she was as safe in his arms as a person ever could be. She wanted him to kiss her, and despised herself for wanting him instead of all the good, solid John Wesleys that Hope Springs had to offer.

"What I want is for you to tell me why you're still here."

He swung his leg off the banister. They were thigh to thigh. Melina felt fever in her blood, leaving her awash in need for him.

With one deft finger he looped her hair behind her ear, brushed her temple where the warm air had touched her with dampness.

"It's hot," he said. "You're damp."

She knew his hoarse words meant more than the obvious. She saw in his eyes that he knew what he said was true. A denial caught in her throat. He pulled her against him, into the hot V of his thighs.

He was hard, straining against her.

It wasn't enough.

He stroked her neck, her shoulder, her upper arm. Her breasts responded, tightening, aching. She lost her concerns that he would detect the differences in her body if they were intimate. She flattened her hand against his belly and felt the muscles constrict and grow taut beneath his shirt. She moved her hand up, sought and found one beaded nipple. He made a ragged sound in his throat.

"This isn't what you want, princess." His voice was a harsh rasp.

"How do you know?"

"Because I know what you want. You want love and security and forever. Things I don't have to give you."

Curse him for being right!

"You think I don't know that?" She leaned over and bit his nipple through cotton, bit and tugged and felt him throb against her belly. "You think I didn't figure that out in London?"

He lifted her face to his. "You want me inside you? You think that's all you want?"

You are inside me. "That's all."

"Liar."

But he kissed her, hard and long and deep, a bruising kiss that couldn't have been too hard or too deep for her. She bit his lower lip, fumbled with his buttons. Her fingers were too clumsy. She tore at his shirt; buttons pinged off the wooden porch. Her hands were on his flesh. He, too, was hot and damp.

He cupped her buttocks and lifted her. She wrapped her legs around his waist, let him hold her, press her against him. She moved against him, felt his lips and tongue roaming her throat and face. With one hand, he reached between them and rearranged their clothing to gain access.

He was hot against her, slipping inside her, moving, filling her. She strained to draw him deeper, harder, faster. The banister groaned with their weight.

Then he exploded inside her, furious and fiery, and she knew this was what she'd longed for. But it wasn't enough.

He was right. He couldn't give her what she wanted. She collapsed against his shoulder, tightened the hold her legs had around his waist.

Right then she knew she would have to let him go.

CHAPTER THIRTEEN

MELINA WAS REMINDED of the night before with a vengeance before she even got out of bed the next morning. She lay still in the first soft light of the new day, reliving those reckless moments in the dark, in his arms. Even now, her skin sang and her blood danced. She remembered the dark, sweet taste of his lips, the powerful bunching of his arms and shoulders, lifting her to him.

Oh, dear.

She jumped out of bed, showered and dressed quickly. What now? How to face him? How to be near him?

"The same way you've been doing it for the last month," she said in a gritty tone of voice to her reflection in the bathroom mirror. "By remembering that it didn't mean a thing."

She cooked breakfast like a person clinging to the edge of a fast, dangerous ride at the amusement park—her breathing felt shallow, her heart raced, her skin felt clammy. Her fingers were clumsy as they popped bread in and out of the toaster, dished up the egg-white omelettes and poured fresh-squeezed juice.

And her tongue was tied when the kitchen table filled. Edgar sat at the head of the table, Emily slouched in a chair opposite her uncle and Ash placed himself directly across the table from Melina. He sat directly across from her every morning. This morning, she couldn't bring herself to look him in the eyes.

For this morning, she remembered the power his body had to overcome her, not by force but by her own willingness to surrender. She remembered his lips damp against her neck, his muffled cry in her ear.

She also remembered that it was just possible that he had noticed that the body he'd held close wasn't the same body he'd gotten to know a few months ago in London.

Oh, dear.

"Sleep well?"

Melina knocked over her juice at Emily's question. "Yes. Of course." She stared at the spreading orange puddle and ordered her body to respond. Paper towels were on the kitchen counter, but she couldn't seem to take the action necessary to get them to the table. She could only register the look of sly speculation in Emily's eyes.

Or was it only a figment of Melina's guilt?

What if Emily had guessed what had taken place last night? Worse, what if Ash now guessed her secret? No, of course not. If he suspected anything, he would speak up. Wouldn't he?

"I thought I heard you up late. On the porch."

Ash was at her side, a wad of paper towels in his hand. He put one hand on her shoulder, used the other to blot up the spill. Why was he being so solicitous?

"I thought I heard you myself," he said.

Why was he covering up for them? Or was he only putting her in the position of having to explain any noises from the night before.

She forced herself to glare at him, already imagining a host of negative reactions to her secret—outrage or anger or noble resignation. Instead she saw uncertainty, a kind of plea. What could that mean? Her mouth went dry.

"No, I wasn't on the porch," she said thickly, reaching for her glass before she realized it was, of course, empty.

"Good," he said, giving her shoulder a gentle squeeze before he backed away. "I was worried something might be wrong."

She stared at her plate. She noticed the simple pattern in the handle of her fork, a single rose, still half-furled, waiting to open. She couldn't eat, couldn't possibly swallow. She needed to get away. But she still couldn't seem to move.

Edgar talked about the heat. Ash talked about the orchards and this year's crop. Emily talked about her plans to bring Kyle and a couple of kids from his class to the farm for horseback riding.

"They can't be mean to him when school starts this fall if he's taken them horseback riding," she announced with fierce determination.

"They're mean to him?" Ash asked.

"Well, not so much now. But they used to be. So he's afraid to like them now."

"Why were they mean to him before?"

"Because they thought his dad was, like, a criminal or something."

"Oh."

Ash's deflated response penetrated Melina's preoccupation with the night before. She looked up. His tanned face had lost some of its color. Melina knew instantly that the reference to a criminal had struck home.

"Hellfire in a broom closet!" Edgar stabbed at his omelette with his fork. "They were blaming Will Travers for beating up one of his high-school teachers back when Methuselah was still in diapers. He never did it and the jury said he didn't do it. But half the blasted town was so all-fired self-righteous they convicted him in their minds anyway. Till we found out right about Thanksgiving time last year who really did it."

Melina watched Ash while Edgar continued. The news of the town's harsh judgment of one of its own took all the light out of his eyes.

Softly, she said, "That doesn't sound like Hope Springs."

"Well, it ain't," Edgar said. "But fear does funny things to a body. That's for sure."

When breakfast was over and everyone rose, Melina wanted to say something reassuring to Ash. She wanted to comfort him. But as Edgar said, fear did funny things to a body. She was afraid of Ash's response. She let him walk out to the barn with Edgar and Emily without making an overture.

Through the screen door, she watched the three of

them—Edgar, trying so hard to befriend Emily, Emily so warily determined to shut her uncle out, and Ash so sure he had nothing to offer any of them. It struck her that Ash looked very different from the suave man in the tuxedo who had swept her away from her old life. That Ash Thorndyke had been cool and sophisticated, unapproachable and unflappable. This Ash was... What? More down-to-earth? More human? Right now, as he walked a half a step behind Emily and her uncle, head down, hands shoved into the pockets of his jeans, he looked painfully human.

Very different from how he'd looked last night.

"Piffle on last night," she muttered, turning away from the screen door. "Last night was sex. Period."

She ran hot water into the sink and began to gather the dishes from the table. Everything was so confusing. She knew she needed to protect herself—her heart—from Ash Thorndyke. But how could she when she knew in that same, vulnerable heart that he was a good and kind man with a past he didn't know how to escape for a future he couldn't quite picture.

Not terribly different from herself, Melina speculated.

For a moment, it occurred to her that the only way either of them could put the past behind them was to face the future together.

Ridiculous. Her baby stirred.

Tears rose in Melina's eyes. "I know," she whispered. "I love him, too. But it's not going to be enough."

Again, her baby stirred.

"No, it isn't enough," Melina insisted. "You deserve better. You deserve a normal life."

She turned to wash the dishes. "We all do."

ASH WAS TOO PREOCCUPIED to pay much attention to what Tood was saying or doing. Ash's body was mucking out the stalls, but his mind was making love to Melina. If it was possible, the feelings between them had been even stronger than they had been in London. Melina had seemed more lush, a softer, fuller woman more in tune with her body than she had been before. But it was more than a physical change. There was something else, something he couldn't put his finger on—

"Your lady seems a mite troubled this morning," Tood was saying from the other stall.

"Uh-huh," Ash said, not bothering to point out that Melina wasn't his lady.

She was last night, came a wry voice in his head.

Last night was—

Magic?

For old time's sake. Memory lane. Nothing more.

"'Course, she seems a little peaked to me all the way around."

"Peaked?"

Emily hung over the stall on Ash's right side. "He means sick-looking."

From the stall on the left, Tood chuckled. "Now, I didn't mean she looks bad. Just a mite pale, especially this morning. Fact of the matter is, I'm a touch mystified you're letting all these local boys beat your time.''

Ash gave a mighty heave with a pitchfork. There was not much he could do about Melina's parade of suitors. Except keep an eye on them. They were not really his business. Unless they had ulterior motives. Unless they knew she was rich and were only interested in her money, and not her sweet nature and her delight in life and her wide, dreamy eyes. Then, they could answer to him. Then, he would... What? Beat them to a pulp? Not likely. Physical violence wasn't the Thorndyke way; that's what Grandfather Thorndyke always said.

''The local boys are not my concern,'' Ash growled.

Emily rolled her eyes at him. Tood just grunted from the other stall.

What was Tood doing in the other stall, anyway?

''What a lamebrain.'' Emily dropped from the stall wall.

Ash stopped and listened. ''Tood?'' There was no reply. Ash walked to the end of his stall. ''Tood, what are you up to in there, anyway?''

Still no reply. Ash dropped his pitchfork. Emily came out of her stall as well. ''Uncle Tood?''

They both moved swiftly into the third stall. Tood half stood, half leaned against the back wall, a shovel hanging limply from his hand, perspiration pouring down his white face.

''Reckon I overdid it just a mite,'' he said weakly. Then he collapsed on the floor of the stall.

TOOD RECKONED the good Lord had a good idea in mind when he'd created comas. Tood hadn't felt this bad the last time, thanks to being unconscious for days. He shoulda gone on ahead and give up the ghost then. Might've, too, if Emily hadn't shown up.

But she hadn't let him get close to her. And hell, who was he to think he could break through the wall around her young heart? She'd had fourteen years of hard life to put it up. Tood didn't have much time left to chip it away. Besides, as old as he was, what right did he have to ask her to let him into her life? Chances were, as soon as she started to trust him and maybe care about his old carcass, he'd get called home to be with Edith. And where would that leave the girl?

He sighed and closed his eyes and listened to the sounds of the hospital.

"Lord, it'd prob'ly be just as good if you take me out of here now," he said.

"Well, that's really stupid."

Tood's eyes shot open. She was standing just inside the curtain that shut off his little Coronary Intensive Care Unit cubicle, her hair barely long enough to form soft curlicues all over her little head and her dark eyes even more accusing than her voice. He couldn't believe she was here after all the trouble she'd gone to avoiding him the last few days.

"Well, Emily, things look different this side of seventy."

"Sometimes things don't look so hot this side of twenty, either."

His heart hurt, and it had nothing to do with arteries and blockages. "Nope. Reckon not. But there's a lot of good living ahead of you, whether you believe it or not. You've got lots to live for."

"Right."

He wanted to tell her so many things, but he knew better than to jump right in and scare her off. This would take time; time he was pretty sure he didn't have.

"You do, too," she said.

He glanced up at her. She'd moved a little closer. "What's that?"

"You've got lots to live for."

He smiled. "Haven't had much to live for in a lotta years."

Except you, he thought, but couldn't bring the words to his lips. What if she laughed at him? Or worse, fled? She'd run away before, hadn't she? Hell, who wouldn't run from an old coot like him?

"You've got Ida," she said.

His niece's words mystified him. "Ida? Why, Ida's just... She's just...got nothing to do with me."

"Grown-ups!" Emily said with disgust. "She's got a case on you. Anybody can see that."

"A case on— Girl, what in tarnation does that mean?"

"It means she loves you. Why else do you think she's always hanging around out there, fussing around and acting like a major pain in the butt?"

Ida. She sure enough had done that. "Why, that's just... She was Edith's best friend. You know that."

"You're hopeless." She turned to the curtain. "I'm gonna get a candy bar. Want me to bring you one?"

He chuckled, but he wasn't really thinking about her parting shot. He was thinking about Ida Monroe. He was thinking about what Fudgie told him, that she'd sat up here in the waiting room day and night until he was out of danger, working those knitting needles of hers like a windmill in a twister. He was thinking about the food she brought every day and the way she nagged him to walk the way the doctors told him to.

Edith would have done the same thing, of course. But Edith was his wife. She had to.

That was a dad-blamed lie. Edith didn't have to. Edith loved him. That's why she stayed on his back all those years to take care of himself. Pure-T love.

Ida Monroe. *Well, if that don't beat all.*

THE FARM WAS QUIET. The cows were silent, the horses neighing only occasionally from the nearby meadow. Birds made the most noise, but there was no sign of human life except for Melina.

Sometimes the quiet felt soothing to Melina. Other times, like now, it felt ominous.

She sat in her room, staring out the second-story window, eyes fixed on the driveway. What would happen, she wondered, if her father found her, suddenly appeared on that gravel driveway? The thought made her heart pound unpleasantly. Or what if the other men who'd been trying to get their hands on her in San Francisco tracked her to this isolated farm?

What if someone did to her what they'd done to Poseti?

Her pulse pounded in her ears. What would happen if Ash and Emily came back from the hospital to find that Melina had simply vanished?

She tried to slow her breath, to bring her heartbeat back to normal. There was nothing to be afraid of. Why, she was never afraid when she was here on the farm with Emily and Edgar and...

And Ash.

No, she was never afraid with Ash around, not even since Poseti died.

But now, alone, the ugly possibilities filled her head far too easily. She linked her fingers across the slight swell of her belly and reminded herself that Ash wasn't her protector, no matter what her silly heart might wish. She might think she could see into his soul, might believe he was the kind of person she could trust. The kind of man who would be a wonderful father, loving and tender and wise. But she had to judge him on his actions. He had abandoned her. He had a past that still held sway over him, a past that would keep him dishonest and cynical and, worst of all, absent. An adventurer all his life, he could vanish like the thief in the night that he was. It was an act she'd seen before, and not one she planned to inflict on her baby.

She heard the rumble of tires over gravel before she could see the vehicle. She tensed, tasting fear again. It could be Neesa. Or Ida. Or Ash. Or someone with the power to wreck her life. She forced herself to breathe. She was being melodramatic. No one had followed them to Hope Springs. They would have known it by now. She waited, eyes growing wider as her heart refused to listen to calm logic.

It was Ash's car. *Their car,* he said. He was alone. The fear subsided but the rate of her heart didn't slow one bit. Melina stayed by the window, watching his loose grace, the glint of sunlight in his sandy hair. He'd picked up the mail when he drove by the box on the highway, and had a plastic bag from the grocer. He was thoughtful, remembering without being told all the little things that needed to be done to keep the household together.

She wondered if the child she carried would look like Ash. She wondered how hard it would be to be reminded of him every day for the rest of her life.

She lost sight of him when he came onto the porch, heard him come through the front door. He was downstairs in the living room, calling her name. She couldn't move or speak to reply. She wasn't up to seeing him, because her longing to see him—to be with him—ran so deep within her. The longing was an ache she felt in her fingertips, in her chest, deep in her loins where she supposed even the baby she carried mirrored that longing. She prayed he wouldn't seek her out.

She heard his footsteps on the creaky wooden stairs. He called her name again. This was foolish. He would find her. The bedroom door wasn't even closed. But she kept willing herself to disappear.

She sensed him pausing in the doorway to her

room. She felt the heat, low in her belly, felt her breasts respond to his presence. She closed her eyes and clutched the armrests of the rocker.

"Are you all right?"

She nodded. Her voice could not be trusted. Why did it have to be this way? Why should she be filled beyond reason with the need to have him take her in his arms and hold her close and love her until she felt safe?

"How is Edgar?" she said, hoping he would reply quickly and go away.

"Hanging on."

"And Emily?"

"Tough as tree bark."

That made her smile. Emily would survive. She could learn a lot from Emily.

He drew closer. Her heart faltered. If he should touch her...

He dropped a large envelope in her lap. "For you."

It was addressed to him, from a post office box in Chicago. He had torn it open. The corners of papers peeked out of the envelope. She placed tentative fingers on the papers. "Is it...?"

"Happy birthday," he said dryly.

With dread, she drew the papers out of the envelope. Her fingers trembled. A California driver's license with her photo slid into her lap. Then a Social Security card, a notarized birth certificate, high-school and college records. Even a passport.

"Welcome to the world, Melody Thompson."

Her longing for Ash was suddenly engulfed by an

overwhelming sense of loss. Melina Somerset no longer existed, her life annihilated in an instant. She felt bereft, and taken aback by her reaction. It shouldn't feel this way, as if she had died. Or worse, never existed. A tear splashed onto Melody Thompson's high-school transcript.

"I never made an A in math," she said, her voice shaky.

"Melody Thompson did."

She covered her face. Then he was pulling her up out of the chair, into his arms, the documents falling in a pile at their feet. She told herself it didn't matter that her safety, his caring, even her very existence, were now only illusion. Just for this moment, in his embrace, she was real. She existed. In a moment, she would let it all go—her name, her past, her ties to real people and real places. In a moment, she would become someone who had only existed in her imagination, living in a place she had only imagined.

In a moment. But for now, Ash's arms were both reality and magic.

CHAPTER FOURTEEN

MELINA PRETENDED to get on with her life in the days that followed. She figured it would soon be a month since she'd arrived in Hope Springs, so she set out to make herself at home.

She went to Neesa's store for an autographing party for a local author whose book on rustic mountain antiques was a bestseller among area tourists. She learned from Libby Travers how to make fried chicken and mashed potatoes the way somebody's grandmother used to make it. And she let Clem show her how to change the oil in the car she might someday own, now that someone named Melody Thompson could trade in her old driver's license for a shiny new Virginia license.

She pretended to take part in all those things one hundred and ten percent, the way she had always gone at life. But the truth was, she was having a hard time shaking the feeling that she was now an observer of other people's lives instead of a participant in her own. She felt like a ghost, except that in this case the rest of the world could apparently see her when she couldn't see herself.

"That's good, Mel." Faith Davenport leaned over her shoulder and studied her knit-two, purl-one stitches. Faith—along with her partners Donna and Kelsy and the four other women in the knitting class at Times Square Crafts—believed in her existence. "Now try to loosen it up a little. Since last week, you've started knitting with clenched fists."

Faith placed her hands over Melina's and demonstrated what she meant.

Melody Thompson, Melina speculated, was too uptight. And who could blame her, arriving on earth a newborn at the age of twenty-six? Her birth had been recorded in Riverside, California, her recent graduation at Cal State. The tense-fingered young woman was an only child with deceased parents. Somehow, Ash's brother had even managed authentic-looking newspaper articles chronicling the deaths of Barbara and Al Thompson, survived by their only daughter.

With her mythical parents lingering in her mind, Tom Somerset also popped into her head. For the millionth time since leaving San Francisco, she thought of the anguish her father was surely feeling at the loss of his daughter. How would he feel, she wondered, if he knew there was to be a grandchild, a grandchild she planned to rob him of forever?

But it was something she had to do. Just as she had to rob Ash of his son or daughter.

What a cruel start Melody Thompson was making in life.

She looked back at her row of knitting. As her thoughts had strayed, the knitting had grown tighter and tighter. Last week, this had been fun.

"Loose," she muttered to herself, and tried to force herself to relax. "Fun. You *will* have fun."

Everyone else was having fun. Faith and her partners, the women in the class. They were laughing at their varying degrees of ineptitude and gossiping lightheartedly about their lives. She would listen to them. She would learn how to *be* again, by pretending to be a part of them.

One day, surely, Mel Thompson would fit in the skin left behind by Melina Somerset.

"So far, so good," Faith Davenport was saying. "Doc Sarah says it's quite likely I'll have to go to bed with this one, because the kinds of problems I had last time often recur. But I'm still on my feet today. Thank goodness."

"No kidding," Kelsy, the young, redheaded partner said. "Do you have any idea what a lousy patient you are?"

"Sean reminds me with great frequency."

"Husbands are always there with an encouraging word when we need them." That wry comment came from Donna, older than the others, but radiating a calm air of contentment that made everyone in the room look up to her.

"The three of you have prize spouses and you know it," said one of the students, an elementary-school teacher who apparently filled her summer break with classes taught by others.

The three partners exchanged smiles. Melina wondered what it was like to be as close as Faith, Donna and Kelsy appeared to be. Wondered if she would ever know that kind of friendship firsthand. How could she, with a phony name and a made-up past and a future that demanded she remain on constant vigil?

"Well, I know I'm the luckiest woman alive," said Kelsy. "How many men do you know who insist on getting up with a crying baby in the middle of the night?"

Ash would, Melina thought. Except that he would never have the chance.

"Girl, he never wants that child out of his sight," Donna said. "He's already got a golf club in her hands and she's barely two years old."

Kelsy laughed. "He said he wants her to caddy for him when he goes on the senior tour. Unless she needs him to caddy for her on the women's tour."

Melina caught a glimmer in the redhead's eyes that could have been tears. The expression that accompanied her damp eyes made it clear that any tears were happy ones. Melina told herself it was just as well Ash wouldn't be around to teach their child the things he knew best.

Like gentleness and compassion, came the mournful little voice whispering into her empty soul.

"Men sure are fools for their little girls," said Donna.

"Little boys make them pretty happy, too," said another of the students, an elderly woman whose proficiency with knitting needles made it clear she was there for the companionship more than the lessons. "Ask Sean Davenport."

"And to think," Faith said, "I used to think I could do it alone."

"You couldn't?" Melina asked, alarmed by Faith's confession.

"Oh, of course I *could*. But having a partner—a real partner—makes it… Well, I only know it's not a struggle, not something I have to survive. With a real partner, every moment is a gift. Even the tough spots."

"The whole is greater than the sum of the parts," Donna concluded.

"That's it."

The three women nodded.

A partner. Melina thought of the nice, safe men her friend Neesa had introduced her to. Solid, steady, dependable. But none of them felt like partners. She didn't feel connected to any of them. None of them would bring tears to her eyes when she talked about them to a roomful of cheerfully gossiping women.

None of them was the father of her baby, or a man who made her feel safe every time she turned to him.

Yes, she loved Ash. But it was more than that. It was the same with him as it was for these three women who were obviously so happy with their lives. No matter what he'd been in the past, Ash was trying to be there for her.

"Look at you three," the elderly woman said, smiling. "Each and every one of you besotted and I remember when all three of you were ready to send your men packing."

All the locals in the room laughed, including the three owners of Times Square Crafts.

"Well, nobody said we were born smart enough to tell the princes from the frogs the first time out," Kelsy said, prompting another round of laughter.

Then the conversation took a turn to bemoaning the frogs each of them had kissed on their way to finding their princes. The stories were funny and the sunny dining room in the Victorian house filled with warm-hearted laughter.

But all Melina could think about was how ready she'd been to label Ash Thorndyke a frog, no matter how thoroughly and convincingly he behaved like a prince. She knew she loved him. She felt about him the way these three friends felt about their partners. So was she making a big mistake? The kind of mistake that ruined your life forever?

IDA TOLD HERSELF she should stay away from the hospital this time. After all, Tood had family now. He didn't need her.

But she couldn't stay away. It was that simple. She knew as soon as she woke up the day after his hospitalization and found herself rejecting every outfit in her closet that she would be heading for the Coronary Intensive Care Unit before the day was over. So she called her part-timer and asked her to come into Sweet Ida's two hours early, made doubly sure her roots weren't showing yet and spritzed a modest amount—barely noticeable, when you came right down to it—of man-tamer fragrance behind her ears. You never knew what a man might be susceptible to.

"You're a ninny, Ida Monroe," she said on her way out the front door. She paused on her front step and replied, "I've been worse. Can't quite think when at the moment, but never mind."

And on to the hospital she went. A quick visit, that's all. Wish him her best and hightail it out of there.

She almost hoped he'd be asleep. Sometimes it was such a trial, guarding the way she looked at him so that what she felt didn't come right out in her eyes for the world to see. But no such luck. He cocked one eye open when she lifted the curtain of his cubicle.

"You again," he said, his voice weaker than it had been two days earlier at the farm. "They'll run you outta here if you brought any of them low-fat cookies."

His gruff teasing set her a little at ease. She still didn't draw too close because she was afraid she might forget herself and place a hand on his arm or brush that wisp of white hair off his forehead.

"Well, heavenly days, you old coot, I know that. I'm saving all that up for when we get you home again."

He grunted, a faint smile on his lips. "Coulda been the last batch nearly killed me, don'tcha reckon."

She smiled. She couldn't think when he'd teased her this much, with almost the same familiarity he used with his cronies from Fudgie's. Her heart felt lighter than it had on the way over here. Even having him treat her like one of the guys was better than having him treat her with the distant respect he usually reserved for his wife's best friend.

"I reckon it was your own mule-headed stupidity that nearly killed you this time," she retorted. "Mucking out a stall. Of all the fool-headed things..."

"You keep nagging me like this, I'll just have to marry you and make an honest woman out of you," he said.

"Don't even think—" His words sank in. Suddenly warm all over, she paused with her mouth wide open.

"Finally figured out how to get you to quit yapping, did I?"

"Well, yes, Edgar, I suppose you did." She tried for some dignity. It was only another of his wisecracks, of course. It wouldn't do for her to overreact and give herself away.

"So, what do you say? Want to get hitched?"

She bit her lower lip and tried to keep smiling. "Oh, stop it, Tood."

"I know I ain't much of a prize. And you're the finest woman I know—now that Edith's gone on to the hereafter. But you'd do me proud to share whatever time I've got left."

"Edgar Grunkemeier, if you're poking fun at me—"

"Oh, hellfire and damnation, woman," he snapped.

''Come over here where a sick old coot can hold your hand.''

She approached cautiously. ''You've got Fudgie Ruppenthal hiding under the bed, haven't you?''

''You're not gonna be satisfied until I sweet-talk you, are you?''

He took her hand in one of his, the awkward move of a man more accustomed to farm work than romancing. Ida's heart swelled. She grew light-headed, as giddy as the girl she hadn't been for plenty of decades.

''I might not at that,'' she said as coyly as she might have once upon a time. ''You've kept me waiting long enough, I deserve a little sweet talk.''

He chuckled. ''You're my kind of woman, Ida Monroe. You've got a sharp tongue and you take no guff and you give as good as you get. But you're pretty as...pretty as...''

She let him falter for a moment or two. ''An orchard in bloom?''

He laughed outright then. ''Yes, ma'am. That's precisely what I was thinking.''

''Why, thank you, Tood. You're a silver-tongued devil, aren't you?''

''A feller my age ain't got much time for courtin'. So if you ain't determined to go outta this life single, what say we tie the knot?''

If this was a dream, Ida hoped the night was young. ''Are you saying I'll die an old maid if I don't settle for you?''

His eyes twinkled. ''Now, Ida, even I'm too smart

to be saying anything like that. But since you've said it yourself…"

"Oh, hush, before I change my mind."

He stared at her for a moment, the twinkle in his eyes softening to something she might have called tenderness. Her heart faltered.

"Sweet Ida," he said, his raspy old voice softer than she'd ever heard it, "you've given a washed-up old man something to live for."

EMILY HUNCHED against the wall outside the cubicle, listening through the curtain. She felt herself getting smaller with every word that passed between the two old folks, as if she mattered less the more they mattered to each other.

Her uncle was going to marry Ida Monroe. That was good. The way it should be. She knew that. It was only happening because she'd refused to sit by while they threw away their chance at happiness.

So why couldn't she feel good about it?

Because she knew now that Uncle Tood didn't need her anymore. She'd had one tenuous reason for being in his life—because he was sick and needed help. And now he wouldn't need her. He would have Ida. He probably wouldn't notice if she just disappeared.

That was good. Now she wouldn't have to hang around waiting for him to croak.

Sniffling, she dragged herself away from the wall. She could hitch a ride back to the farm for now. The way she saw it, she had one more little job to do before she blew this taco stand. She tried to imagine the look on everybody's face when the truth came out.

And she wouldn't let herself wonder if the day would ever come when she mattered so much to somebody else that she gave them a reason to live.

In her dreams.

ASH WAS WORRIED about Melina. She hadn't been her usual upbeat, enthusiastic self since the day the package had arrived from his brother. Even the news from the hospital late this afternoon—that Tood and Ida had set a wedding date, if one could imagine—hadn't brought the old Mel back.

Her smile was gone and he missed it.

"I don't suppose they'll want a big wedding," she said as Emily cleared the supper dishes from the kitchen table. She seemed merely to be making conversation. Ash saw no sign that she cared what kind of wedding the elderly couple had.

"Oh, right," Emily said. "I can see Uncle Tood in one of those monkey suits."

Come to think of it, Emily was stranger than usual, too. She'd been edgy ever since she returned from the hospital, jumping up every two seconds, chewing fingernails that were already gnawed to the quick and staring from him to Melina as if they held great fascination.

Women. He didn't get it. He supposed he never would.

"From what Ida said, I suppose they'll opt for

something simple and soon,'' Ash said. ''I don't think they're interested in all the trappings.''

''Yeah.'' Emily spun her glass in a circle, sloshing milk onto the table. She stared glumly into the spreading white circle. ''Do you want all the trappings, Mel?''

Melina looked startled and confused. ''Me? Well, I... It's... I'm not getting married. So—''

''Maybe you ought to be. Getting married, I mean.''

Ash noticed that the vague edge in Emily's voice had suddenly taken on sharp focus.

''Well, no, I don't think so. Not...not any time soon.''

Melina's voice, on the other hand, held a nervous uncertainty. Ash knew for sure now there was some female subtext here that he was ill equipped to read.

''But that's why Neesa's fixing you up, isn't it? So you can get married? So your baby'll have a father, right?''

''My...''

Ash looked at Emily. He wondered what had prompted her unpleasant little joke. Then he looked at Melina. She'd gone deathly pale.

''I mean, it's *got* a father, right?'' Emily looked pointedly at Ash. ''But you're shopping around, I guess. To make sure you get the best deal in dads.''

Ash still couldn't figure out the joke. Teenagers, he reminded himself, were strange. ''Emily, what are you talking about?''

Then she looked him right in the eye and said,

"Your baby. Mel's baby. How far along are you, any-way, Mel?"

Exasperated, Ash looked at Melina to see if she understood what Emily was doing. She looked shell-shocked. "Mel, I don't—"

Then the truth hit him somewhere in the region of his solar plexus. This wasn't a joke. This wasn't some weird teenage game. Emily meant what she said. And Melina wasn't denying it.

CHAPTER FIFTEEN

ASH COULD ONLY STARE at Melina as she lurched out of her chair and said to Emily, "You had no right!"

Then she ran out of the house without even a glance in Ash's direction.

He was numb. It was true. Melina was pregnant. And if all of what Emily said was true, the baby belonged to Ash.

But how could that be? It had been mere days since they'd been together that one crazy night. Granted, she could be pregnant. But how could Emily know, how could anyone know, so soon?

London, of course. Four months ago in London. Melina, pregnant. A renegade thread of elation ran through his initial tremor of foreboding. A baby.

"Oh my God," he breathed.

"Pathetic." Emily snatched her milk glass off the table and stalked to the sink. "I hope I never grow up, if it makes people so pathetic."

Ash jumped up and grabbed her arms. "You're sure about this?"

"Duh. Have you ever heard of morning sickness? Have you ever heard of, like, gaining weight so your jeans don't fit?" She rolled her eyes in that distinctly expressive way she had. "Like anybody with half a brain couldn't have figured it out a month ago."

Of course. He thought back over the six weeks since San Francisco and realized he'd had all the clues a man should need—her womanly roundness, some morning sickness. But he'd been oblivious to it all, because he'd never in his life been around a pregnant woman.

No, because he hadn't wanted to see it.

A baby.

He wondered if this was what it felt like to be in shock. "Okay. You're sure. There's definitely a baby. But that doesn't mean...that is, somebody else could be...you know..."

"Oh, nice. Now you're going to try to weasel out of it. No wonder she didn't want to tell you."

Ash squeezed his eyes shut. His head was spinning, the idea of Melina pregnant whirling in his mind. Him, a father. A man with responsibilities. He took half a dozen big gulps of air.

"Now I suppose you're going to hyperventilate?" Emily snatched a handful of paper towels and turned to clean up the puddle of milk on the kitchen table. "Get a grip, for cripe sake. It's a baby. People have babies all the time. Especially when they fall in love. Now, if you can't figure out what to do next, well, I just don't know. Maybe you're hopeless after all."

"Next?" He was supposed to do something now. But what? He'd never been a father before. A father-to-be, rather. What did a father-to-be do? Buy insurance? Baby formula? Cigars?

"Next. As in, go after Mel and make nice."

"Go after her?" The thought paralyzed him.

Emily rolled her eyes. "Do I need to write a script here?"

"And make nice?" His mouth felt dry.

She crammed the wet paper towels into the trash, took him by the arm and turned him in the direction Melina had run. "Go. Now. And repeat after me. Melina, I love you."

"But—"

"Do it." She gave him a shove in the direction of the back door.

"Melina, I love you."

"Not very convincing, pal. Work on your delivery while you're looking for her, why don't you?"

All Ash could think to do was follow orders. He'd been brought up to handle himself smoothly in any eventuality, never to be at a loss for clever, convincing words, to think on his feet and respond in a flash. Why was it that a lifetime of training kept failing him when it came to Melina?

Melina *and* a baby. Could he really be that lucky?

He went out the back door. Behind him, he heard Emily call out, "Add this. With all my heart."

He nodded absently. Was it lucky? Could he be sure it was lucky?

"Did you get that, Ash?"

"Got it," he said. "With all my heart."

Even with Emily's coaching, he wasn't sure he could handle this. His mind had shifted into reverse.

He found her in the far meadow, where the orchards started fanning out toward town. She sat under a tree, her knees drawn to her chin. The last of the sunlight touched her hair, cast a rosy glow over her pale face. She took his breath away, and not just because she was beautiful. But because she was wonderful—strong and bold and funny.

And he did love her. With all his heart.

But how did he dare tell her that?

He dropped to the ground beside her. Her eyes were red and puffy. She'd been crying. His fault. His heart wrenched in his chest. He wanted to touch her, to comfort her. But she didn't want his comfort. She'd run away from him. Worse, she'd hidden this from him for months. He might love her, but the feelings clearly weren't mutual.

He was going to lose everything. Melina. The baby. His second chance. He knew it. And he resented it before it even came true.

"Why didn't you tell me?"

She looked at him, misery shining in her damp eyes. Her words held more than a touch of bitterness when she spoke. "When I first found out, I didn't know precisely how to get in touch with you."

He deserved that. "Okay. You're right. I screwed up in London. But since then... We've been together for weeks. More than a month. We made love. We—"

"We didn't make love. We had sex."

Her words were like a slap. But what if she was right again? They had mated with passion, but maybe their coming together hadn't been an expression of emotion. Not because the emotion wasn't there—at least, for him—but because he'd been afraid to express it. Afraid of scaring her off. Afraid of…something bigger than he was.

He wondered what reasons she had.

"Were you ever going to tell me?" He found himself dreading the answer, felt the heat of anger beginning to spread in his chest.

Her voice sank to a near whisper. "You're not exactly father material."

The news sank in a little deeper, cut a little more sharply. She hadn't told him and she never intended to tell him. Okay, it was over. He would deal with it. He would… What? Die from the emptiness inside him? "That's why you kept telling me to leave."

She didn't deny that, either.

Ash felt sick fear in his gut. This woman carried a baby they had made together and she would have kept it from him. He wrestled with anger and self-contempt. Could he really blame her? He had abandoned her. And when he next saw her, she'd learned exactly what kind of man he was.

He didn't like self-contempt, so he let the anger win out. Better to be angry with her than to blame himself for being the kind of man no woman would want around to help raise a child. Not even a woman who is alone and penniless.

He hated himself. He hated every rotten choice he'd ever made in his life. He hated her for coming along and forcing him to see his life for what it was, then stealing his best chance to do something about it.

He stood abruptly. "You'll never want for anything." He could do that much. He *would* do that much. Surely she couldn't deny him that.

She stared up at him, her expression forlorn. "All I want is a normal life for my baby. Can you give us that?"

The answer damned him to hell. He turned without answering and stalked back to the farmhouse.

"WE MIGHT AS WELL well head for the car."

The professor always gave up too easy, that was his pal's opinion. "Give it some time," he said.

The professor looked at his watch. "We've been in this one-horse town for two hours already."

"Yeah. And we can spend another two if we need to."

"She ain't here. Everybody told us so."

"It don't smell right."

The professor jingled the keys in his pocket. "The woman at the bookstore said no way Melina Somerset's been here. The girl grease monkey said the same thing. The clerk at the dress shop, too. Now, what does that tell you? A woman like Melina Somerset's gonna need a new dress or two, don't you think?"

"I think their little stories all sound like somebody told 'em all what to say. That's what I think." He paused in front of a little shop that had a pink-and-white-striped awning and ice-cream parlor tables inside. "Come on. I'm thirsty."

"There's a bar at the other end of the street."

He looked at the professor. "Yeah. I'll bet Melina Somerset spends a lot of time hanging out in rat-hole bars." He gave the brim of the professor's hat a yank. "You stupid mug, she ain't that kind of dame. She's a tearoom kind of broad. Can't you see that?"

"Well, why didn't you say so?"

They ordered tea and carrot muffins from the ditzy-sounding woman who introduced herself as Ida. That made her the owner, judging by the name of the shop. They chatted her up, remembering to watch their grammar. They talked about the weather and the tourists and they finally gentled her around to the reason for their visit to this mountain burg.

"Say, we heard you've had a pretty famous visitor here this summer," the professor said.

"Oh, we always have famous visitors in Hope Springs," Ida said cheerily. "Why, once the president came and brought his family. Oh, it was a madhouse for days. Secret Service, you know. And the news media. You know, the members of the media are not always on their best behavior."

"I imagine you're right about that," the professor said. Had to hand it to the professor, he knew how to turn on the class when it was called for. "But we heard this year was particularly exciting."

Ida leaned closer and adopted a conspiratorial tone. "Did you?"

The professor leaned closer, too, and dropped his voice. "Melina Somerset."

Ida's eyes doubled in size. For an old lady, she was

actually kind of cute. "Melina Somerset? You heard that?"

"Yes, indeedy."

Ida tapped him on the shoulder with her pencil. "And they thought they were being so clever. But I knew who she was right away, of course."

He tensed, unable to stop his reaction. At last, somebody who wasn't lying like a dog to cover up the truth.

"Hard to disguise a face like that," the professor said smoothly. Thank goodness for the professor.

"Absolutely."

"They, uh, still around?"

"Oh my, no. They were going to…oh, where was it? Oh, I know. The Keys. The Florida Keys. In a little sports car. I thought at the time it didn't look like a very comfortable car for such a long trip. But her companion—she was with a very charming young man, you know."

The professor glanced at his pal. "Yeah, that's what we heard."

"Well, he said it was the perfect Florida car. A convertible, of course."

"Of course."

The professor couldn't leave it at that, of course. He had to play out the charade, finishing up their tea and chatting up the old lady some more, while his pal sat there itching to jump in their own car and map out the best route to the Florida Keys.

Ida smiled as they left, walking them to the door and asking them how long they would be staying in

Hope Springs. The professor promised to stop by the next day for another chat. His pal was ready to brain him by the time they got away. Melina Somerset and Ash Thorndyke had a three-day jump on them, and the professor was swapping recipes with a little old lady who ran a tearoom.

MELINA STARED into the dresser drawer in the bedroom she'd been using.

"You're packing."

She glanced at Emily, who stood in the half-open door, looking jittery and guilty.

"There's nothing to pack," Melina said.

Emily frowned. "What do you mean?"

With a heavy sigh, Melina slammed the drawer shut. "Everything I think is mine, he gave to me."

"Oh. Yeah."

Emily slipped into the room and closed the door behind her. Melina sat on the edge of the bed, the teenager slid her back down the door until she landed on the floor. "I guess I screwed up, huh? Letting the cat out of the bag, I mean."

"It's my own fault. I should have left a long time ago. I should have…" She shrugged.

"I thought he'd marry you if he knew."

Melina stared down at the girl who was so street-wise, but not very heart-smart. She saw no point in telling her that she'd decided to tell Ash the truth and that things might have worked out differently if she had.

"I don't think Ash is the marrying kind."

Emily seemed to pause to digest that, then gave a world-weary nod. "He'll leave, too, I guess."

"You won't be alone. You'll have Edgar and Ida. You'll have real family."

Emily shrugged, a who-cares gesture that didn't fool Melina. She was too deep into that act herself not to recognize it in her young friend.

"He won't mind if you take your stuff," Emily said.

"I don't need it. I have…" Nothing. Nothing but her new, empty life and her name that meant nothing. "I have everything I need."

"Where will you go?"

"To Neesa's maybe. Or Clem's." Neesa would take her with nothing. Clem Weeks would take her with nothing.

"Or the Davenports," Emily added, allowing enthusiasm into her words. "Or the Travers family. Any of them would be glad to help."

And Melina knew it was true. Any of the people just named would help her out if she asked. She knew that about Hope Springs and it gave her precisely what the town's welcome sign promised—hope.

"See," she said with a faint smile. "I do have everything I need."

"Will you still be my friend? Even after I screwed up?"

Melina walked over and dropped to the floor beside the girl, putting her arm around a pair of narrow shoulders. "I'll always be your friend."

"No matter what?"

And that, Melina thought, was the difference between her and Ash. Between the people of Hope Springs and Ash. "No matter what."

But the sad truth was that, when she got on the phone seeking a place to stay for the night, everyone had an excuse. Everyone she'd thought she could depend on hemmed and hawed, as Edgar would say.

"Um, I'd love to, Mel, just not tonight. Why don't you stay out at the farm one more night and I'll pick you up sometime tomorrow. Or the next day. I'll call, okay?" That was Neesa, sounding hesitant and embarrassed. The rest sounded about the same.

By bedtime, Melina was discouraged and despairing. She would spend one more night here, but that was it. She turned toward her room. And there, at the top of the stairs, was Ash. His face was closed and cold.

She thought of all the times she'd felt so lost and unsure of herself these last weeks and how he was always there with precisely what she'd needed. She thought of the comfort of his embrace, where more than once she'd found a safe haven to shed tears. Maybe he was thinking all those same things, and brooding on how she'd been deceiving him all those same times.

The words *I'm sorry* quivered on the tip of her tongue. But they were so inadequate.

He brushed past her without a word and disappeared into his room. She felt the chill of his anger as he passed.

THE NEXT DAY Ash and Emily did their best to make Tood's second homecoming even more festive than the first, especially in light of the good news about him and Ida. Even Melina came down for the first time that morning and pretended everything was just as it had been before. It wasn't, but Tood and Ida didn't need to know that yet.

The women were on the porch, talking wedding plans. Tood asked Ash to accompany him for his walk that afternoon. Getting away from the house, even for a few minutes, sounded good to Ash.

"Got some things to say," Tood said when they cleared the corner of the house and got out of earshot.

"I'm listening."

"First, I've got to get off this farm. Doc Sarah says I can't manage it no more and Ida says I can't manage it no more and I reckon they're right. But I can't stay here and stop doing the things I've always done. Been doing 'em all my life and I'm too set in my ways to change. So I'm moving to town, as soon as me and Ida tie the knot."

"That sounds like a fine plan."

He saw the way the old man's gaze swept over the familiar land. Ash didn't know what it was like to stare at trees and barns and a house where you'd spent an entire lifetime, but he got a hint of it in Tood's pensive old eyes.

"Reckon so. Anyway, I want Emily to have the farm. I want her to know she's got a place that's hers, where she'll always belong. So I talked to Sean Davenport yesterday. He's the local lawyer. He's drawing up what he called a trust. For Emily.''

Ash nodded. He wasn't sure why the old man wanted him to hear all this; maybe he just needed support or encouragement or somebody to tell him he was doing the right thing.

''And I want you to be the one to oversee everything. Take care of stuff till Emily's old enough to do for herself.''

''Me?''

Tood put a hand on Ash's shoulder. ''You're the man for the job. Steady. And good with the girl.''

''But Tood…''

Ash was stunned. How could he explain to Tood that he wasn't the kind of man you ought to trust with anything, much less a young girl's future. Just ask Melina. She'd been able to figure out that much. And here he was blaming her for what he knew himself to be true.

''Don't go bashful on me, boy.''

''Tood, I'm not… I don't know how to farm. And I don't… As far as being a family man, I…''

''You'll do fine,'' Tood said with the air of a man who'd made up his mind and wouldn't be swayed.

''No, I won't. You have to believe me, Tood.''

He hoped it wouldn't come down to telling his whole life story to the trusting old man. Life had never been this complicated. First there was Melina and the baby. His baby. Then there was his ailing father to worry about. And he had to confront his own dissatisfaction with the life he'd been living. Now this.

No wonder the Thorndykes preferred a life of classy crime. Anything had to be easier than real life.

"And one more thing," Tood said as they turned back toward the house.

Ash didn't have room on his shoulders for one more thing. He was sure of that.

"Ida tells me some men came through town yesterday."

Ash instantly focused on Tood's next words.

"One big old husky feller, looked like a prizefighter who broke his nose one too many times. And the other one kind of schoolteacherish. Odd looking pair, everybody said."

Ash had thought so, too, when they hired him to kidnap Melina. The blood rushed to his feet, leaving him with a momentarily spinning head.

"Looking for Mel, turns out. Showing her picture around. Called her Melina Somerset." Tood gave him a sly smile. "'Course, everybody in town allowed as how there'd a been a big ruckus if somebody as famous as Melina Somerset showed up in Hope Springs. Most folks told 'em straight out they hadn't seen no Melina Somerset in these parts."

"Most folks?"

"'Cept Ida. You mighta noticed, Ida's real helpful."

"Yes?"

"She gave them fellers a real good description of

the car you two were driving when you left here headed for Florida.''

"She did?"

"That she did. They was real grateful, too. Took off in a great rush, she said. Headin' all the way to Key West. Reckon that'll take 'em a while, won't it?''

IDA WAS TEACHING Melina the fine art of turning cucumbers into pickles. It was hot work and it left the air smelling of vinegar, but Melina didn't mind. Not one bit. Especially when Ida explained that a jar of homemade pickles would be one nice way of proving to everybody in town that they'd been right in insisting that the Mel they knew couldn't possibly be the richest young woman in the world.

"Why, dolly, Melina Somerset never made a pickle in her life," Ida had said. "You could wager good money on that."

Melina stared at the gauge on top of the huge pressure cooker where the canning jars full of cucumbers and vinegar and dill right out of the garden simmered. Her eyes watered and it wasn't the vinegar. She understood now why none of her friends would let her come into town and stay with them the night before when she'd wanted to run from the farm. Every last one of them wanted to make sure the two men who were looking for her were long gone. And they wanted to do it without tipping her off that they knew who she was, so she could keep up her charade as long as she wanted. No questions asked. Just unconditional loyalty. From an entire town.

Even cynical Emily had been awed by the news.

Melina turned away from the pressure cooker to the sinkful of cucumbers still to be washed and sliced for Ida's famous bread-and-butter pickles. Her heart was full. With so many loving friends, she would hardly miss Ash once he was gone.

She set to work on the cucumbers.

When they'd received word that the men who wanted to get their hands on Melina had tracked her to Hope Springs, Ash had redoubled his efforts to contact his grandfather. He'd finally reached Findley Thorndyke, who had promised to come up with a plan for putting those men out of business. Ash had seemed to relax then. Nobody, he had assured Melina, was better at plotting schemes than Grandfather Thorndyke.

Soon, he had promised, it would be over. They could get on with their lives. He hadn't mentioned the baby again.

But she remembered how relieved he'd looked when he said they could soon get on with their lives.

The first batch of pickles was finished, according to the gauge on the pressure cooker. She turned off the burner and took a glass of iced tea out to the front porch to cool off before starting the next batch. She wouldn't think of Ash. She would think of her joy in the baby whose growth was beginning to be noticeable and the satisfaction of learning everyday chores that would help her create a normal life for the two of them. She would think of baby clothes and teddy bears and teething rings.

She had just settled into a rocker when she heard the rumble of a vehicle on the gravel driveway. Tensing slightly, she relaxed when she saw it was only an old truck, probably one of Tood's friends.

The truck came to a stop in front of the house. The driver's door opened. Tom Somerset got out.

CHAPTER SIXTEEN

LOVE AND DREAD mingled in Melina's heart, bringing her to her feet, then freezing her in place. She wanted to fling her arms around the father she adored and missed; and she wanted to snap her fingers and make him disappear before he ensnared her life once again.

Her father appeared equally conflicted. He stood beside the battered truck for long moments, staring up at her, his arms tensed at his sides.

"Father." She sighed the word, a breath of anguish and yearning escaping her so softly the man in the yard couldn't have heard it.

She felt a hand on her shoulder and knew who it belonged to—the other man she held in her heart with both anguish and yearning.

"I'm here," he said softly. "There's nothing to worry about."

And she knew it was true. With Ash's support, she could get through anything. She nodded and walked across the porch, down the steps and toward the man she'd been trying to get away from for years. Her legs wobbled. But she held on to the courage she'd drawn from Ash's presence.

Tom Somerset looked old and gray. Her heart broke.

"Thank God," he said, his voice quavering.

In her entire life, Melina had never seen her father cry. He had surely wept when his wife and daughter were taken from them so brutally. But he'd never allowed Melina to see it. Now she saw the tears collecting in his eyes and trailing along the crevices beneath his eyes and along his cheeks. She wanted to run to him and throw her arms around him and tell him everything would be okay now.

But she knew the price for his peace of mind. She refused to pay it any longer.

"I thought we'd never find you. Especially after—"

He looked down, but not before she saw the pain in his eyes. She knew what he had been about to say. Especially after Poseti died.

"I hired the best I could find. Because...because I wanted to tell you how sorry I am." His voice cracked and his eyes pleaded with her. "This is all my fault. Can you ever forgive me?"

Confused, Melina frowned. "What?"

"You told me." He paused, appeared to be calling up control that remained elusive. When he spoke, his voice continued to crack and fade with emotion. "You told me...a hundred times how...miserable my fears were making you. And I never listened."

Melina's reply caught in her throat. How could she love so much and still harbor so much ambivalence? Ash came to mind, and her brew of conflicting feelings for him. It was possible. Oh, it was painfully possible. "No. You never listened."

"My fears...they were valid. They were...justified. But holding you hostage to them, that wasn't. That was wrong."

Hope fluttered in Melina's chest, clearing a path for the love for her father. "I...I just wanted to...live. To have a life."

He pulled a handkerchief from his front pants pocket and wiped his eyes. The handkerchief was wrinkled, obviously well-used. "I see that now. And I came to say I'm sorry. That's all. I won't blame you if you never want to see me again. But I had to come."

She ached to be caught up in one of her father's familiar hugs. She ached to let him know she was happy now and didn't harbor any resentment for him. But she held back, afraid yet that he would set in motion some trickery to force her to return to the isolation that set him free.

"I'm sorry my leaving hurt you," she said, and meant it.

"As long as I know you're okay." He stuffed his handkerchief away again. "I only came to see for myself that you were okay. And...to tell you face-to-face that I want you to lead whatever kind of life will make you happy. Because I love you more than anything in my life."

The fluttering in her chest broke free, the feeling of her heart being released from its cage. Tears rose in her eyes and she fought, as her father had, to blink them back.

"But please let me help," he continued. "I'll do anything you say."

She wanted to tell him she could take care of herself. That she had more people than she had ever imagined willing to help her and teach her how to live a normal life. But she didn't. Because he was her father and he loved her and he deserved the chance to learn how normal fathers loved.

She deserved it, too. And so did her baby.

She smiled at the thought of the gift she could give him in return for the gift of her freedom. "I'd like that," she said. "Your grandchild would like that, too, I think."

"My...?"

"Grandchild." She nodded, allowing herself a hopeful smile.

He buried his face in his hands, his tenuous grasp on his emotions obviously gone. She went to him then, and touched one of his trembling hands. He swept her into a crushing hug. Melina buried her face against her father's chest and cried with him.

She was happy and free and she had her father back.

ASH STUCK to the periphery of the flurry of activity on the farm the rest of the day, and hoped no one would notice him. He didn't know how to be a part of all the joyous feelings filling the air as Melina and her father reconciled and as last-minute plans for the next day's wedding took place.

The poignant moments between Melina and her father reminded him that time was running out for his own father. Bram Thorndyke was dying, alone and in prison, and Ash hadn't been able to see him or hold his hand, hadn't managed to do a single thing to make his father's dying a little easier.

But now that Tom Somerset was on the scene, he had confirmed that the men who'd hired Ash were neither government agents nor had Somerset hired them as Ash had fleetingly wondered when he realized Melina wanted to get away from her father. Whoever they were, at least for the moment they were caught up in a wild-goose chase to Florida. So maybe with them momentarily distracted, he could risk trying to see his father. A call to the minimum-security prison outside Washington, D.C., where his father served his time, turned up some disturbing news.

"I'm sorry, Mr. Thorndyke," said the very efficient young man who responded to his inquiry, "but Bram Thorndyke is no longer at the prison hospital."

Panic lanced through Ash. Could his father have died? Surely Forbes would have contacted him about that. Had the men who'd hired Ash to kidnap Melina done something to his father in hopes of luring Ash into a trap? He tried to still the clamoring voices of fear in his head. "What do you mean? Where is he?"

The sound of rustling papers came across the telephone line. "Well, according to the file, he has been…moved to another location."

"What location? Where?"

"I'm afraid I can't provide that information over the phone."

No matter how hard Ash pushed, no more information was forthcoming, not from the young man or from the sharp-toned higher-up who replaced him on the telephone when Ash persisted. Bram Thorndyke was no longer at the prison or the prison hospital. They couldn't—or wouldn't, Ash thought bitterly— tell him if his father was alive or dead.

He dialed Forbes immediately. But instead of hearing the ringing of a phone in Chicago, he heard a recording that let him know the number had been disconnected. Chicago directory assistance told him there was no longer a listing for Forbes Thorndyke. Ash's knees began to shake.

He was almost too upset to call his grandfather. He wasn't ready to let his father, his brother, his family, go. *Not yet,* he prayed. *Please, not yet.*

As the overseas call went through, Ash leaned against the wall beside the kitchen phone and listened to the murmur of laughter and conversation coming from the front parlor. Melina's voice and her father's. Then Tood's voice and Ida's. He remembered the ache within him when he'd watched father and daughter embrace in the front yard an hour earlier.

He needed to see his own father. He needed to be there for his father.

Grandfather Thorndyke's raspy old voice filled him with relief. "And a good day to you, young fellow. I suppose you're growing impatient to hear my plan."

"Where's Dad?"

"Why, he's fine."

"You've seen him?"

"Well, no, I haven't seen him. But he is... Well, I'm not at liberty to say at this time. But you can rest assured, he is in good hands."

Relief seeped through Ash. "I want to see him."

"In due time, my boy. Be patient."

"I don't want to run out of time, Grandfather."

"I quite understand. You will hear from me within the week. I have an excellent plan and you'll know everything in time."

Ash reminded himself that his grandfather always liked to play things close to the vest. He loved the theatricality of keeping everyone in the dark. Pressing would only strengthen his determination. Well, if Findley Thorndyke wanted a little drama, Ash would give it to him.

"Grandfather, I want out."

"Out? I don't understand."

"Out of the life."

There was a long silence from Monaco. "Oh, my boy, you don't mean that."

"Yes I do."

"First Forbes. Now you." Ash heard the puzzlement in his grandfather's tone.

"Where is Forbes?" he asked.

"I'm afraid I haven't the foggiest notion. It was Stacy's idea, you know. I dare say this is all about your young woman, too. You can bring her along, of course. Women can often add an element to our work that—"

"No." Ash broke into the little speech. "No, I can't. She wants a normal life." He hesitated, but he knew the words that followed were the plain and simple truth, no matter how much trepidation they caused him. "So do I."

"Oh, my." Disbelief and regret tinged his grandfather's voice. "How remarkable. Well, my boy, we'll straighten that out when I get there."

At last, a slip-up. "You're coming here?"

Grandfather Thorndyke chuckled, a comfortingly familiar sound as charming as it was sly. "As soon as this young widow I've befriended loosens her hold on her...er...valuables."

Ash laughed in spite of himself. As his dashing grandfather aged, it sometimes seemed to Ash that the elderly gent's interests were shifting from relieving wealthy women of their jewels to relieving them of other valuables.

"Watch she doesn't steal something of yours, Grandfather."

"Oh, no. I've a firm grip on myself. Especially in matters of romance."

Ash thought, as he hung up, that it was too bad he couldn't say the same for himself. But he heard the laughter from the parlor once again—hers light and pure—and knew that she'd stolen his heart.

He didn't even want it back.

BABY-SITTING KYLE was a better deal than getting caught up in all the sappy stuff that was going on at the farm today. Didn't take a genius to figure that out, Emily thought as she led the boy into the barn to see a new colt.

The colt had been the only draw strong enough to get Kyle to leave his friends today, Emily had discovered. The realization that he had listened to her advice and begun to bridge the gap with his schoolmates made her feel good in one way, but more alone than ever. She had no father, no mother, no one. Even Mel had real family again. Sometimes Emily wanted to cry. But she had to hang tough. She would be out of here soon. Maybe tomorrow. Or the next day. Right after the wedding. That would be a good time to blow this joint.

"Cool," Kyle said, hanging over the stall and gaping at the spindly-legged chestnut. "Can I touch him?"

Emily didn't know the answer to that, but she wasn't about to let a nine-year-old catch her exhibiting ignorance of anything. "Not yet. He's too young."

"Oh." Two minutes of staring at a colt pretty much exhausted Kyle's attention span for things not yet interactive. He dropped from the stall wall and glanced at Emily. "Maybe you oughta be helping with wedding junk."

He spotted an old saddle in a dark back corner of the barn and started fiddling with its buckles and straps.

"No way." Kyle had been her ticket out of discussions about wedding cake and flowers and stuff like that. "I might not even go."

Kyle looked at her. "Go where?"

He wasn't even paying attention to her. Even Kyle didn't need her now. "To the wedding, you goof."

Kyle had apparently spotted a bale of hay, sized up the situation and decided it would make an excellent substitute for a horse. He began tugging the saddle in the direction of the bale of hay. Emily didn't offer to help.

"I like weddings," Kyle said between huffs and puffs.

"Right."

"I do." With a mighty heave, he flung the saddle over the bale of hay. "My dad and stepmom's wedding was way cool. Nobody even cried."

Emily doubted that would be the case when Uncle Tood and Ida tied the knot. The whole town would probably blubber. Sometimes, it even made her feel a little choked up, thinking about it. She wasn't sure if that was because she knew that after the wedding nobody would care what became of her, or if it was something else.

Either way, she didn't plan to make a fool out of herself getting all runny-nosed over somebody's wedding.

"Weddings are dumb," she said in response to Kyle's assessment.

"Nope." He was riding now, slapping the sides of his hay-colored stallion with an imaginary tether. Ride 'em, cowboy. "Weddings make families. That's cool." He stopped and stared at her. "You oughta know that. Now you'll have a family."

The words were like sharp little pinpricks in her

heart. She began to feel them behind her eyes, too, and knew she had to get out of here. She wheeled and headed for the barn door. "Oh, shut up," she muttered.

Maybe Kyle was right, in some cases. But not in this case. Not when it came to Emily. Family wasn't an option for her.

When she reached the barn door, she almost ran over her uncle in her haste to get away. He put his trembly old hands out to catch her and Emily was seized by the desire to fling herself into his arms.

"Whoa, there, girl."

"Stop it!" she said fiercely, scrunching up her face against the tears threatening to fall. "Let go of me!"

But he didn't. Instead, his grip tightened on her arms. She found herself looking into his eyes, which seemed to be smiling right at her.

"Don't reckon I'm gonna do that," he said. "Don't reckon I'm ever gonna let go of you, Emily, girl. I'm gonna hold on for dear life."

It was too late now. The tears were there, pooling in her eyes, almost ready to spill onto her cheeks. The old geezer! It was going to be his fault if she made a fool of herself.

"No," she said. "No you're not!"

"Sure I am," he said, and his voice was so gentle it pushed her tears right over the edge. "You're family, girl. Come tomorrow, nothing's going to change that. Family always has room for one more."

She was crying, the tears ripping through her and

hurting so bad she thought she had to sob or fly apart. "No," she whimpered. "No."

"Oh, yes," he said, and took her into his arms. "It'll break my heart to have it any other way. And you know, girl, I'm thinking we've both had enough broken hearts for this lifetime. What say you?"

She couldn't say a word. She collapsed against his chest and breathed in the smell of hay and coffee that clung to his overalls. She clung to him, too, and wondered if it could possibly be true that losing her would break his heart.

She cried in his arms until she had no more tears. Then he dried her eyes with the sleeve of his faded shirt and took her by the hand and said, "Thanks for coming home, Emily."

CHAPTER SEVENTEEN

IN ALL OF HOPE SPRINGS, only two places were large enough to hold all the guests expected for the Saturday wedding of Tood Grunkemeier and Ida Monroe.

One place was the ballroom at Heritage Manor, and all the townspeople—especially Fudgie and Eben Monk and the rest of the barbershop gang—agreed that Tood Grunkemeier and the gilt-edged ballroom simply weren't a fit.

So Silver Lady Meadow it was.

Invitations weren't mailed and none were needed. Folks simply understood that everyone was invited. And everyone showed up.

Silver Lady Meadow overlooked the Blue Ridge Parkway. It spread for acres at the foot of Silver Lady Falls, green and lush and dotted with wildflowers. Bitsy's Flower Bower added an arbor, woven with sweet-smelling honeysuckle vines, for the wedding party to stand under. Church elders brought folding tables and chairs from the fellowship hall and food was provided in the usual way: Ginny Bryant's sweet-potato pie, Esther Hurd's tunnel-of-fudge cake, cider from Tood's farm, chicken and dumplings from Cindy Martin and chicken and dressing from Mandy Powell, plus Norma Featherstone's hummus, which nobody had liked when it first started showing up at covered-dish dinners but was now tolerated by most and enjoyed by quite a few.

The boys from Fudgie's served as ushers, which they'd been reluctant to do until they learned that the groom would be wearing new overalls from Hurd's Hardware. They all matched, down to the little red boutonnieres pinned to their denim straps and the smart blue-and-white-striped shirts they wore beneath the overalls. Most of them had even thought to shine their work boots and Fudgie contributed shaves and haircuts all around. Whiskey Rowlett hadn't touched a drop in three days—he couldn't wait for all the folderol to be over so he could slip away for a long-overdue nip—and Eben promised to wait until after the ceremony for his first dip of snuff. The old gang looked sharp and they knew it.

The bride wore a gauzy dress the color of ocean waves and Mediterranean skies, with a wreath of tiny pink tea roses in her silver-blond hair. She looked decades younger than she had looked in, well, decades, proving that smiles may well indeed be God's natural face-lifts.

Children ran the meadow until they were tired enough to sit still during the ceremony. Kyle led a reconnaissance mission to the foot of Silver Lady Falls, where their spiffy Sunday best fell prey to attack by rushing water. But the grown-ups were too preoccupied to notice. As many folks watched from quilts and blankets spread on the grass as from the rows of chairs set up by the church elders.

Music was provided by the community band, which was thankfully still short a bass drum player, with a vocal solo by Marcia Moondancer, who had been a saloon singer in her previous life as Marcia Greenberg. She could melt hearts with a ballad. If the sweet old couple exchanging vows didn't open up any tear ducts today, everyone agreed that Marcia Moondancer's rendition of "My Funny Valentine" would. It could wring tears out of a rutabaga.

Melina took it all in from one of the folding chairs in the front row. Her father sat on one side, Emily on the other. She held her father's hand and responded when necessary to Emily's excited chatter—the girl's veneer of hardened cynicism seemed to have cracked in the last twenty-four hours.

But Melina's real attention was on Ash, who sat with the ushers.

"Guess what I get to do?"

"Hmm?" Barely acknowledging Emily's enthusiasm, Melina thought Ash looked grim. Maybe he was unhappy about taking part in something so life-affirming. But no, that wasn't fair. Ash was—

"You're not listening!"

Emily's accusation caught Melina's attention. She didn't want to get caught mooning over Ash Thorndyke. "Sorry. What do you get to do?"

"Live in town *and* on the farm. Whichever I want to do. Uncle Tood said Ida's house and his house will both be my home. Isn't that cool?"

Melina smiled, momentarily distracted by the face

that she'd never seen look so childlike and excited. "That's wonderful, Emily."

"Yeah. I was thinking, it might be cool to just, you know, like, fit in."

"Yes. I'm looking forward to that myself."

"I guess he's not so much into fitting in, huh?"

Melina followed the course of Emily's gaze and found herself once again looking at Ash, the only one of the ushers not wearing a pair of overalls.

"No, I suppose not," Melina said.

If only she knew how to make Ash happy with a wife and a child and a small-town community, her life would be perfect. She had her father's love and support. She had loyal friends who didn't care one whit about her inheritance. She had a baby on the way.

But she had to let Ash reach his own decisions. She wouldn't cajole or beg. She wouldn't betray any of her mixed feelings. He had to decide for himself. Staying with her, being a father to their baby, had to be what *he* wanted. Not just what *she* wanted him to do.

So she sat and listened to the sweet, familiar vows taking place between a couple who didn't want to waste a single moment of the time they had left. She listened and held back the tears, afraid if they started she wouldn't be able to stop them. And when the words were over and the blushing couple had exchanged awkward pecks on the cheek and the townspeople had cheered, Melina heaved a sigh of relief.

She'd gotten through it.

Her heart felt heavy. But she told herself it was the child inside her growing heavier each day.

And that was a reason to rejoice.

ASH HAD ATTENDED some of the most elegant soirees ever seen by the world's upper crust. Nothing stood up to the spread that came together in Silver Lady Meadow without months of planning or small fortunes placed in the hands of professional caterers.

He'd filled and emptied three plates of food and still hadn't sampled everything he wanted to sample. He contemplated one more plate.

After all, eating was a better occupation than worrying about Melina.

He'd pretended to pay her little attention today. She had her father. Ash's protection was no longer needed. In fact, he realized that Tom Somerset might not appreciate the presence of the man responsible for his daughter's pregnancy—and he suspected from the speculative gazes leveled on him that Tom Somerset knew exactly who was responsible.

So Ash steered clear of the two Somersets. He even steered clear of Emily, because it was obvious she and Tood had connected. She no longer needed Ash, either.

But no matter how he tried, his thoughts and his gaze continued to stray to Melina throughout the afternoon.

She wore a loose-fitting, rose-colored dress that brought out the peaches in her creamy complexion. Emily had explained that Melina's dress was loose-fitting so as not to upstage the bride and groom by revealing her pregnancy on their wedding day.

"Tomorrow," Emily had announced importantly, "she comes out of the closet."

He'd wanted to ask Melina if she intended to name the father. He'd wanted to ask how she felt about letting the world in on a secret that some might not approve of. But he didn't.

If Melina wanted to have anything to do with him, she would let him know. And who could blame her for wanting nothing to do with him.

Instead, as in previous days, he kept his distance and an eye on her. He tried to watch her surreptitiously, telling himself he was only concerned about her safety. It was habit now, after all these weeks.

But it wasn't habit. It was wishing and hoping and trying not to despair of ever being back in her life. It was seeing the tidy upturn of her nose and knowing he had no right to be brought to a smile by the sight. Would he ever again kiss those full, soft lips? Would she call his name in labor, the way she had called his name in passion?

He turned abruptly and ran into Tom Somerset, who had been standing beneath a nearby tree and, apparently, studying him.

"Another wedding in the near future wouldn't be amiss," Tom said with quiet persuasion. "I've been watching the two of you, young man, and it isn't hard to see what's going on here."

Ash suppressed the urge to loosen his tie, which

suddenly felt remarkably like a noose. "I can't quite see her agreeing to a shotgun wedding."

Tom nodded. "And she's the one you'd have to point the shotgun at, I suppose?"

"She's not one for being pushed into things."

"So I've learned. The hard way." Tom's smile was rueful. "But I notice you're still hanging around. I notice the way you look at her."

Ash wondered if hanging around had earned him a point or two in Tom's book. He decided, regardless of the consequences, it was time for all-out honesty. "I love her. I just found out about the baby, but…I want a chance to love this baby, too." He hesitated. "There's more."

He told Tom Somerset about the plot to kidnap her, about the men who had followed them and tracked them to Hope Springs just days before. He saw the set of Tom's mouth growing grim as the story unfolded.

"So she is in danger." Tom's jaw began to work as the full import of the story sank in. "And you were hired to do the dirty work. Who are you exactly, anyway?"

Any points he might've earned weren't going to be nearly enough to get him back into Tom Somerset's good graces after this one, Ash was convinced of that. But there'd be no hedging. It was time for honest answers.

"A cat burglar. Fourth-generation."

The words came out like a thwack from the executioner's blade, painful but unfortunately not fatal.

He had survived the blow to suffer other consequences.

"Playgrounds of the rich and famous, mostly," he said, taking in the icy look coming into Tom Somerset's eyes. "My father's in a federal penitentiary right now. His freedom was my price for taking part in the little scheme to start with."

"I see." Tom's voice was tight and grudging. "But you fell in love with her instead?"

"Actually, I fell in love with her four and a half months ago. In London. Before I even knew who she was. This was all, well, an incredible coincidence, I suppose."

Tom studied him for a long time. "Then I guess your…professional background…is to thank for my daughter's safety."

Ash kept silent while he waited for Melina's father to continue.

"And what's in this for you now?"

The words smarted, but Ash answered clearly. "If I'm lucky, Melina and our baby."

He could almost see the words *over my dead body* flashing in neon on Tom's forehead. "And if you're not lucky?"

"If all I get out of this is the incentive to go straight, I guess I can't complain."

And he wouldn't complain. He also wouldn't explain the plans he'd already set in motion to pay back what he owed whenever possible. The truth was, he would probably be broke before the year was out, but it hardly mattered. The money didn't matter, because it would never buy him the things that really counted. He knew that now.

He attempted a smile. "If a broken heart is my payment for all the years I lived on the wrong side of the line, well, I guess that's fair enough."

"Sounds awfully noble."

"It's a little late for nobility, I'm afraid."

"The old man seems to trust you," Tom said, nodding in the direction of the groom, who was posing for a wedding photo between his bride and his niece. "I understand he's placed the farm in trust for Emily. You're to oversee the farm and administer all the girl's finances. I expect there's a nice little payoff there."

The news stunned Ash. "He *did* that?"

"You didn't know?"

"I told him it wasn't a good idea. I never..." Ash closed his eyes. "I'd never betray Tood. Or Emily. Never."

"Why not?"

"Because..." How did you explain a code of honor that allowed you to take from people who could afford it—especially if the one you were explaining it to was one who could afford it?—but staunchly prohibited betraying those who trusted you or needed you? Ash knew it was hopeless. "Because it would be wrong."

Tom's skeptical look was to be expected. Even to Ash's ears the words sounded incongruous. He supposed he would spend the rest of his life trying to atone for the way he'd lived the first part of his life.

And not everyone would accept his good intentions. He knew that; he'd have to handle it.

His gaze swept the meadow until it landed once again on Melina. She was at the center of a handful of the women in town who had become her friends. They were laughing and she looked content. Seeing her that way gave him a good feeling, even while his heart was breaking. He'd brought her here, where she had a chance at a normal life. Maybe that was all he would gain from this, the satisfaction of knowing he'd helped her achieve her heart's desire.

He repeated his words softly, "Because it would be wrong. And because I love your daughter enough to change everything I've ever been or done."

He knew as he said it aloud for the first time that the statement was true. Being with Melina and seeing her courage to turn her life around had shown him what was possible, had given him the conviction he would need to change his own life.

Tom Somerset studied Ash's face for a long time. Ash thought he saw something change in the older man's expression. "Have you told her that?" Tom asked at last.

"Not in so many words."

"Well, then, I suggest you do. The worst she can do is send you packing. And she's doing that anyway."

MELINA WAS TIRED—physically tired from the long afternoon of celebrating and emotionally tired from feigning high spirits.

The wedding celebration had continued until late afternoon. Just an hour ago, Tood and Ida had left for their honeymoon, with speculation about their destination ranging from Hawaii to Ireland to the honeymoon suite of the Towering Pines Bed-and-Breakfast between Dogwood Avenue and Old Oak Street in Hope Springs. The best money was on Towering Pines B&B, because Faith Davenport swore the narrow Victorian mansion had always been Ida's favorite spot in town.

When Melina and the others reached the farm, dusk still hadn't fallen. But the sun had dipped low behind the ridge of trees that shielded the house and barn from the road. The shadows were deep. Parked in the gloom was a late-model, dark blue sedan. Melina sensed Ash and her father tense as soon as they saw the car.

"Back out," her father said. "Get out of here now."

"Too late," Ash said, slowing the car. "Whoever they are, they've already seen us. And we'd never outrun them in this thing."

Emily snapped off her seat belt and hunched forward to look between the two men. "Oh, cool. A car chase. Let's do it, Ash. I've never been in a car chase before."

Ash glanced at the girl. "Don't you start, too."

Emily giggled. But Melina stared straight ahead as two men in dark suits started for the car.

"Feds," Emily said. "Look at the clothes and the haircuts. Gotta be feds."

One of the men approached the driver's window. "Ash Thorndyke?" He flashed what Melina assumed was some kind of identification, although she couldn't see it from the back seat. "Agent Ted Burnes. Your grandfather said to tell you he sent us."

"I knew it," Emily said triumphantly. "Feds."

"I want a better look at that ID," Tom Somerset said to the agent who had approached from the passenger side.

Both agents complied. Melina watched as Ash and her father studied the badges, then exchanged a glance.

"Look authentic to me," Tom said.

"Yeah, but I though that once before," Ash replied.

"Hear us out, Mr. Thorndyke," Agent Ted Burnes said. He then opened the car door behind Ash and smiled at Melina. "Miss Somerset."

He had such a bland smile. If he'd been trying to con them, he would have made a bigger effort with his smile, Melina told herself. Nevertheless, her heart raced. She had seen the gun holster when he pulled out his identification to show Ash. What choice did they have?

They gathered in the living room. Emily squeezed into a chair with Melina, excited but still seeking safety with an adult she trusted. Ash stood in front of the fireplace, arms crossing his chest defiantly. Tom Somerset perched on the arm of Melina's chair.

Ted Burnes and his sidekick sat on the edge of the sofa, elbows on their knees.

"Your grandfather brought this to us and—"

"Grandfather Thorndyke? Why would he do that?"

Burnes pursed his lips. "We're here to execute the plan. We're not privy to the deal he cut."

"He'd never cut a deal with feds," Ash said.

Melina understood Emily's need to draw comfort from someone else's closeness at a time like this. Ash's decisive tone, his no-compromise stance, stirred in her the need to draw close to him.

The two strangers glanced at each other again. "It had something to do with the release of a Mr. Bram Thorndyke."

"Yeah, I've heard that before, too."

Burnes stirred as if to rise. "You really should listen, if Miss Somerset's safety concerns you."

Ash caught her eye. She read the ferocious protectiveness in his gaze. Her heart grew strong with the knowledge.

"Ash, I want to hear this," Tom said.

So did she, Melina realized. She almost welcomed whatever showdown must come.

Ash nodded, and Burnes launched into a clipped and concise story about two minor players from the underworld who had been hired to kidnap Melina Somerset, and who had subsequently hired Ash to do the dirty work. Nabbing the two men who had hired Ash was critical because only they knew who was behind the plot.

And Melina Somerset was the key to nabbing the two men.

Tom's fingers tightened on Melina's shoulders, signaling his instinctive reaction.

"You're looking for a decoy?" Ash said.

Melina glanced at him. His shoulders seemed to sag with the burden of this news.

"She's the only bait we have," Burnes said.

"She's not bait," Ash said in a menacing tone that made even Melina shiver. "Use one of your agents. You don't have to put a civilian at risk."

"They'll be leery of a plant. Would you fall for some veiled woman?"

Emily sat up straight. "I think we should stay right here and shoot it out with the bad guys when they show up."

No one acknowledged the teenager, except Melina, who threaded her fingers through Emily's.

Ash set his lips grimly and shoved his hands into his pockets.

"This is the only way to get to the man behind the plot," Burnes said. "The only way to put an end to the danger."

"I won't have it." Tom Somerset stood. "Send me. I'm the one they really want."

"Maybe. Maybe not. But they know the only way to be sure they have you over a barrel is through your daughter," Burnes said.

Tom still shook his head dubiously.

"No way," Ash said. "You'll have to do better than this. We don't even know for sure that you're who you say you are."

The four men argued, all of them speaking at once

in calculated but combative tones. Their voices escalated and Melina's anxiety increased with the noise level. The decision, she knew, wasn't Ash's or even her father's. The decision was hers. Only she could decide whether to put herself—and her baby—at risk.

As the heated discussion raged, Melina listened to a dozen voices in her head and heart, some of them the voices of her fear, others the voices of her fearless determination to take charge of her own life. She was on the verge of making up her mind when a new and unfamiliar voice came into the room and broke quietly through the others.

"My, my, my," said the soft but compelling voice. "I told you gentlemen it would never do to show up here without me. Now look what a ruckus you've created."

Melina, as well as the others in the room, looked toward the voice. A lean and stately elderly gentleman wearing a burgundy-colored cravat and resting lightly on a pearl-handled cane stood just inside the front door. He had a thick mane of snow-white hair, a neatly trimmed mustache and a benignly gentle face that the devil himself would trust.

"Grandfather!"

Ash and the newest newcomer to Hope Springs embraced tightly. And with much chastising, Findley Thorndyke verified that the two men were, indeed, federal agents and their plan was, indeed, the best shot at putting out of business the people who were so determined to get their hands on Melina Somerset.

"Have you told them the rest?" Findley Thorndyke asked Ted Burnes.

Burnes, who now stood almost at attention at the end of the sofa, shook his head. "No. We're really not sure that's a good idea."

Thorndyke waved dismissively. "Of course they should know." He looked from Melina to her father and back again. "They are fairly certain, you see, that the man behind this is the same one responsible for the deaths of Thalia and Justine Somerset."

Melina went rigid, felt the bite of her father's fingers in her shoulder as he, too, reacted to the news.

"Who?" Tom Somerset said. "Who is it?"

The two federal agents protested, but Findley Thorndyke ignored them. The man he named had once been Tom Somerset's partner, a friend in his youth who had disagreed with Tom about the direction of the company. Melina glanced up at her father. His face looked gray and slack.

"He was my friend," Tom whispered. "But after we went our separate ways, he didn't do well. I did. He came back several times, wanting help, then asking for 'his share.' He'd received his share, but at first I gave him more. Out of…concern. Finally, I…" He looked at Ash's grandfather. "They're sure?"

"As sure as we can be until we get our hands on him," said Agent Burnes. "We have information which suggests he had the means to commit the earlier crimes. Once we have our hands on him, we believe we can link him to forensic evidence in that case. And we know he's been in contact with the two men who were after Miss Somerset in California. But we need them to lead us to him.''

A long silence filled the room as the news sank in that the man who had already damaged the Somerset family wasn't satisfied with the destruction he'd already committed.

Burnes continued. "And we need Miss Somerset to help us get to them."

"So, my dear," Grandfather Thorndyke said at last, approaching Melina and taking her hand in his. His smile comforted her and made some of the voices in her head grow silent. She realized it was Ash's smile she saw in his face. "The decision is yours, of course. These gentlemen assure me the risk will be minimal."

Both Ash and her father pressed closer.

"That's not—" Ash began, at the same time Tom Somerset said, "You can't—"

Melina stood and clasped the old man's hand tightly. "I'll go."

CHAPTER EIGHTEEN

AFTER THE HOUSEFUL of people finally slept for the night, Melina crept down the stairs and out the back door. Pulling her robe tighter against the mountain air, she walked the farm that had been the first place to feel like home since her mother died.

She smelled sweet hay and the sharp fragrance from the nearby stand of pines. She listened to the velvety swish of night air through those pines. She accepted the protection of the calico cat, who stepped out of the barn to accompany her on her farewell walk.

Perhaps it wouldn't be farewell, of course. She prayed she would return safely. She hoped she would see Hope Springs and Emily and the others again. She dreamed of raising her baby here.

She even still cherished the wish that she might one day love Ash and receive his love in return.

But none of that was possible, she knew, as long as this threat hung over her head. She recognized the truth of her father's fears now. This threat had hung over them both for fourteen years. She felt a huge welling of anger and hatred for the man who had torn her life apart. But as the nuns at the convents had taught her years ago, after her mother and sister were killed, hate wasn't a healing force.

But claiming her right to determine her own life and her baby's, that was affirming and that's what she would do tomorrow.

And there was only one way to do that—she had to be willing to risk everything. Her heart beat wildly against her ribs when she thought about the danger, especially the danger to her unborn baby.

She reached her favorite meadow, the one where the mares and their colts frisked during the day. She could see the house from here, and hear the soft trickle of a nearby creek. A full moon wrapped a silver luster around all that was green. The night felt magic, but what was most magical of all was her knowledge that in small towns like Hope Springs, nights like this were not uncommon. In Hope Springs, magic was an everyday occurrence.

She dropped to the ground beneath a spreading oak and tried not to think about tomorrow. The cat circled Melina's feet until she found the perfect spot of meadow grass, then curled up in a purring ball. Melina smiled. Despite what might happen, she felt a measure of peace tonight.

Melina heard footsteps behind her and knew instinctively who besides the barn cat had followed her. She didn't turn, but waited for Ash to sit beside her.

"Don't go," he said softly.

His voice had never been so tempting. "I have to," she replied simply.

"We'll work out something else. We'll…" He

floundered in his obvious effort to offer hopeful alternatives.

"We'll what, Ash? What choice do I have?"

"We'll think of something."

His hair was slightly ruffled, maybe where he'd tried to sleep. Shadows fell into the sharp hollows of his jawline and beneath the ridge of his sandy eyebrows, highlighting the discouraged look he tried to cover with his words. His attempt endeared him to her, made her appreciate all the ways he had tried to make her life better these last seven weeks. She wanted to smooth his hair, wanted to feel the coarse tangle of it. She clenched her fist against the impulse and shook her head. "I know it's dangerous. But my mother and sister deserve justice. And if the trade-off for my safety is a life of virtual captivity, well, that's not an option. Not for me. Not for my baby."

He touched her then, a soft caress that drew her face toward his. His eyes were dark and troubled in the moonlight. "I'll take care of you. You'll always be safe."

She smiled. "That was my father's answer."

He cupped her face between his hands. "Would it make any difference if I said I love you? That I can't do without you?"

Her heart twisted sharply in her chest. How long had she wanted to hear those words? And how desperately did she want to disbelieve them now, when hearing them made her conviction that much harder? She swallowed back the emotion clogging her throat.

"If you mean that, if you really love me, you'll understand that I have to do this."

He closed his eyes, still holding her face between his hands. He lowered his lips gently to hers, drawing her into a kiss so poignant it brought tears to her eyes. She could feel the love in his kiss and the call of it was almost stronger than her resolve to be free. Almost.

"You're right," he said against her lips. "I do understand."

Tears spilled from her eyes. He brushed them off her cheeks with his thumbs, kissed the tracks they left behind.

"It's why I love you," he said. "How can I ask you to do anything different when this is the very reason I love you?"

She laid her head on his shoulder and snuggled against him, smiling at his familiar scent. "You love me because I'm stubborn?"

"I love you because you have a bold heart. Because you make me want to have a bold heart, too."

Being so close to him felt good, too good. It felt like forever and she had to remember that maybe their forever was only for this moment. "What would you do if you had a bold heart?"

He continued to caress her face with one hand, holding her close against him with the other arm. "I'd stay here."

That sounded good to her, as good as his nearness felt. She liked what it said about him. He could change; he was changing. "Is that bold?"

"For me it is."

"And if you didn't have a bold heart?"

"I'd stay anyway."

"You're going to do it? Stay and run the farm and take care of Emily?" She waited for his answer with a thumping heart, although she knew what he would say before he spoke. It was hard, in the face of what he was saying, not to be swept up in hope. His words said she had been right about him, and that he was beginning to see the things in himself that she'd always believed were there.

"I'm tired of running, too, I guess."

Contentment trickled into her heart, a quiet balm to her previously racing thoughts. She rested her hand on his chest and felt the steady thump of life within him. He would be a good father. Oh, it was hard not to hope. "Is that what you were doing when you left London? Running?"

"The way I felt about you scared me. Just thinking about going straight scared me. Wanting to do things I didn't think I was a decent enough person to do scared me."

"Why on earth did you think you weren't decent?"

"My whole life said so."

"No," she insisted. "I'd never love a man who wasn't fine and decent."

His hand stilled against her cheek.

"If he was very good at pretending to be something he's not..."

"Which you aren't." She smiled against his chest.

God was giving her a wonderful going-away gift—the gift of Ash's redemption.

"Oh, but I am. I've built a career on it."

"I can see right through you, Ash Thorndyke. You're a softy and you have principles and you have staying power."

"Me?"

"You haven't cut and run on Emily. Or on me, not this time around."

"But before, in London—"

"That was then." She glanced up and smiled. His face was puckered in a frown. "This is now."

He studied her face, a lingering gaze. His frown began to ease and she saw his intention to kiss her again. He lowered his lips to hers and swept her up in a long, slow kiss, a kiss that was all heart and soul. A kiss that was not a prelude to anything else, complete all by itself.

When the kiss drew to a reluctant close, he said, "I have something for you."

"A going-away present?"

"Don't say that."

She sat up and looked at him. His smile was a little boy's hopeful smile. In that moment, she felt certain their baby would be a boy. And it would look just like its father. "For luck, then."

He made an attempt at a brave smile. "Yeah. For luck."

He took something out of his pocket then and began to unwrap it. Beneath the soft cloth lay the wedding pendant that had belonged to her mother, the piece she had hocked the day they met in London. It glistened in the moonlight. She touched his fingers where they held the tissue. "Oh, Ash."

"I love you, princess."

"And I love you."

He placed the pendant around her neck, settled the moon-kissed stone into the hollow of her throat.

She clung to him.

"Make love with me," she said, knowing she wanted that closeness tonight, in case it was their last chance.

"When you come home. I'll make love with you then."

"But—"

"No buts. You're coming home. And when you do, I'll make love to you for the rest of our lives."

As hard as she'd tried to avoid it, she let her heart jump on those words and ride them to the stars. "Will you, Ash?"

"I promise," he said.

They walked back to the house, hand in hand, the calico cat setting a lazy pace. No more words were necessary. Ash's promise echoed in the night.

But when Melina left early the next morning with the two agents, headed for a private airstrip outside Washington D.C., she saw in Ash's eyes that his confidence was slipping away in the harsh light of day.

He, too, was thinking about the two men who waited to exchange a suitcase full of money for Melina Somerset.

He, too, was wondering what would happen if he could never fulfill his final promise.

ASH PACED. He paced in his room. Then along the lane that split the meadows and pointed the way to the wooded path into town. Then up and down the porch. He kept looking at his car, jingling the keys in his pocket. He checked his watch. An hour they'd been gone.

Then ninety minutes.

He kept taking a step in the direction of his car, then checking his impulse.

He kept thinking of Melina, at the mercy of two men who wanted ill for her and two others whose concern for her safety was purely professional.

"Don't do it, boy," Grandfather Thorndyke had said to him after breakfast was eaten and one trip up and down the lane was completed. "You'll get in their way. Botch the whole operation. Physical confrontation is not your forte, need I remind you?"

Ash paced some more.

Emily clutched the old barn cat to her chest and stared at Ash, her eyes as unblinkingly accusatory as the cat's. "I think she needs us."

Ash knew what that meant. It meant how could he ask Emily to trust him if he couldn't be there for Melina when she needed him.

"We'd tip off the guys who want to get their hands on her," he protested.

Her expression said she wasn't buying it.

Tom Somerset sat on the porch, his hands clasped

in a death grip between his knees. He had sat in silence all morning, struggling, Ash imagined, with his anguish over once again being at the mercy of the man who had already robbed him of two of the people he loved most.

"How long will this take?" he finally asked. "Will they call when it's over?"

The answer to Tom's question, Ash knew, was that it was a long ride to Washington D.C., with plenty of opportunities for wrong turns, some of which led to dead ends.

"Oh, assuredly," Grandfather Thorndyke responded. "I say, Mr. Somerset, I know the timing is all wrong. But sitting here, it has occurred to me that this farm could be a gold mine, used properly. See what you think of this."

Ash almost smiled at his grandfather's barely veiled attempt to distract Tom. The two retired to the kitchen for a game of pinochle and began hashing over a couple of ideas for converting the farm into ready cash, when Ash decided he could take it no longer. Without a word to anyone, he went to his car, started the engine and headed down the lane to the highway.

They had a two-hour head start. He wondered how fast the car would go.

He'd gone twenty-three miles down the Blue Ridge Parkway when he heard rustling in the back seat.

"I'm not sure we should've left them there alone with my farm," Emily said, rising from the floorboard behind the driver's seat and climbing over into the front seat. "Uncle Tood's gonna be pretty ticked if he comes home from his honeymoon and finds out they've conned us out of the farm."

Ash automatically slammed on the brakes. "What the—"

"You'll never catch them if you turn back now," Emily said as she buckled herself in.

"Emily, this isn't a lark. This is—"

"I know what it is, Ash. I'm going. In fact, I've probably got more experience with this kind of hood than you do. So why don't you just forget the fatherly lecture and let's go after Melina."

Ash sat in silence for a few moments, resisting the impulse to smile. "Somebody's got to give you a fatherly lecture every now and then."

She put her feet on the dashboard, crossing her ankles. "I suppose the next thing, you'll be wanting to tell me about the birds and the bees."

"Ah, actually…ah…"

"Don't worry. I already know all that stuff."

"You do?"

"Sure. Got any questions? Need any pointers?"

Farm. Teenager. Parenthood. He was in deep water and he didn't even know how to float. Who was he kidding?

"You know," Emily said, "movie heroes are never at a loss for words."

He glanced at her. She was grinning, eyes trained on the highway.

"Of course not, wise guy. They've got scriptwriters and I don't, as you've already pointed out."

"Maybe we should get you one."

"Maybe I'll just leave the clever one-liners to you."

She nodded. "Okay. But who does that leave to handle the action scenes?"

"I know tae kwon do," he said.

She rolled her eyes. Even from the side, he could tell that.

"You're a regular killing machine, aren't you? Lucky for you I brought the gun."

He held out his hand. "Hand it over."

She hesitated, then slapped it into his palm. "Have you ever nailed anybody?"

"If you're smart enough, you don't have to nail anybody," he said by way of avoiding her question.

"I didn't think so." She played with her bony kneecap. "Can you if you have to?"

"If it's them or Melina."

"Or your kid."

He glanced at her again. "Or either one of my kids."

"Don't get ahead of yourself. You've only got one so far."

"One here with me," he clarified. "And one on the way."

She went very still. "Yeah?"

"Yeah."

DUSK HAD FALLEN when they reached the airstrip. A small private plane was the only one on the runway.

Two cars, five people visible in the lowering darkness.

They had parked a few miles away and were creeping closer in the cover of the metal hangar. Ash hadn't even tried to bully Emily into staying with the car. It would have been wasted breath. Besides, she was as good as he was—maybe better—at this stealthy stuff.

Close enough now to hear the murmur of voices, Ash didn't like the grip one of the federal agents had on Melina's arm. He was holding it awkwardly, probably too tightly. If there was a bruise on her, he'd see that they paid. He'd—

"Something's wrong," Emily whispered.

He shushed her. But he studied the tableau a few dozen feet away. She was right. The man grasping Melina's arm at such an awkward angle wasn't Ted Burnes or his sidekick. It was one of the men who had first hired Ash to kidnap Melina Somerset. Ash almost came out his skin. Something had gone awry.

"They've got her," Emily said. "Ash, they've got her."

And they were backing toward the plane, guns pointed at the two federal agents. Ash had to think and he had to think fast.

There wasn't time to think. With a bloodcurdling yell, Emily was already charging the five people on the tarmac. There also wasn't time to worry about the fact that gunfights and fistfights weren't Ash's strong suit, as Grandfather Thorndyke had so encouragingly pointed out. Emily had tipped their hand. He had no choice.

He charged with her.

Their appearance at least had the element of surprise.

Even Ash was surprised.

So surprised he forgot to pull his gun.

But he did add his voice to Emily's unearthly shriek and the five people a few yards away on the tarmac reacted with confusion. One of them whirled in a circle, searching for the disturbance. Ted Burnes quickly took advantage of the distraction to leap on him. And Ash, one thing on his mind, bulldozed into the henchman who had his fat fists around Melina's arm. He hit with a crunching thud and heard the other man grunt. They all three went to the ground.

The thug's grip on Melina broke when they hit the ground. Ash realized that Emily had also lunged at the thug at the same time he did. She was wrapped around his head, pummeling him with her fists. The man struggled blindly, but Ash's litheness paid off. He maneuvered his knee into the big guy's gut and grasped both hands around the hand that held a gun.

From the corner of his eye, he noted that two federal agents had wrestled the other man to the ground.

"I'd love to break your fingers one by one." Ash hoped he sounded convincing. "So just hang on to that gun and give me an excuse, why don't you?"

THE TERRIFYING MOMENTS were over almost as quickly as they began. Melina sat on the tarmac, shaking, as the federal agents slapped cuffs on the two men who had gotten the drop on them moments before. She couldn't take it all in. One moment she'd been full of dread, her worst nightmare coming true, and the next—

Ash lifted her gently, favoring her aching arm, cradling her in his embrace.

"You're hurt," he crooned. "Oh, princess, you're hurt."

"You came for me." She breathed deeply, absorbing his comforting presence.

"I was afraid Burnes and his buddy weren't as committed as I was to giving us another chance to make love."

She felt his lips against her hair. She smiled weakly.

"Besides, Emily's already running a little late on having a baby brother or sister," he said. "We had to make sure nothing went wrong with this one."

She looked into his eyes and once again saw the promise in them. And knew it was more than a promise. It was a commitment. One she could count on.

EPILOGUE

"WHERE SHOULD WE GO for our honeymoon?" Ash held her in the circle of his arm.

They were lying side by side, so he couldn't see her. But he knew what she looked like, lying here in the old four-poster bed in the upstairs bedroom with the moonlight spilling through the open curtains. She looked fair and fragile, her dark hair flowing across his arm, a faint smile on her lips.

Of course, she wasn't fragile. Farm wives weren't fragile. Especially not a farm wife who helped harvest a record crop of apples in her eighth month of pregnancy and then gave birth to a sturdy eight-pound baby boy.

"We've been married seven months," she said. "It's too late for a honeymoon."

"No, it's not. We had to wait for the baby to come. And for harvest to be over."

"And for your father to finish his treatment. You know, I think he's going to be in remission for a long time."

"Babies might be a better treatment than radiation," Ash said. He'd never seen a sick man blossom as Bram Thorndyke had the day they'd placed the not-so-little Thomas Jefferson Thorndyke in his arms.

Ash said a little prayer of thanks every day that his father's request for early parole to pursue more aggressive treatment had finally been granted—thanks to some of Findley Thorndyke's machinations, he suspected. "So what do you think? The Mediterranean? Bali?"

She yawned and snuggled deeper into the curve of his arm. He loved it when she did that. It made him think he might still have it in him to wrestle crooks to the ground, even now that he was a steady, reliable father and a gentleman farmer.

"Ash, you won't mind terribly if I've had all the adventure I need for a while? At least until Emily's settled in school."

"Mel, she's settled. She had seven girls over for a sleepover last weekend."

"I know. Wasn't it wonderful?"

It was, actually. The shrill laughter, the muffled laughter, the absolutely giddy girlish laughter led by a girl who hadn't known how to laugh when they first met her.

"Not to mention two boyfriends," Melina added.

"Yeah— What?" He felt an instant protective alarm. "Two *what?*"

"Boyfriends, Ash."

"Isn't she a little young for boyfriends?"

"She'll be fifteen in a month."

"It's not that boy with the earring, is it?"

"Oh, Ash, you're a wonderful father. Paranoid and overprotective and *so* conservative."

He smiled at her fond needling. "I did pick it up rather quickly, didn't I?"

"I knew you would."

"You did not. You thought I didn't have it in me."

"No, I thought *you* thought you didn't have it in you."

The faint sound of a baby beginning to fuss reached his ears. Melina stirred. "Tommy wants his mother."

"Actually," he said, slipping his arm from around her and tucking the covers back up to her chin, "I think that's his 'I want my daddy' whimper."

He looked down at her, her lids at half mast over her enormous eyes, looking so contented and lovely and normal. Everything he'd ever wanted in life was right here, on this land, in this house.

She smiled up at him. "Now that you mention it, I think you're absolutely right."

He stepped into his slippers and went down the hall to the nursery. His son was beginning to cry in earnest when he reached him and bent to pick him up.

"You wet? Hungry? Or just feeling left out?" He cradled the plump cheek against his neck and was rewarded when Tommy began to gurgle contentedly. "I'm right here, little guy. Your old man's not going anywhere."

HE WAS GONE SO LONG Melina began to worry that something was wrong. She slipped out of bed and made her way down to the nursery, taking care not to waken the rest of the house.

And the house was full. Besides the three of them,

there was Emily, who had helped the Las Vegas police track down the man they were looking for. Her adoption would be final in time for her birthday. Plus Grandfather Thorndyke, who had become the king of the roost at Fudgie's in the few months since he'd settled in Hope Springs; they all hoped his temporary lay-off from the life of crime would become permanent. And, of course, her father-in-law, yet another suave but kindhearted Thorndyke gentleman whose health problems had resulted in a change of heart regarding his career. Her own father, too, as often as his schedule allowed. And his schedule seemed to have relaxed a bit; Tom Somerset seemed less driven now that the man responsible for the murders of his wife and daughter had been brought to justice. He seemed content to be part of their growing family. Especially on Sundays when Tood and Ida came out after church for an old-fashioned southern Sunday dinner.

Ida swore Melina must have southern blood in her veins, she fried chicken like a native.

She peered into the nursery and smiled. Both her men were sound asleep, Tommy cradled in Ash's arms, Ash's head drooping against the back of the rocker. She wondered if it ever occurred to him how perfectly suited he was to his new life as husband and a family man, not to mention owner of a home security consulting firm catering to all the wealthy people building resort homes in the nearby mountains.

She kissed him on the forehead and he stirred. He smiled up at her.

"I was thinking," he murmured.

"And I thought you were dreaming," she teased.

"This little guy's going to need a brother."

"Or another sister," she said.

"Both, maybe."

"Then we'd better get busy."

They tucked the sleeping baby into his crib and went back to bed to work on their all-American family.

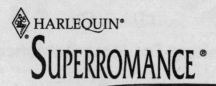

HARLEQUIN®
SUPERROMANCE®

From July to September 1999—three special
Superromance® novels about people whose
New Millennium resolution is

By the Year 2000: CELEBRATE!

JULY 1999—*A Cop's Good Name* by Linda Markowiak
Joe Latham's only hope of saving his badge and his reputation is
to persuade lawyer Maggie Hannan to take his case. Only Maggie—
his ex-wife—knows him well enough to believe him.

AUGUST 1999—*Mr. Miracle* by Carolyn McSparren
Scotsman Jamey McLachlan's come to Tennessee to keep the
promise he made to his stepfather. But Victoria Jamerson stands
between him and his goal, and hurting Vic is the last thing he wants
to do.

SEPTEMBER 1999—*Talk to Me* by Jan Freed
To save her grandmother's business, Kara Taylor has to co-host a
TV show with her ex about the differing points of view between men
and women. A topic Kara and Travis know plenty about.

By the end of the year,
everyone will have something to celebrate!

HARLEQUIN®
Makes any time special ™

HARLEQUIN®
SUPERROMANCE

IN UNIFORM

THERE'S SOMETHING SPECIAL ABOUT A *WOMAN* IN UNIFORM!

WINTER SOLDIER #841
by Marisa Carroll

When Lieutenant Leah Gentry—soldier and nurse—went overseas as part of a team that provided medical care for those in need, she expected long days and hard work. What she *didn't* expect was to fall for Dr. Adam Sauder— *or* to become pregnant with his child.

Watch for *Winter Soldier* in June 1999 wherever Harlequin books are sold.

HARLEQUIN®
Makes any time special ™